José Sotolongo

THE OPTIMISTIC CUBAN
A NOVEL

HISTRIA
FICTION

Histria Fiction

Las Vegas ◊ Chicago ◊ Palm Beach

Published in the United States of America by
Histria Books
7181 N. Hualapai Way, Ste. 130-86
Las Vegas, NV 89166 USA
HistriaBooks.com

Histria Fiction is an imprint of Histria Books. Titles published under the imprints of Histria Books are distributed worldwide. We appreciate your support of copyright by purchasing an authorized edition of this book and for respecting intellectual property laws by not reproducing, scanning, or otherwise distributing any part of it by any means without permission. You are supporting authors and enabling Histria Books to continue publishing books for everyone.

All rights reserved. No part of this book may be reprinted or reproduced or utilized in any form or by any electronic, mechanical or other means, now known or hereafter invented, including photocopying and recording, or in any information storage or retrieval system, without the permission in writing from the Publisher. No part of this book may be used or reproduced in any manner for the purpose of training artificial intelligence technologies or systems.

Certain characters in this work are historical figures, and certain events portrayed did take place. However, this is a work of fiction. Names, characters, places, and incidents are either the product of the author's imagination or are used fictitiously. Any resemblance to actual persons, living or dead, is entirely coincidental.

First Edition

Library of Congress Control Number: 2025930518

ISBN 978-1-59211-606-5 (softbound)
ISBN 978-1-59211-607-2 (eBook)

Copyright © 2025 by José Sotolongo

> "Hope" is the thing with feathers—
> That perches in the soul—
> And sings the tune without the words—
> And never stops—at all—
>
> — Emily Dickinson

> Accept the things to which fate binds you, and love the people with whom fate brings you together, but do so with all your heart.
>
> —Marcus Aurelius, *Meditations*

1

1956

An ominous, laden Caribbean air gathered over the university as the students assembled on the steps to protest. The Romanesque arches over the portico blurred in the humidity, as if they too wanted to hide. Fernando felt an immobilizing fear that moistened the hair in his armpits and his groin, something akin to paralysis but more toxic, like venom in his veins.

The brume engulfed the architecturally mixed neighborhood surrounding the university, typical for the city. Many stately homes had fine, elaborate masonry, and yet some blocks were nothing but collapsing hovels with tin roofs. Fernando watched as dozens of students arrived and began milling around in groups, overflowing the sidewalk of the wide boulevard. Some of the students sat on the grand marble steps that led up to the university's front terrace. A few of them carried signs they weren't holding up yet, waiting for the protest to start in earnest. There was no laughter among them today, the hum of their voices subdued and tense. The traffic nearby was the dominant sound, with the horns and sputtering buses.

Like most of the demonstrators, Fernando was in the school of law, where the ideals of democracy had lit the most fuses in the student body. And they all had one thing in common: they wanted democracy, which meant free elections, an uncensored press, and an honest government that didn't extort businesses, no matter how small, for the right to operate. There were students who had a defined ideology, such as socialism or communism. But most of them, like Fernando, just wanted the dictatorship gone.

He moved away from the crowd and stood aside on the fringe, watching, worried about what was coming and trying to remain inconspicuous. Still, he knew he stood out. He was taller than most of the people around him, and his wavy light brown hair, always shiny, was more so today because of the oily sweat pouring out of his scalp. His beige linen shirt was soaked and stuck to his chest and back. But he stayed.

There was going to be blood again today. He could see it coming. There had been a few protests over the past year, but they were becoming more frequent, and the police were responding with more violence than before. And the crowd's agitation was growing, the crescendo of the pitch and cadence of their voices signaling a readiness for conflict.

Green military buses arrived. Havana municipal police, heavily armed, began to pour out of them, and fast behind them came trucks with military personnel wielding rifles and clubs. Some of the soldiers carried tear gas guns. Power sprouted from coercion, not consensus, in this country, and the armed forces were at the direct and immediate service of the president. Fernando had seen a less menacing version of this before—students being controlled by a handful of police or a dozen army soldiers. It had been going on like this for three years, since 1953. But this was frightening him; the number of armed forces like nothing he had seen. The government's suppression of the students had become more ruthless and bloody, even lethal, with each passing month.

Fernando moved away from the crowd because he didn't want to get hurt. There was too much to do that required his well-being, his physical strength, and his ability to come and go. He didn't want to risk his health or his life in a violent demonstration that he saw as short-sighted, a gesture that would result in nothing of lasting consequence.

Fernando knew that trying to overthrow the government placed him at risk for torture or even death. Still, in his mind, achieving a just society took precedence over his individual safety, and overthrowing this dictatorship was the only way. All his life, he had seen people all around him in dire poverty. The children he had played with in the park were often barefoot, their naked chests nothing but ribs covered by parchment-like skin, their eye sockets hollow. He had asked his mother why some of his friends looked as if they were sick, why they begged him for food. "Some people are poor," is all she had said. The unfairness of it nagged him, the suffering of the playmates who had been so important to him.

Especially Gustavo. He and Fernando were the same age, ten years old, when they met in the park. Gustavo taught him how to wield a baseball bat correctly, what to watch for when the ball was pitched. "You have to eat more beans," he said when Fernando had trouble swinging the bat with enough force. Gustavo's skinny brown arms were sinewy and powerful. "This country has many good things," he said, "but especially baseball players. So you just have to practice, because you have to be good." Fernando remembered Gustavo holding his bony shoulders back and pushing his bare chest out in an exaggerated display of pride. "We're Cubans," he said. "We're always good at what we do."

It was the first time Fernando had thought of himself as belonging to a specific nationality, and he absorbed the concept as an integral part of who he was.

And now, standing in front of the university, he saw Gustavo carrying the shopping bag. Few students in the school of law had skin as dark as Gustavo's, and he was easy to spot walking toward the crowd. Fernando waved and hurried to him, away from the throng of students that now numbered over a hundred.

"Everything good?" Fernando asked.

"It's all there," Gustavo said. "Fifty copies."

Fernando didn't look at the bag. Gustavo put it down on the sidewalk as planned.

"Are you staying for this?" Fernando asked, indicating the demonstration with a swing of his head.

"Of course. I have to. That's why I wanted to meet you here."

"Okay." Fernando picked up the shopping bag. "Be careful," he said, and saw his friend join the other protesters.

Fernando crossed the wide avenue, away from the university steps and the crowd of fellow students. Passersby slowed their steps just enough to look at the assembling protest. They had seen it before, or certainly would have read about it in the paper, or heard of it from their neighbors. The pedestrians on the sidewalk were well-dressed, the women in tailored outfits with subtle prints, the men, some with fine fedoras, in pleated trousers and ironed shirts. The economy might not be what it had been once, but there were still people who could and did adhere to a certain style.

Standing across the street from the university and the growing crowd of students, he saw Gustavo carrying a sign someone had given him that said "Down With the Dictatorship." Fernando Leal didn't want Gustavo to see him watching, holding the shopping bag like a timid old lady, not taking part in the mounting uprising, and he turned and walked down the avenue.

2

The walls of the dining room were a pale yellow, like a faded lemon, and the table and chairs were laminated in brown and chartreuse. Luis sat reading the newspaper, his cup of café con leche nearby. He held a slab of lard bread slathered in butter that he ate without looking away from the paper.

"Where's your brother?" his mother Elena asked, just in from the bedroom down the hall. She was already in a housedress, ready for morning chores.

"I don't know. He left before I got up." It was nine o'clock.

"Why does he have to leave the house so early every Saturday?"

Luis looked up from the paper and shrugged. His thick sienna hair was still a tangle from bed. "Have you asked him?" he said.

"Of course, but Fernando doesn't like to talk about where he goes," she said, and left the room.

After he finished breakfast, Luis left the scattered newspaper next to the cup and went to get dressed.

From the kitchen, Ines heard Señor Luis leaving the dining room, and she went in to tidy up. She folded the newspaper carefully. The tall black letters on the front page meant nothing to her almond-shaped black eyes. She could read only if she sounded out each word, which took time, and she had things to do: go to the market, make lunch, do a load of laundry. It was the laundry that took the most time, the hardest part of her day. She had to heat the water on the stove because there was no hot water in the kitchen, only in the bathrooms. Then she had to fill the outside slop sink with it, add the detergent, all the laundry, and rub the clothes against the washboard. Her hands were raw at the end, but still she wrung everything out, one garment at a time. Ines was only fifteen, short and wiry, but she was already strong, her forearms sinewy. Doing the laundry was tedious and exhausting, but it was one of the chores she was paid to do.

Ines took the newspaper and Señor Luis's cup into the kitchen. She brought her nose close to the rim, smelled the drying coffee and the souring milk, and tried to find where the young man's lips had touched. There was no trace of the brownish beverage he had sipped on the edge of the cup. She resisted the urge to put her lips on the rim.

She made her way to the neighborhood bodega, where she could get the thin steaks she would sauté for lunch and the chicken she would stew for dinner. There was always plenty of rice and all kinds of dried beans in the kitchen, but she needed to buy garlic and onions. As she waited her turn at the counter, she saw several people reading the newspaper. She wondered why so many people, including Señor Luis and the rest of the household, were so interested in reading the news every day. What was so important in those written words? She felt left out, as if she were missing a part of the world that so many people paid attention to.

Working on her parents' tiny farm just outside Havana had replaced school when she had turned ten. Rows of coffee, mangoes, and tamarind had to be tended, and the pigs and chickens needed to be fed, their waste scooped out of their pens so they wouldn't sicken and die.

There had been three older brothers, two of them now dead from illness, she didn't know what. A fever, a rash, and they were gone. There was no doctor they could afford to see, and even the local *curandero* in their neighborhood charged something. Her parents couldn't afford to part with the chicken the man demanded, and prayed for the health of one son first, then the other a month later. The third son, Ernesto, the youngest of the three boys, had a fever but survived, and then left to live in Havana at the age of sixteen. He had not been in touch with the family since two years ago, around the same time Ines started working houses in Havana.

Ines cut the chicken up into quarters, chopped the garlic the way her mother had taught her, the way she had done already, even at this young age, hundreds of times back home while her mother worked the fields. She cut the lime, squeezed the juice over the chicken, and added the salt, garlic, cumin seeds she had toasted and ground into powder. Her mother had taught her all the tools she used to make a living now, and she would make sure this family would keep her and not tell her *go away, you're no good, go back to Bauta*. Her mother's brusque manner didn't seem so bad now, no longer a source of resentment. It had made her absorb useful knowledge.

Ines went into the living room. "Señora, I'm leaving," she said to her employer.

It was six o'clock. Ines would wait for the bus two blocks away, then change buses and be in her village in an hour.

"The beans just need to be warmed and the chicken has another half hour on the stove," Ines said.

Señora Elena looked up from the magazine and laid it on her lap. Ines noticed she had changed into one of her old pastel housedresses, a blue one today. The lipstick she had put on that morning had faded. "And the rice?"

"It's ready. It's still warm."

"Until tomorrow, then," the woman said, and resumed her reading.

"Tomorrow is Sunday, Señora."

"Ah," her employer said with a quick nod. "Until Monday, then."

At seven, Elena went to the kitchen and turned on the burner under the pot of beans. Ines had already set the table. She went back to the living room to read until the beans were warm, then called out "The food is ready" to her husband and two sons, as she did every evening, and brought the loaded plates out from the kitchen. "I wish the house was big enough for a live-in maid," she said out loud, even though she was alone.

3

Antonio was forty-three, four years younger than Elena. They had been married twenty-two years, but he still dressed and undressed in private in their bathroom. He never failed to comb his hair and change his shirt for dinner. Elena walked into their bedroom just as he was starting to button his shirt, and he turned around so she wouldn't see his chest.

"You will never learn to knock," he said.

"Oh, Antonio, please." She paused. "You have to talk to Fernando. He disappears early Saturday mornings before anyone is up. He's looking nervous about something, and he doesn't talk about where he goes or what he does. And he comes home late from the university several times a week. Something's going on with him and I'm worried."

"I hope he's not getting involved with these student groups we read about in the papers," Antonio said, raising his voice as if Elena were to blame. "I have friends whose sons and daughters disappear for two or three days and they come back with horrible injuries from torture."

"That's exactly what I'm worried about." She paused. "What a terrible country this is," she said, and she sounded dejected.

Just down the hall, Luis walked into Fernando's bedroom. He sat on the bed, which was covered carelessly with a blue chenille bedspread. Fernando was putting away clean laundry that Ines had folded and left on his bed.

"Mom's been asking where you go on Saturdays," Luis said.

Fernando didn't look at his brother. "She's asked me too."

"And what did you tell her?"

Fernando closed the underwear drawer. "To a study group."

"She doesn't believe you."

Fernando shrugged and nodded and said, "Well, I guess you're right because she insisted that I tell her the truth."

Luis stood up. "So what's the truth?"

Fernando shrugged again. He didn't want to lie to his older brother, but he saw no reason to worry him. "It has to do with school."

"But it's not study."

"No." Fernando paused and looked at his brother. It was more than just a glance, and then he added, "It's almost time for dinner. I want to go wash up." He started to walk out.

"You need to be careful. Mom shouldn't have to be worried about us at our age."

"I can't help that. I have to do what's important. What I do has nothing to do with drugs or anything illegal."

"So what is it?" Luis said.

"It's better if I don't tell you." Fernando went out to the bathroom.

Antonio was already seated when Luis entered the dining room. "Where's your brother?" he asked. Elena was bringing plates of food from the kitchen.

"He's washing up for dinner," Luis said.

"He's like a ghost," Antonio said. "He disappears on Saturdays and no one knows where he goes. What's going on?" His fists were clenched and he sounded angry, as if it were Luis's fault.

"I don't know, *Papá*," Luis said.

"How can you not know?" Antonio's voice rose. "He's your younger brother."

"He doesn't tell me."

"He's full of mystery," Elena said, and sat down just as Fernando came in. He sat at the opposite end of where the family had clustered at the long table for six. Antonio glowered at him from the head of the table.

"You and I have to talk," Antonio said to Fernando.

Fernando nodded and remained silent as the others started commenting on the food. The three men had remarked often on what a good cook Ines was, despite her youth.

"The chicken is especially delicious today," Antonio said a few minutes later, his annoyance at Fernando apparently forgotten. "I wonder how she made it."

"It's my recipe," Elena said. "It's marinated in cumin, garlic, and lime juice. I taught her how to make it."

As they finished their dinner, Antonio turned to Fernando. "Let's you and I go out to the porch for our talk," he said.

"I'm going to the movies with Gustavo."

"This is important. You can go to the movies tomorrow."

"How old is Ines?" Luis asked his mother, seemingly oblivious to the conversation.

"Fifteen," Elena said. "She's just a girl."

Fernando looked at Luis, who was smirking at him. Fernando didn't return the smile. He knew what that smile meant, and he didn't approve.

As they got up from the table, Antonio said to Fernando, "Come with me."

The young man considered standing his ground, going to meet Gustavo despite his father's demand. He was nineteen, after all, old enough to be treated like an adult. But he knew that Antonio had been brought up in a traditional Spanish household where respect for your parents overruled everything else, and the man expected nothing less from his family.

It was not a large house. There were three bedrooms, two bathrooms, an open dining room, and a modest living room. A small kitchen was in the rear, with a door to the backyard. There weren't too many options for privacy for their discussion, except the cramped bedrooms or the living room, where Elena would be watching TV.

On the porch were two metal rocking chairs and a small table. Antonio took the green chair and pointed to the red one, but Fernando stood, with his hands in his pockets.

"What are you involved in?" Antonio asked.

"What do you mean?"

"Don't play games with me." Antonio kept his voice low, but there was a tone of anger.

Fernando hesitated, then said, "On Saturday mornings I meet other students. We talk."

"You meet just to talk? Talk about what? What's the discussion about?"

"Things that are going on."

Antonio looked away as if he had gotten all the information he needed. He stood up and tilted his head up to address Fernando. "Just remember you're only nineteen, but the police and their gangsters don't care how old you are. You and your friends, whatever you're up to, can be jailed, tortured, or killed. You know that's happening, right?"

Fernando looked over his father's shoulder and nodded. The man was standing too close to look directly into his eyes, a confrontation. And his father had a point. Several students had been found in ditches in Havana the past few months, shot through the head. Those had been the lucky ones, Fernando thought. The tortured ones were permanently disfigured. He suppressed the fear elicited by his father's words.

"You have two more years of university. Don't ruin your future," Antonio said, less authoritarian, more counseling. He didn't go back in the house, as if he wasn't done with this exchange, and instead looked out at the darkness over the tiny garden just visible from the light on the porch.

"What's wrong with our country?" Fernando said. His father had not made himself available for a private conversation very often. In fact, he couldn't remember the last one, and he wanted to prolong this one. "Why do we go from one dictatorship to another?" He knew the nation's history, but he really didn't know the root cause of decades of authoritarian governance.

"It's a long story. It's a leftover from Spanish rule. Once we were no longer a colony, we weren't prepared for independence. It's always been chaotic." Antonio's voice had not risen, but it had a sharp edge of outrage. "There was no Constitution, no guidelines. By the time the Constitution was written, cheating and stealing was the way things were done."

"Like an undisciplined child who becomes a disaster as an adult," Fernando said.

"Worse," Antonio said. "At least that adult can still be a good citizen. This country is hopeless."

"No, *Papá*, I don't think it's hopeless. We have so many riches here."

"Of course," Antonio said. "The Spanish saw that too when they first discovered the island. They went back to Spain and described the fertile land, the beauty of the rivers and the mountains, and that's all it took for the Spanish to turn it into one of their colonies. Pure exploitation. They didn't care enough about us, their own descendants, to guide us into democracy."

The Optimistic Cuban

After his father went inside, Fernando stayed and sat in the dim yellow light of the porch. The conversation had left him dejected, but he wasn't out of hope. The land was so abundant in natural resources and the people were clever, spirited. He was convinced that Cuba could be one of the best countries on the planet if only an honest government were in place with leaders who would honor democratic rule.

4

Fernando called Gustavo to let him know he had not left on time and would not be going to the movies. He decided to go into his room to read, maybe study. He had exams coming up in one week on the Constitution. He touched the cover of the book. Constitutional law. A theory in books only, not practiced.

Fernando closed the textbook. He went over what his father had said, that a newly independent country without accountable politicians would descend into a race for wealth and power. But after sixty-two years of independence, not only had there been no progress, Batista was the worst president ever. Had things ever been this bad?

Corruption had tattered the economy, and people like his brother Luis graduating from university had little luck finding employment. With a few months to go before receiving his degree in finance, Luis had no job prospects. And most of Fernando's friends who already had law degrees were unemployed. Forty percent of university graduates couldn't find work.

Out of frustration, he had channeled his energies into anti-government activities. When Gustavo mentioned the student movement in passing, Fernando had asked him about it. Gustavo demurred at first, then admitted he was involved. But he still tried to dissuade Fernando.

"You know what they did to Nico?" Gustavo had said three months ago, trying to discourage him, when Fernando first asked. "Just because he recruited students from the school of business? They threw him in jail for three days. When he came out, he had cigarette burns on his balls, a broken leg, and part of his ear was missing. They just sliced it off."

Fernando had recoiled, but his mind was set. He couldn't stand by while his brother, closer than he was to graduating, complained there were no jobs, sometimes with a break of misery in his voice that startled him because it was so atypical of his driven, self-confident personality. Being involved would at least give Fernando hope. Some students planned to leave the country right after graduation—Spain, the United States, Mexico. But he couldn't give up on his country so easily.

He loved the landscapes, the music, the positive outlook of the people. It was what he knew, where he belonged. He had understood that since age ten.

"I don't care about the risks. Let me be part of it," he told Gustavo that day. And now he was.

5

The gray light of dawn squeezed in between the window frames and the ragged pieces of burlap her mother used as curtains. Ines could hear her father snoring just a few feet away. In the shadows she could see her mother standing at the table, noiselessly putting coffee in a tin strainer. It was Sunday, a day off from her job in the Leal household, but not a day of rest. Soon it would be time to feed the chickens and the pigs. The threads from the frayed sheet covering her thin body tickled her cheeks and nose. When her mother went outside to start the fire, Ines got up and pulled on a faded but clean dress she had found in the garbage in Havana. She went to the icebox and poured herself a glass of milk.

"You didn't need to get up so early," her mother said as she stoked the charcoal. Ines knew her mother was about the same age as Señora Elena, but she looked as if she could be her employer's mother, the skin of her face brown and cracked from the sun, hair stringy and gray. Señora Elena's cheeks were smooth and her hair was always a shiny mahogany.

"I have to feed the animals before I go to the field," Ines said.

On her way to the rows of coffee plantings, she saw scattered pages from a newspaper on the pebbled path. Despite the dirt, she could see photographs of well-dressed men on the front page, one with his finger up in the air as if he was saying something important. She didn't know who the leaders were in the government. Her father spoke of the thieves in the presidential palace, but she didn't understand what he meant. Ines picked up the newspaper and put it under a rock so it wouldn't blow away while she hoed the weeds between the rows. She would try to read it later, when she was done with work.

At one o'clock it was time for the main meal, and on her way back to the house Ines picked up the old newspaper. She washed her dusty arms at the well's spigot and saw her father riding his horse home from the sugarcane fields. She patted the horse's neck, the rough white hair familiar and comforting, and the animal nuzzled her shoulder. The horse's show of affection made her smile deep inside her chest, although her face remained expressionless.

Ines sat with her parents at the table inside. Her mother pulled back the makeshift curtains on the four windows, one in each wall, so the light could come in. The one light bulb hanging overhead was used only when absolutely necessary, after sunset. They shared a quarter capon that her mother had wrapped in banana leaves and roasted outside over charcoals. The capon was tough, cheaper than a young chicken, but it was flavorful with garlic and the bitter oranges that grew wild near the house.

In the afternoon, they rested outdoors near the cooking pit, sat on their found chairs. Ines's father played the guitar as her mother mended one of his torn shirts and listened to the radio tucked on a windowsill. Ines took the newspaper she had saved from the field and brushed off as much of the dirt as possible. She sounded out the headlines. *The President Promises Order*. Order for what, she wondered. She recognized the word "students" at the beginning of the article but didn't read the rest of the sentence. She wished Señor Luis could read the article to her. Maybe one day she would ask him to explain what was in the paper that he found so interesting. After a few minutes, Ines went inside to comb her hair. Then she changed into a clean dress to get ready for the man who was coming from a nearby neighborhood, the man she was supposed to marry.

6

Six o'clock. Fernando turned off the alarm. The sun was already bright and hot through the window. He turned the overhead fan off and got dressed. The shopping bag of newsletters that Gustavo had given him yesterday was hidden behind his hanging shirts in the closet, and he took it with him into the dim kitchen. It was Sunday and the family was still asleep.

He made coffee quietly and warmed up some milk, drank the café con leche quickly, and rinsed the cup so it would be easier for his mother to wash when she arose in an hour.

The bag held the mimeographed sheets Gustavo had picked up from Enrique, the student in their political group who worked in the law department and had access to the office after hours. Fernando, Gustavo, and three others wrote the newsletter every Wednesday afternoon, and Enrique ran the sheets on the mimeograph when he worked alone on Friday evenings. But it was Gustavo who picked up the copies from the faculty office and got them to the other students on Saturday mornings. This week it was Fernando's turn. Enrique ran the mimeograph, but he was terrified of being caught with subversive, anti-government material that detailed the torture of students, the abysmal corruption, the unemployment rate of the graduates.

Fernando's first stop was the nearest bodega, which was several blocks away and would still be closed. He left twenty or so copies on the store's dominoes table, weighed down with a rock. His next stop was a church, and he entered after the last of the six o'clock worshippers had left and before seven o'clock Mass. He scanned the nave to make sure he was alone and placed a pile of the flyers by the offerings box in front of a large crucifix. Next was a pharmacy that he knew would be open at this early hour, the "on-call" druggist for Saturday night and Sunday. He left the papers on a shelf among the hangover remedies, out of sight of the pharmacist behind the counter.

The locations varied and only repeated after five or six weeks, but in no particular pattern to avoid detection. The dance with any potential government observers had been choreographed by Gustavo, with input from Sonya, Maribel, and

Cristina. The three young women delivered the flyers most weeks, Fernando once a month. It was easier for the women because they would be less suspect of taking part in political acts and could carry the newsletters in purses or shoulder bags. Of course, Enrique wanted nothing to do with the distribution, and Gustavo was Black. "They'll shoot me if they see me carrying a shopping bag in a white neighborhood," he had said, attempting to make light of it. They all tried to laugh, but it was true and frightening, and all they could do was look at him and shake their heads.

Fernando was intrigued by Maribel. She was an avowed communist, seemed to always be on edge, brusque and to the point, and showed no pleasure in the camaraderie of their meetings. The others joked with each other, perhaps to relieve the tension of what they were doing, but Maribel was impatient, almost angry when the rest of them bantered. Her huge black eyes reflected a mysterious light, a flash when she interrupted their small talk. The fine down on her arms was as intriguing to Fernando as the cascade of black hair that fell on her shoulders. He wanted to run his fingers from her wrists to her elbows.

They all knew each other's schedules at the university to make communication easier in case it was necessary. The prior month, Fernando had waited near Maribel's classroom at the end of a period. He wanted to ask her out but didn't want that to enter into the political meetings of the group. When she came out into the hallway, she saw him but didn't acknowledge him, as if she had never laid eyes on him before. Still, Fernando caught up with her as she made her way out of the building.

"What do you want?" she hissed, her eyes glinting, when they were on the side terrace, near the steps that went down to the courtyard.

Fernando hadn't expected this hostile reaction. "I just wanted to talk to you," he said.

"Not here," she said and turned her back, then strode away briskly, almost at a run.

He watched as she went down the steps to the courtyard, where students on break congregated in small groups around the fountain. The dress she wore that day was loose, but Fernando remembered the well-rounded hips that stretched the fabric of the snug skirts she wore sometimes. He watched as she joined two female students sitting on the edge of the fountain. The three women talked, laughed, gestured. He had never seen Maribel so relaxed, had never even seen her smile.

More than anything, he wanted her to be that way with him. He went down the stairs and sat at the opposite edge of the fountain, where he could watch her pretend she hadn't seen him.

7

Perfect. His mother was out for the afternoon, playing canasta or something, his father at work, and Fernando in school. Luis had the house to himself, except for Ines, busy wringing and hanging laundry out back. He had another class at the university, but it wasn't for another two hours.

Luis waited until he heard Ines back in the kitchen, and he went in.

"Is there anything you want?" Ines said. She was peeling potatoes for dinner.

Luis said nothing, but he smiled and got closer. He could see a spark of alarm in her widening eyes, the dilated pupils, but he had seen her looking at him when she thought he wasn't aware. He brushed his fingertips on her arm from elbow to shoulder. Luis heard her gasp as the paring knife stopped in midair, and she turned her head so he wouldn't see her face. He expected resistance, at least at first, but he wasn't discouraged. He got closer and pressed his groin to her hip bone, wrapping his hand around her narrow, still child-like waist. Ines let out a moan that to Luis sounded like fear, but he hoped that if he persisted she would give in. He had been thinking about doing this for weeks.

The previous two girls his mother had hired had seemed too self-confident for him to approach. Luis suspected they were already sexually experienced, and he wanted no part of that. He needed to explore and get initiated with someone like Ines, who was, if not a virgin, then shy and probably not as skilled in lovemaking as the other girls had been. If he was clumsy, he was sure Ines wouldn't make fun of him, if she even noticed. And Ines was pretty. Her slanted black eyes, rounded pink cheeks, and curvy lips reminded him of the dolls he had seen in shop windows in the Chinese neighborhood. He vaguely wondered whether she had any indigenous blood, although he knew that was rare, the native population of the island had been largely wiped out by the early Spanish settlers.

Luis pushed his groin in harder and held her waist with both hands, even though he wasn't aroused. He was just going through the motions. Ines turned away and pulled his hands off.

"I'll win eventually. You'll see," he said, and left. By the time he got to the porch, he had forgotten about Ines.

Luis would be seeing his girlfriend Anita tonight, after dinner. But of course the date would be limited to sitting on her porch while her mother lurked just inside in the living room, listening to everything through the open window. She was a sentinel who would snap to attention if the conversation stopped for too long, suggesting kissing or straying hands. Luis hated the old woman, but Anita was worth the unpleasantness of dealing with her parents. He thought that Anita's looks, with her hazel eyes and smooth pink skin, were marvelous. She was the image of the wife he thought he should have one day. At nineteen, she was two years younger than him, and she wasn't allowed out on dates without a chaperone. Her younger sister Conchita was a clinging presence when the three of them went to the movies or a dance.

Luis had felt Anita pressing her breasts against him once at a party while they danced in dim light. He was taken by surprise at her daring move and did not nuzzle her neck, as many other men were doing to their dates on the dance floor. Conchita had been sitting on the sidelines and evidently did not see Anita's clinging embrace or her flushed cheeks, because she made no chiding comments afterwards in her high-pitched nasal voice.

They weren't engaged yet. Luis had spoken to Anita's father once, a few months ago, about his intention to marry her. She was the only girlfriend he had ever had, and he thought that once he turned twenty-one it would be time to start thinking about being married. "Do you have a job arranged for when you finish university in May?" the man had said. He was much older than Luis's parents and looked at the young man through bushy eyebrows.

"No," Luis said. "I've been looking, but I haven't found anything."

The man shook his jowly head. "Why are you asking for her hand, then? What are you going to live on?" And then he added with a derisive chuckle, "Are you going to live with your parents after you get married?"

"No." Luis's voice had shrunk.

Another shake of the jowls, silent this time.

Some of the students in the university's business school had succeeded in at least making a promising connection with a company, an industry. The lucky ones found an American employer. But fewer and fewer opportunities were becoming available each year, even here in Havana. In six months he'd have his diploma, and it would be worthless.

Luis and Fernando had talked about this. What was their future? Their father, Antonio, would be of no help in the business world. He worked as an agent in a shipping company that had lost much of its business to competitors willing to pay bribes to officials who controlled the transport permits.

"What are you going to do when you graduate?" Fernando had asked his brother recently. Luis had not been able to get an appointment for an interview at a bank or any other commercial firm.

"I have no idea," Luis said. "Maybe you'll have better luck next year, when it's your turn."

But Fernando shook his head. "Nobody graduating this year from the school of law has a job," he said. "I just don't know what we're supposed to do with our future."

8

It happened in early November, right after All Saints' Day. Seven months before Luis's graduating class of 1957 was to receive their essentially useless diplomas, a peaceful protest was organized by Rogelio, the president of the student council. This would be followed by a week-long student strike. Gustavo was a member of the council, and he alerted Fernando, Maribel, and the rest of the group. "Tomorrow will be the last day of class for a week," he warned. "Rogelio will make the announcement in the afternoon, in front of the school of law," he said on Wednesday during their weekly meeting.

"But we should still do the flyers this week," Cristina said, almost a question.

"Of course," Maribel said. "The people need to be informed."

"Try to be there at the rally tomorrow afternoon, four o'clock," Gustavo said. "I'll be by Rogelio's side." His onyx skin glistened with the slick of worry. He had friends who had been tortured by the police and had seen the after-effects: thumbs amputated, eyes blinded by acid, permanent scars from cigarette burns disfiguring young women's cheeks. He always recounted the torture in quick snippets, as if that would lessen his horror. "They don't like to kill us," Gustavo said with a forced chuckle. "They want us to be living warnings to the rest of the students."

Had it been raining that Thursday afternoon, there might have been less chaos. But the gray sky was flat and indifferent, with no engorged clouds in sight. Fernando stood on the plaza at the bottom of the steps. He could see Gustavo clearly on the terrace at the top. He had seen Cristina on his way here from his last class, but no one else from the group.

Fernando would have felt safer standing close to the rest of his collaborators, as if they could shield one another, although he knew that was absurd. Being near his group would be no protection against an attack by the government. And he reminded himself that being together was impossible. It had been decided at the outset that they would not socialize or even speak outside of their Wednesday meetings. His attempt at approaching Maribel between classes and her quick rejection had been a sharp reminder. And yet more than anything now he wanted her at his side to protect her if things got dangerous, although he didn't think she was the type to look for or even accept protection.

It was nearly four o'clock and the crowd grew, not in clusters of socialization but in a restless, scattered congress attentive to the terrace at the top of the white marble steps. He saw Gustavo talking to Rogelio, easy to identify because of his unruly mass of curly brown hair. Even from this distance, Fernando could see Gustavo's dark forehead glistening with sweat. Somebody handed Gustavo a megaphone, and he passed it to Rogelio. It looked to Fernando as if the megaphone had been shaking in his friend's hand.

Nothing was happening. Fernando looked around for a familiar face, a law school classmate, a friend, but the crowd had thickened with students from other faculties. The heat in the crowd, although it was November, was suffocating, and he could feel his chest dripping. In a crowd this size and this dense, an onslaught from the police and army would turn into a crushing stampede.

Rogelio turned on the megaphone. "Good afternoon," he said. And then he began the litany. *No free elections. No job prospects. No political freedom. Torture and assassination of students. Corruption.* A few minutes of this and then he stopped, looked left, to Fernando's right. Rogelio's mouth dangled open in disbelief. Fernando heard gunfire and screams, and the multitude began to churn and move with overwhelming force away from where Rogelio's eyes were riveted.

9

From the terrace, standing next to Rogelio, Gustavo watched as army buses blocked the wide avenue and all traffic stopped. Soldiers and military police poured out of the armored vehicles wielding pistols, machine guns, and clubs.

Gustavo watched, paralyzed with fear, mouth agape. Rifle butts cracked craniums, tear gas canisters flew, swinging clubs broke ribs, gunfire felled young bodies. Some of the students fled, shoving and trampling, and some wrestled with the police. Gustavo stood behind one of the marble columns and stuck his head out every few seconds to monitor the melee. He wanted to keep an eye on the troops in case they started up the stairs to the terrace, where he stood along with the rest of the student council. His face faded to gray when he saw the mass of green uniforms start to climb the steps. "Let's go," he heard Rogelio say, but he was already through the doors as the group scrambled into the building. They ran down the stairwell to the ground level, where back doors led outside to the faculty parking lot. As they ran down the marble steps, Gustavo could hear the stomps of booted feet in the great hall above, just inside the terrace. The group of students cannonballed down the last flight and through the back doors. Once they reached the parking lot, they dispersed without a word.

Gustavo's heart pounded into his neck and ears. He ran as fast as he could down the unremarkable narrow avenue that abutted the rear of the huge university building. The thought of his mother having to nurse any wounds he might sustain, or worse, bury his corpse, made the panic flow through his veins and fueled the muscles of his legs. He flew down the avenue and slowed down only when he could no longer hear the gunfire and explosions of tear gas. Gustavo hoped his friends at the demonstration, especially Fernando, had escaped the mayhem unhurt. Fernando meant the world to him. He was the one white friend Gustavo had who went to his house and liked to spend time with him outside of their political activities. They went to the movies, the beach, parties. *God protect him*, Gustavo prayed.

10

On the university's plaza, at the bottom of the marble steps, a sudden violent push from the multitude toppled Fernando. His hand was crushed by the stampede, but he scrambled upright and staggered away from the teargas and the screams and the gunshots.

He held his throbbing hand up against his chest and managed to stumble to a bus stop two blocks away. His shirt was torn, the buttons missing, and his hand was purple and bleeding. There was a tear at the knee of his white trousers, filthy with dirt and blood, maybe his own, because his leg was hurting. When the bus finally came it was crowded, but he managed to climb on. The other passengers murmured and chittered and made way for him. One elderly woman, wearing a white hat and a blue paisley dress, stood up and said, "Sit down. What happened to you?" Fernando just shook his head. The kindness, the humiliation. He thought he might cry if he tried to speak. He sat and rested his forehead on the back of the seat in front of him.

When he got home, only Ines was in the house, and more than anything he wanted her to help him, but he was still dazed and didn't even know what to ask for. He went into the kitchen to rinse his bloodied hand in the sink, and Ines gasped. "But what happened to you?" she said. He had never heard her raise her voice above a murmur. She cleaned the torn skin gently and quickly with peroxide, bandaged it with a clean towel, and made him sit in the living room while she made him a café con leche.

He heard his mother's car pulling into the driveway, tried to get up to go to his room and avoid questions and an emotional scene, but he was still shaking and his legs wouldn't cooperate. Elena's mouth dropped open when she saw the bandaged hand and the torn, bloodied clothes. When she asked what had happened, her voice a squawk, all he said was that a demonstration at school had turned violent and that he wanted to go to bed. He tried to stand but couldn't. Elena put her arm around him, hoisted him up to his feet, and helped him to his bedroom.

Gustavo called him in the afternoon, wanting to know how he was. "The government has closed down the university until further notice," he said. "So just lay low for now."

11

1957

The government kept the university permanently closed following the demonstration in November, and neither brother had the prospect of getting a degree anytime soon. On that day, while Fernando's hand was being crushed and fractured in three places, Luis had been in the university library, where he could hear the gunfire. That morning, news of that a demonstration had spread, a call to action to insist on government reforms. But Luis had midterms in the school of business and he had work to do. He would ignore the demonstration, because he didn't think that student rebellions would have any real impact, and his own future came first. Still, at the sound of gunshots he went to a side window from where he could see the military trucks grouped near the university building and the teargas smoke, but not the throngs and the violence. He considered going to the front of the school, where he'd be able to see the crowd and look for Fernando in case he had been part of it, but he wasn't going to risk it. Luis did suspect that Fernando's evasiveness about his activities might mean that he was involved, but he really didn't know for sure. He gathered his books, went down the back stairs, and exited through one of the rear doors just seconds before Gustavo and the rest of the student council did the same.

"Why were you in the middle of it?" Luis asked his brother the next day. Fernando's hand was in a cast.

"It was important. It's our future. Yours too."

"It wasn't going to accomplish anything. And your hand has been turned into hamburger meat for nothing."

"It's not for nothing," Fernando said.

Luis shook his head and tucked in his chin. "My little brother," he said, putting his hand on Fernando's shoulder. "You need to learn to take care of yourself. You come first. Remember that."

Out of school now, all these months later, Fernando was bored, uneasy with what he saw as sloth, and he wanted to work. Other students with financial means had resumed their studies in Spain, or in Mexico, but he had no interest in going to another country, did not want to live in another culture. He felt a loyalty to the university in which he had begun his studies, the Universidad de la Habana, in his own city. It was where he belonged.

He went to law firms, but nobody was hiring, especially without a degree. He didn't want to drive a bus or be a sales clerk or deliver mail. Luis had gotten a job as a bank teller that hardly paid anything. He was overqualified for the position, but at least it was clean work.

"I'm thinking of leaving the country," Luis said one night at dinner.

Elena's fork stopped in midair. "To go where?" she said.

"To the North."

She put her fork down on the table with a snap and said, "You're crazy. You don't know what it's like there."

"This is your country. You'll never fit in anywhere else, not in the same way," Antonio said.

"This country is garbage," Luis said. He wanted to say more, but he knew better than to start an all-out argument at the dinner table. The outburst, he realized, would sour the atmosphere in the house for days.

Elena picked up her fork again, waved it at him, and said, "You'll be making a very serious mistake."

"But you love it there," Luis said. "You love going to Miami Beach."

"Going on vacation for a week is one thing," Antonio said. "It's a totally different thing to live there."

"It's a very materialistic place," Elena said. "They're very nice people, but everything is money, things. And their hygiene and morals aren't very good. They don't use bidets, and the women are very loose."

"That doesn't matter. I have no future here," Luis said, and looked at Fernando. "And what do you say? You think there's a future here?"

Fernando thought a moment. "I don't know, but I'm not ready to leave."

"That may be fine for you," Luis said, "but what about me? We're talking about me leaving. There's nothing for me here."

Elena shook her head. "What a thing to say. Your family doesn't count?"

Antonio wiped his mouth with his napkin and brought his fist down on the table with a thud. "I don't want to hear anything more about this," he said. "If you want to go, go."

There was silence until Fernando said, "At least you have the bank. I can't find anything." His voice was small, as if he didn't want anyone to hear. He immediately regretted saying anything, creating the suggestion that he was pursuing an argument, but the words had sprung from a dismal well of disappointment.

Luis didn't look up from his plate. "It's a crappy job," he said.

Afterwards, Fernando sat on the porch. He chose the red rocking chair, which was old and rickety. He left the new green one vacant in case Luis wanted to join him, smooth over the spat at the table. The light was dim, the February sun well below the horizon. He didn't want to turn the porch light on and attract insects. He'd have to go back in soon, before the mosquitoes found him and riddled him with welts.

He didn't want Luis to go. Of course the relationship was not symmetrical, Luis acting selfishly towards him as he did with everyone else, but Fernando loved him and trusted his judgment, and looked to him for guidance. Luis had the drive to succeed that he wished he had. With his male friends—Gustavo, Enrique, Rogelio—there was the political angle, and everything, every interaction, was colored by that overriding mission. They could not be used as comparisons for professional success. The same was true for Cristina and Sonya, more so because they were women, and there was the prevailing idea that they were not reliable mirrors of men's aspirations and dreams. And of course with Maribel it was much more complicated, because his attraction to her and the confounding feelings of rejection displaced any sense that she was only an academic peer.

He didn't have any other friends, really, just acquaintances from school whom he couldn't use to define himself, because most of them just wanted to get by, were not really dedicated to their professional futures. But Luis was determined to make something of himself, and Fernando wanted that same roadmap. He had consulted with Luis about the type of law to pursue, what career path to follow after graduation. "Constitutional law," his brother had said. "It's supposed to be the foundation of our country," he added with a snicker, and Fernando had followed his advice, hoping the country would actually live by that document one day. Antonio and Elena cared, but they were too focused on their own lives to give Fernando's doubts much consideration. "It's up to you," they would say when he asked their opinion. They just wanted him to follow the expected pathway: school, career, marriage, family. How he got there, the variations along the way, was not anything they could help him with.

12

Everywhere she went—the butcher, the bodega, the fisherman's stand—Ines saw people reading the paper, stopping to engage in loud discussions, pointing at the newsprint, heads snapping in argument. There had to be something important they were all talking about. Again and again she had tried to practice her reading, but it took too long and she didn't have time.

She straightened out the living room, emptied the blue glass ashtray Señora Elena liked to use in the afternoon while she read or watched TV. Afterwards, Ines would dust, then sweep before mopping the green ceramic tile floors. She would polish the windows after lunch.

Ines heard the bell of the vegetable vendor and looked out the window to make sure the horse-drawn cart had stopped. The customers, all women, came out of the nearby houses to gather around the wagon of produce.

Some of the women were like her, hired housekeepers who did everything that needed to be done in a home. Some, from the wealthier households, were dedicated cooks, and at the other end of the social spectrum were housewives without the means to hire anybody. There was a mix of large turreted mansions and modest stucco homes on this block.

Most of the women around the cart were dressed like Ines: faded cotton blouses, frayed skirts, rubber or leather sandals. But one of the women was always in a starched white uniform, spotless. Ines knew her name was Caridad because the other women gossiped about her when she wasn't among them. "Where's the grand lady?" they would snicker. They ridiculed her stout figure, resented her because she didn't chit-chat with the rest of them. Caridad stood aside and waited until it was her turn, then bought the produce without asking the price of anything, as the rest of the women had to do. Ines imagined Caridad knew how to read, and she knew that the woman didn't have to take a bus every day to the large two-story house that resembled a French château. She had her own room there, one of the other women had said. The rumor among the ladies was that Caridad even had her own assistant.

"What's your wish today, Señorita?" the vendor asked Ines. She didn't know his name. The other women had an easy familiarity with him, either because they had known him much longer or because sass and double entendre were the currency they used with men in general. But Ines had only seen him a dozen or so times. He had a heavily lined face and dull gray hair under a faded baseball cap.

Ines asked the price of the onions, potatoes, and malanga before she bought them. She asked for six eggs. The vendor wrote all the prices down on the paper bag with a stub of pencil sharpened roughly with a knife. Ines had trouble reading, but she knew numbers. They were easy for her. Señora Elena had given her one peso, and the total came to ninety-seven centavos. Señora Elena would check the produce and the figures on the paper bag later. "Give me the change in parsley," Ines said to the man, and he stuffed a bundle of bright green fronds in the bag.

Ines turned away from the vendor and saw Caridad waiting her turn, standing away from the group that clustered near the cart, as if getting too close to the other women might soil her pristine uniform. Ines looked at Caridad and smiled. The woman's strong square face, capped by tight brown curls, relaxed and allowed a small smile in return, and she dipped her head slightly in a subtle nod. Ines was too shy to speak, though she wanted to say something like "Good day." She wished her clothes weren't so shabby. In a remote part of her brain, she suspected that a connection with this woman might hold for her a better future than she was destined for. But how could she chat with Caridad looking the way she did, not being able to read or even speak properly?

13

Antonio didn't drive, had never learned. He had grown up in an old-fashioned household in the old district in Havana, where cars were an unnecessary burden. His family, headed by his taciturn Spanish father, was formal in its daily life, his Cuban mother's spirit and love of music suppressed. Antonio's father had never left the bedroom without a tie, even in the heat of summer, ceiling fans the only relief.

Antonio went to his job at Cargo Cuba by bus, then walked five blocks along the seawall to the two-story brick building at the edge of the city. His office in the shipping company looked out over the ocean, and across the bay he could see the imposing Morro Castle. On the days when he had an early meeting with a client not located near a bus route, Elena drove him in her pink 1954 Ford Fairlane.

"Where's my mother?" Fernando asked Ines. He needed the car. It was eleven o'clock and his mother should have been back from dropping his father off.

"She's not back yet. She said she had to do some errands."

Fernando would have to take the bus to Cristina's house for this week's meeting, and he was going to be late.

He needed to be at this gathering. The group had continued to meet regularly, despite the closure of the university, now going on four months. They were still writing and distributing the flyers, but only every two weeks, because with the university closed, Enrique could no longer make the mimeographs in the law department. It was being done by Sonya now. She had found a job as a teaching assistant in a small school and used the mimeograph there, but she had to work in short spurts, when she could produce the fliers without any of the other teachers nearby.

The group was becoming dispirited. They saw no change in the government's violent oppression, nor any lessening of the corruption, and had begun to question the entire point of putting themselves at risk with the flyers. There was no sign that President Batista was going to open the university again, because he saw it as the cradle of communist student unrest, although, in fact, specific ideologies for most students were unimportant. The main goal of the country's youth was having a new, democratic government.

Stepping up the pressure on the dictatorship was necessary, Maribel had argued recently, and she wanted to throw Molotov cocktails at the presidential palace in the middle of the night. Fernando had spoken up. "It's just too risky," he said. "This won't be jail for a few days with torture. It'll be execution by a military squad." They all knew that to be true, and that there would be a perfunctory trial with a predetermined outcome. It had happened more and more frequently in the past year as student unrest escalated and the activist youth was made to pay dearly.

Fernando heard the quick crescendo of the Ford's engine in the driveway and rushed to the porch.

"I need to borrow the car," he said to his mother as she got out of the driver's seat.

"Where are you going?"

"To see a friend about a job," Fernando said.

"Who?"

"Gustavo," he lied again.

Elena gave him the keys to the Ford. "Does he have a job, then?" she asked.

"Yes," Fernando said. Another lie, but because Gustavo was Black, Elena didn't know his mother, wouldn't have socialized with her. She'd have no access to the truth.

Fernando arrived late to Cristina's house, where they had been holding morning meetings since the closure of the university. The house was large, with a spacious covered patio where they could meet even if it rained, and where her parents couldn't hear the discussion.

"Where's Sonya?" Fernando asked.

"She dropped out of the group," Gustavo said. "She's afraid this is getting too risky. So now we don't have any way of making mimeographs."

"She dropped out because of the Molotov cocktails?" Fernando asked, and Maribel shot him a look. He didn't care. It was an absurd idea, even if she was beautiful and he wanted to kiss her.

"Probably," Cristina said. "I think we have to be careful with that."

Maribel's fists clenched. "The flyers haven't done anything. They closed our university and they have no plans to reopen. We have to do more," she said, her voice on the verge of a shout.

Fernando looked at Gustavo, who said nothing.

Cristina said, "What do you think, Gustavo?"

The man hesitated, his smooth dark skin looking like polished ebony in the diffuse light of the patio. "I think we're doing what we can. I don't think it would be a good idea to attack the presidential palace."

Maribel pounded the arm of her aluminum chair and said, "Why keep meeting, then? What's the point?"

Fernando left an hour later. Nothing had been decided. Maribel had kept pushing for violent action, relentless, and at some point Fernando's attraction turned into annoyance and a wish that she too would leave the group.

Disappointment and despair accompanied him on the drive home. No work, no chance for finishing his education, and a bleak future for his country. He rarely smoked, hadn't done so in months, but now he really craved a cigarette. He knew his mother kept a pack in the car, and at a traffic stop he opened the glove compartment and grabbed blindly because the light had turned green. He put the pack on his lap, along with something else he had scooped up. At the next red light he looked down and saw, resting on his thighs, his mother's cigarettes and a pack of condoms.

14

She had done laundry on Tuesday as usual and didn't really need to do one until Friday. But Ines was going to be busy anyway because she wanted to prepare a special meal for Friday dinner. It was going to be Señor Luis's birthday, and she would have to start preparations two days before, as Caridad had recommended.

Ines had finally become friendly with Caridad. It had taken several months of building up courage, but she had spoken to the matronly cook as they stood by the vegetable vendor. On that morning, Ines waited her turn several feet away from the cart and the loud, chattering women. They flirted with the vendor and made jokes about the size of the horse's genitals. Ines felt her face flush, and saw that Caridad was looking at her with either sympathy or agreement about the crassness of the women. Ines moved farther away from them and closer to Caridad, who said, "What trash they are," to Ines in a low tone.

The next time she saw Caridad by the produce cart, Ines stood near her, half expecting the reserved woman to move away or ignore her. Instead, Caridad said "Good morning" to her. They talked about the vegetables, about which looked good, which didn't. It was a tentative but easy conversation. Caridad volunteered that she wanted to buy baby onions to make coq au vin for the head of the household's birthday.

"What is that?" Ines asked. She had never heard of the strange-sounding dish.

"It's a French dish. Chicken stewed in red wine."

"I wish I knew how to make something special like that," Ines said, thinking of Luis's upcoming birthday.

"I'll bring you the recipe," Caridad said. "But you have to make it the day before so that it rests in the Frigidaire overnight."

Ines planned ahead. It would have taken her forever to read the recipe, despite having practiced her reading by looking at the newspaper every day. She asked Caridad to describe the technique when the woman handed her the recipe the next time they met, and she repeated it to herself on the way back from the vegetable cart.

Ines had never made a festive meal for anyone before. She didn't even know the rest of the family's birthdays, but she had made a note of Luis's after hearing the date in passing from Señora Elena.

In the late afternoon on Friday, Ines realized that making a special dinner for Señor Luis might give away her interest, which she had been careful to disguise. To her relief, Señor Luis had never approached her again as he had that day in the kitchen, despite his threat that he would. That lack of follow-through had only made him more attractive to Ines, as if he had repented his indecent pass.

Before she left for the day, Ines went into the living room to find Señora Elena, as she always did around this time.

"Is there anything else you need?" Ines asked.

"No. Is dinner ready?"

"Yes." Ines realized she sounded hesitant, and she cleared her throat. "I made a birthday dish for Señor Luis."

Señora Elena cocked her head. "Really? What did you make?"

"A French chicken stew. Coq au vin."

Ines saw a sparkle in her employer's eyes, a restrained, perhaps skeptical, smile. "Oh, so that's why you bought the baby onions," Elena said. "Thank you. Thank you very much, Ines."

The young woman saw that Señora Elena had arrived at some conclusion, an opinion, that had nothing to do with gratitude. Ines blushed. She was mortified that her secret might be out.

The next day, Saturday, Elena said to her, "Ines, the chicken was delicious. Thank you."

"Did Señor Luis like it?" Ines asked.

"Oh yes, very much. He cleaned his plate, which he doesn't usually do." Elena paused. "He smiled when I told him you had made it especially for him, but he didn't say anything. I'm sure he'll thank you the next time he sees you."

As she went around her chores that day, Ines thought back to Pedro, the rough man she was to marry. He was a clean, honest man, and kind, but his skin wasn't smooth and pale like Señor Luis's. His hands were red and callused, and her skin wanted to shrink away when he touched her arm or held her hand. She wondered what it would be like to have Luis's hands on her body. He had never returned to the kitchen when she was alone. Sometimes she wished he would, although she wasn't sure how far she would let him go. She thought she should save herself for Pedro, although she was not sure she would have anything to do with him if she had another choice.

15

In Havana, only American tourists went to the beach in winter, but now the April days were getting warm, and Luis missed the sand and the numbing thrill of the waves. It was Saturday and he called his old friend Joaquin. Luis liked going to the beach with a male friend. It made it easier to evade the groups of older American women who sometimes made suggestive overtures when he went alone.

Luis and Joaquin had been friends on and off since childhood. They had grown up in the same neighborhood, indeed, the same houses they lived in now with their parents. Joaquin hadn't gone to university, instead joining his father's lucrative jewelry business in Old Havana right after secondary school. Although months would go by when they didn't see each other, they fell back into the old, solid friendship easily. Now they were twenty-one. Men. One of them had a secure future and the other did not. They rode to the beach in Joaquin's 1956 gray Aston Martin, last year's model.

Joaquin was shorter and more muscular than Luis, darker, with a block of black hair, ochre eyes, and the olive skin of southern Spain. His teeth were perfectly straight and sparkled behind full lips. Today, he had an inward alertness that was new to Luis, an edge, although the smile was unchanged. He seemed to be on the brink of making an announcement or a declaration.

They hadn't seen each other since the university had been closed by the government, five months ago, because Luis had refrained from socializing. He had become unsure of his future, preoccupied with his lack of a college degree, with no prospects for meaningful employment beyond his menial job at the bank. That interval of isolation, Luis thought, had created the distance he was feeling now. What he saw as Joaquin's skittishness was probably a result of his own awkwardness; his friend had never been remote before.

"So tell me. Catch me up. What's going on in your life?" Luis asked in the car.

"What's going on?" Joaquin said, as if mulling the question over. "Let's see. I have news. I'm engaged."

A jolt of pleasant surprise with a dose of despair passed over Luis, like the moving shadow of a cloud. He had a vague feeling of uneasiness. "No way," he said.

"Who's the girl?" He couldn't understand what was making him uncomfortable about the news.

"You don't know her. Gilda."

"How did you meet her?" Luis asked.

"She's the daughter of my father's business associate," Joaquin said.

Something, perhaps Joaquin's tone of voice, or how he had met this woman, put a doubt in Luis's head, a doubt about Joaquin's enthusiasm for the engagement. And why wasn't Joaquin spending his day off with her?

"I'd like to meet her sometime," Luis said.

"Of course. How about you? You still seeing Anita?"

"Yeah."

"Serious?" Joaquin asked.

"I don't know. Her father is a son-of-a-whore who doesn't like me because he doesn't think my job at the bank is good enough."

Joaquin nodded. He said, "I wish we had a place for you in our company. If something becomes available, I'll let you know."

Luis felt the pang of being on the receiving end of charity, or worse, pity. Either way, he didn't want it, but he said nothing more about his job prospects.

At the beach club they went into the locker room, where several men were in various degrees of nudity, some pulling bathing suits on or off, or walking to or from the showers with a lack of modesty consistent with the prevailing macho culture. Luis undressed, and while fully naked, opened his beach bag and found his trunks. As he pulled them on he saw Joaquin, still in his briefs, watching him. His friend then averted his gaze and turned away from Luis to lower his own underwear and pull on his bathing suit. Luis didn't remember this unusual display of modesty in Joaquin throughout all the times they had come to this locker room, and he wondered what had changed.

On the beach they stretched out on towels, walked, had beers in the open-air bar sitting on stools under a thatched roof. They talked about movies they had seen and the economic situation. A few beers and a plate of pork rinds substituted for lunch.

Luis noticed a young couple sitting at a nearby table. The woman was blond and the muscular man was badly sunburned. "He's not used to the sun," Luis said, and nodded his head in their direction.

"They must be Americans," Joaquin said.

"She's really something," Luis felt obliged to say, because it was inescapable. "Beautiful. And those big guns up front."

Joaquin laughed and said, "Yes. She's got an impressive *promontorio*." He paused. "And the guy is very handsome." He stopped smiling at their exchange about the woman's chest and was now staring at the man.

The jovial bantering suddenly stopped. Joaquin looked down at his beer and said nothing more.

Luis wanted to neutralize the awkwardness; he grinned and in a jokey tone said, "Don't tell me you're swinging both ways nowadays."

Joaquin smiled and shrugged. He looked out at the people in the bar, on the surface an empty gesture, and said, "I can tell you that I've had some fun times recently in unexpected situations. A complete surprise."

Luis nodded, and with a slight smile and raised eyebrows he took a swallow of his beer. Nothing more was said of it, but the barely discernible barrier, that sheer veil that had been present between them since the morning, simply evanesced.

The day became a touchstone of sorts for Luis. He replayed it in his head again and again as he thought about Anita and the humiliating hurdle he felt he had to jump for her father in order to be deemed a desirable son-in-law. Somewhere inside he sensed that this hurdle would become irrelevant.

16

Maybe Maribel is right, Fernando thought. What's the point of this? It was seven o'clock on a Sunday morning and he was out with his shopping bag full of hand-printed flyers. Now that they couldn't be produced in large numbers, the group had decided on short announcements decrying the government, written out by Cristina in block letters. These one-page flyers were taped to lampposts and telephone poles near the same businesses where they had left the propaganda previously.

The first thing he felt: arms grabbed above the elbows, being yanked back, toppling. In a flash he saw a man in a baseball cap, a club in his hand rising and coming down on his head so fast the pain replaced everything. Then again and again, and then nothing, darkness and a void, until he woke up on the hard ceramic floor of a room with a desk and a chair. The light through the shutters said it was midday. He struggled to his feet, his eyes and ears pulsating in pain, his neck bruised and his throat feeling as if it had been crushed. He collapsed on the chair.

He was desperately thirsty. The desk was bare, and there was nothing else in the room. He held his head, elbows on knees. He went to the door and tried the knob, which clicked but didn't turn. And then two men opened the door and came in.

The questions. *Name. Why. Who else?* A brass knuckle punch to the face at his answer that he worked alone, blood now flowing from his cheek, eyes flooding uncontrollably at the pain. A club to the ribs, the shins, the knees. He felt as if bones were being broken everywhere, his breath shallow and difficult from the agony of the splintered ribs. His hand, still deformed from the fracture during the student uprising, was clubbed on the desk again and again until he blacked out once more. Cold water on his face revived him. More questions. When he answered that they were just students who wanted change, they punched him in the face, as if they wanted to hear something more sinister. He didn't even have time to consider divulging the names of the people in the group, because he was knocked off the chair with a blow to the head. His fingernails were pulled from their beds with pliers, a pain so intense his lungs couldn't expand to let out the screams. The club to the head again, again, and again, then out.

What he didn't see but heard from Luis a few days later: Elena hearing a car from inside the house later that Sunday, the clang of the gate opening, her animal roars as a black sedan sped away, she and Luis and Ines carrying him in from the driveway, stripping him, putting him in the shower to revive him, washing the blood off his hands and scalp.

When he came to he was naked, sitting on the floor of the shower, his back against the cold hard tiles. He couldn't see because his vision was gone and would remain so for hours, but he heard his mother's agitated voice, felt her hands rubbing him with towels, drying him, reviving him like a mother dog licking a moribund pup. When he was more alert but still unsteady, Luis and Elena lifted him and carried him to his room, and with Ines's help, laid him on the bed, and called the doctor to come see him.

Police violence couldn't be cared for in a hospital. No emergency department wanted any part of it for fear of government payback. So it was in Batista's Cuba in 1957.

17

He was by now half-hearted about the whole thing, but Luis called Anita and said he would be over to visit her on Saturday afternoon. He had stopped going out with her anywhere that required the presence of Corita as a chaperone, circling them like a pestering gnat with judgmental eyes. For weeks now he and Anita just sat on her porch, or walked around the neighborhood, the nearby park, the wide avenue with shops. His time with her was boring him.

He no longer pictured her in his future. The conversation with Joaquin and the sense of mediocrity her father instilled in him had destroyed his interest, which he now saw had been merely lukewarm and not based on any real attraction. And why hadn't Anita ever spoken up? Why couldn't she sit down with her father and tell him how much he meant to her, if indeed that was the case? Could it be that she was of the same mind as her father, that unless Luis had a good enough job she was not so enthused about being engaged to him, the ultimate goal being a life of comfort?

But it was more than just Anita in particular not being a part of his future. Luis had lost interest almost entirely in finding someone to marry, an undefined existence taking shape. Why had he even endured the humiliation of begging her father? The old man had actually chuckled when Luis told him of his new position as a bank teller, asking him if that changed his mind about allowing the engagement. "No," he had said. "It's not enough." Well, Luis thought now, no, Anita is not good enough for me either.

Luis didn't want to sit on her porch today. He suggested the park, where Corita's presence wouldn't be needed. The afternoon was dim, the sun behind massive gray clouds, and it wouldn't be too hot. He didn't want a scene on her porch, or at a café, or ice-cream parlor.

The park was small, a quarter of a square city block, with straight paved walkways and scant landscaping. Tall, scrawny trees dotted the area and provided spotty shade. A few people strolled leisurely, but most of them just traversed the space to get someplace else.

His dark mood silenced him, and Anita looked at him quizzically. "Something's going on with you today," she said.

He didn't answer right away. Finally, he saw that there was no point delaying the news. It wouldn't be fair to her. No matter what, he had felt deep affection for her once, or so he had thought. He couldn't be sure if it had been affection or just a need to be in a relationship with someone. He said, "I'm thinking of leaving."

Anita stopped walking. "Where are you going?" she said.

"The United States." He smiled and said it in English to make light of it, hoping it wouldn't sound so annihilating to what they had, although indeed ending it was what he wanted.

Anita's sudden intake of breath made a sibilant sound, air through a narrow space. Her eyes widened. "When?" she asked.

"Sometime this year. Maybe October," Luis said. The worst was over.

"And us?" There was fear in her eyes.

"I don't know. Maybe once I'm there, making money, I'll come back." He didn't say "to get you," or "to marry you," and the words not uttered were the harshest part of what he had said. He could see it in her eyes, the lids so swollen with emotion they looked like slits.

A break in the clouds appeared and they were standing now in full sun. Luis's shirt was beginning to stick. He wanted to go out of the hot, ugly park and back to his own house. He didn't see any point in going on. But she said, "Are we waiting for each other, then? As if we were engaged?"

"It's all so uncertain," Luis said. "I don't know what kind of shape my future will be."

She said, "So you're saying that you and I are finished."

Luis turned and looked away. "I'll take you home."

They walked the two blocks in silence. When he glanced at her, he saw no sadness, just anger. Her eyes had remained dry and she looked dangerous, capable of savagery.

At her house, they paused on the sidewalk outside the gate that led to the small garden. Anita looked at him, her eyes steady, the jaw set. She turned and walked through the gate. Luis remained on the sidewalk a few seconds while she stepped up onto the porch, but left before she entered the house. He'd be gone by the time she looked out the window, if she did.

18

"Two cracked ribs," Dr. Ramirez said after he examined Fernando, hours after the government henchmen dumped him in the garden. The dignified, graying physician didn't send Fernando for X-rays. The hospital staff would have been suspicious because of his fractured ribs, bruises, and cuts on the face, the state of confusion from the cranium bashings. The physician, fortunately, had a busy general practice and twenty years of experience and knew how to apply a cast, even for a hand. He was able to confirm just two broken ribs, not three, which would have required hospitalization for observation. He gave Elena strict and detailed instructions to watch him for worsening confusion or loss of consciousness for the first twenty-four hours, which might indicate a dangerous subdural hematoma.

Fernando was mostly confined to the house for three weeks, healing, regaining his mental faculties. He was at first unable to read or hold a conversation for long before becoming confused. He could only sit on the porch, listen to the radio, or watch TV in the living room with Elena. After a few days, he complained about the string of American shows she liked—*I Love Lucy, Fury, Perry Mason*—that played incessantly on all three channels.

After two weeks he began to recover, at least mentally. He woke up without rib pain three weeks after the beating. His mother had gone out in the car, Ines said to him that morning when he awoke feeling well. From the sofa in the living room he heard the sound of the engine in the driveway around eleven o'clock.

He remembered the condoms in the glove compartment, had tried not to think about them all these weeks. Vaguely, he had concluded, without much thought, that he must have been wrong about his father's aversion to the use of condoms. He chose not to question why they'd be in the car if that was the case, and didn't dwell on the fact that the car was used almost exclusively by his mother. Luis, like Antonio, didn't drive, so the condoms could not be his.

Elena was dressed in the style Fernando had seen when she went out with her friends to play canasta or for lunch, in a tailored, flowered dress and heels. Her hair, however, needed combing.

"Where did you go so early?" Fernando asked.

Elena hesitated. "Eh ... the dentist."

"Everything all right?"

"Yes. Fine," she said. "I'm going to change."

On his way to the kitchen, Fernando heard the shower in his parents' bathroom. It was the family's habit to shower in the evenings, before dinner, not in the mornings. He didn't want to think of the condoms or where she had been that morning that she needed to shower now.

In the kitchen, Ines was making lunch. "How are you feeling?" she asked. She had let her dark hair grow long and had it pinned above the nape, which he noticed was smooth and pale.

"Much better, thank you."

"Would you like some coffee?"

"No, thank you. I'm going to make a guava shake."

"I'll make it and bring it to you."

"Thank you."

Fernando went out to the porch. He didn't want to sit with his mother in the living room. At this time of day she would want to watch her *novelas,* with their melodramatic plots and exaggerated acting, instead of the American shows he had grown to at least tolerate. He chose the rocking chair he liked, the old metal red one instead of the green one, and listened as his mother changed the channel on the other side of the window.

His mother had been a force of nature these past three weeks while he healed, constantly vigilant of his condition, calling the doctor in for follow-up at home. She hadn't wanted Fernando to be seen in public or at the doctor's office recovering from a beating, arousing suspicions. She had changed his dressings, re-taped the ribs after each shower, and taken his temperature constantly the first week, like the doctor had said. And following the man's instructions, at night she had gone into his room to awaken him every two hours to make sure he was stable and not succumbing to a brain bleed. Never a complaint or a reprimand or criticism for his political activities that could have placed the whole family in jeopardy.

He had heard his parents attribute his willingness to indulge in risky behavior to his relative youth. That reasoning was simplistic, he thought, a discredit to his conviction that what he was doing was necessary for the good of the country. It seemed to him that he was the only one in the family with that degree of passion for the political well-being of his birthplace. His parents and Luis just focused on the material, the vicissitudes of day-to-day life. He wanted more for his country, for himself.

His father had only scowled and shaken his head every time he saw Fernando's bruised and broken face, but his mother had anointed him with nothing but concern and compassion. He did not want to be disappointed in her. And yet he was.

19

Ines had an idea of what was going on. She understood just from that one time with Pedro, when they had gone to his mother's house on a Sunday afternoon when she was out, might be enough to make her pregnant. He had asked her to marry him immediately afterwards, and she didn't answer yes or no because she wasn't sure what she really wanted to do. She just stalled and said, "When?"

"Soon," he had said. Nothing more. No date.

Señora Elena had asked her to stop working on Saturdays, and her salary was cut. From the kitchen, Ines had overheard the family discussing their financial problems. Señor Luis was not making much and Señor Fernando had no job at all, scarred from the police beating, afraid to leave the house. And she had heard Señor Antonio use words like "bankruptcy" and "catastrophe" when he talked about the shipping company he worked for. Only Señora Elena's voice sounded firm and unperturbed. "We'll get by however we can," she always said.

Ines used her Saturdays now not only to help her parents around the small farm but to practice her reading. She read old newspapers that the owner of the ramshackle bodega near her house let her have for free.

One afternoon, a customer standing at the bodega's counter asked her why she wanted the old newspapers. She was a round woman with short black hair; *a man's cut*, Ines thought. Her simple brown dress was intact, had never been mended, and wasn't even frayed. "Are you making something out of papier-mâché?" the woman asked.

Ines had no idea what the woman was referring to and only answered, "No. I'm practicing my reading. Any newspaper is fine."

The woman nodded. "Aha," she said. Then she added, "Can you cook?"

Ines was puzzled at the question, but she said, "Yes." She remembered the coq au vin that had turned out so well, and she was not shy about asserting her skill in the kitchen.

"I'm a teacher and I can help you with your reading on Saturday afternoons if you cook Sunday dinner for my husband and me. Something out of the ordinary."

It had gone well right from the start. Margo told Ines that she was surprised by how quickly the young woman progressed. Within weeks she was reading slowly but steadily and could finish any newspaper article she started.

"Where will we live?" Ines asked Pedro. A few days ago she had agreed to marry him, two months after her last period.

"There's a small house not far from your parents," he said. "It needs work, but we can rent it cheap and fix it up."

How would she be able to help her parents financially and on the farm if she had this other commitment, paying rent on their new house? And how would Pedro help his mother, a widow, with her expenses?

"Let's not worry about that," he said. "We have to live our lives. They'll be okay."

She had no solutions, no ideas, only worries that Pedro wasn't thinking things through.

"Besides," Pedro said. "They're saying there's an armed revolution in the east winning battles against the military."

She had read something about that in the newspaper. "So what?" she said.

"Everything will change. They're fighting for us, the poor. The revolutionaries have taken land from the rich and given it to the peasants."

She had not seen anything about the Revolution benefiting the poor.

When she next saw Señora Elena, she waited until they were alone in the house and went into the living room, where the woman was watching TV.

"What is it?" Señora Elena said, not unkindly. Even now, with the tension in the household higher than Ines had ever seen it, her employer was direct but never harsh.

Ines picked at her cuticles. She felt foolish, maybe even presumptuous, approaching her employer with a question that had nothing to do with her work in the house, as if the woman were a relative or a friend.

"I've read there's a revolution in the east, in Oriente?"

Señora Elena gave Ines her full attention. Her eyes showed alarm. "Yes, I've heard that too."

"There are rumors that it's to help the poor," Ines said.

"Yes, but who knows. They're just rumors. And revolutions aren't usually good for anybody."

Ines nodded. "Would you like some coffee?" she asked.

"Yes, please. With lots of milk and sugar."

In the kitchen, Ines boiled the water and heated the milk to a low simmer. She had learned this from Señor Luis, who always said that milk tasted better that way. He had been gone a month and she wondered how he was, wished he hadn't left for the United States.

Ines brought the coffee out to the living room. She had placed a chocolate cookie on the saucer. She knew that her employer liked sweet things when she was upset, and the mention of the Revolution had seemed to alarm her.

"Have you heard from Señor Luis?" she asked the señora.

"We had a letter yesterday," Elena said. "He's fine. But that's only what he says. Who knows how he really is or what's really going on."

"Where in the United States is he?"

"In Florida. Not Miami. He's working for a sugar company owned by Cubans," Elena said, and took a big bite out of the chocolate cookie.

20

"It's for you," Elena said to Fernando, telephone handset in her hand.

"Who is it?" He wasn't expecting anyone to call him.

"Maribel. Who is that?"

Fernando took the phone and whispered, "I'll tell you later."

"So who is Maribel?" Elena asked Fernando after he had hung up. She had remained within earshot of the conversation.

"Somebody from the university. From my study group."

Elena tightened her lips. "She sounded a little abrupt," she said. "Almost rude."

"She wants to come visit," Fernando said. "This afternoon."

"Who's coming with her?"

"She didn't mention anyone else."

Elena shook her head. "What type of young woman visits a man in his house by herself?"

"It'll be okay," Fernando said.

"It's not okay. But that's her problem. I hope if she comes again after today, she brings somebody with her." Elena started to walk out of the living room, then stopped and said, "Why does she want to visit? Does she know you're injured?"

"Yes. She said Gustavo told her," Fernando said. He had no idea how Gustavo had found out he was hurt.

"Ah, yes. Gustavo," Elena said. "He called right after the assault because he said you had missed a meeting of the study group. I told him you couldn't talk because you had been in a car accident."

Fernando was angry that he had been made the subject of a lie to his friend. He would have to be complicit or tell his friend the truth and reveal his mother to be the liar. But no, he would have to level with Gustavo, tell him and the rest of the group what had happened. They needed to know how dangerous things had gotten. He stayed in the living room to wait for Maribel while his mother went to the kitchen. When he heard the clanging of the front gate, he went to the door.

Maribel was wearing a brown skirt and a white blouse, looking not unlike a nun. Her black hair was tied back into a ponytail with a white ribbon. She said a brief hello, as if they had seen each other a few uneventful days ago, and didn't smile. She declined going inside when Fernando invited her in. "Let's stay on the porch," she said.

It had been just over a month since Fernando's abduction and torture, and his face showed a scar running from his cheekbone halfway down his cheek. The sutures had left red cross-hatches and his left hand was still in a cast. The fingernails of his right hand, which had been pulled out with pliers, were still missing, the bare nail beds raw and bruised.

"Take the green rocking chair," Fernando said. "It's more comfortable." He took the old red one with the rust stains.

After a moment of silence, during which Maribel avoided his eyes and looked out at the tiny front garden, she said, "I came to see how you are." Her tone was soft, not the usual brusque one.

"Here I am. On the mend," he said.

"I'm very sorry this happened to you," she said, looking at his hands. "I feel partly responsible."

"What do you mean?" Why would she feel responsible for a car accident? And then he said, "Do you know what happened?"

"Gustavo called a few weeks ago. Your mother told him you were in a car accident. But we talked about it at the next meeting, and we had our suspicions that you were attacked by government thugs. And now that I see your hands ..."

Fernando just nodded. He wished he could hide his disfigured hands, his face. He felt as if it were his fault the attack had occurred, as if he just hadn't been careful enough.

"I wish we knew how it happened, how they identified you," Maribel said.

"They watch. Maybe the people in the neighborhoods I visited talked," Fernando said.

"I don't know where we go from here," she said. Her forehead displayed an intense frown, as if she was going to blow a fuse, and her lips were puckered in a knot of nuclear energy. Her hands gripped the arms of the rocking chair.

The old Maribel he knew was back. Fernando could see her commitment to political reform oozing through her skin. When Gustavo had excused himself from distributing flyers because of his dark skin, the rest of the group had made good-natured fun of him, but she had defended him as if they were serious. She knew no humor, was all blind passion.

Something shifted in him. The superficial desire he had felt for the various parts of her body—the smooth cheeks, the curved lips, her round, firm buttocks—-morphed into a camaraderie for which he wanted to be strong. Not to protect her, but to work alongside her and her irritating, almost deranged militancy. It didn't matter that she was a communist. They all had the same goal. And her passion gave him reassurance that he was going to be okay, because of course he had to be, so he could continue the fight. He did not regret his involvement with the group despite what he had been through.

"Give me some time to heal," Fernando said, his voice almost inaudible, in case Elena was in the living room, just on the other side of the open window. "Then we'll make plans."

Maribel smiled, the first time he had ever witnessed that expression directed at him. She stood up, and before she started down the steps to the garden she placed a hand on his upper arm. He could see that her eyes focused on the scar on his cheek.

21

Fernando didn't call Gustavo right away after Maribel's visit. He wasn't ready to meet with him and be seen in public. If his physical appearance had made what had happened clear to her, so it would be to anyone else who laid eyes on him. It was obvious that he had been the victim of an assault, political until proven otherwise, and he needed to put his socializing and his activism on hold for the time being. He should try to find a job, subsist in his parents' house with any income he could get.

His search through the classified ads yielded nothing, the scant listings limited to mechanical and manufacturing positions, and he wanted to work in some aspect of the law.

When he felt well enough to venture out, he avoided spending much time in his neighborhood, where the attack had started, as if the same men might be lurking in the entryways of hardware stores, bodegas, and pharmacies. He looked out the window of the living room before he stepped out. Walking to the bus stop, he turned his head to look behind him every half block. He dressed well and took the bus to the center, in Old Havana, and walked the narrow but carefully landscaped streets, the colonial buildings with their balconies adorned with potted plants. He wanted to work and belong here, be able to look out his window and see all this beauty, and he made note of the law offices that looked especially substantial, with impressive signs and lists of partners. He went into some of them and presented himself to the receptionists without an appointment but was always turned away, although some of them took his name and number. Later, from home, he'd look up the firms' phone numbers and call them, offering his services for free as an apprentice, a clerk of sorts. He hoped that entry would lead to employment until the university reopened and he could finish his law degree. Not one of the law practices was interested.

He finally called Gustavo one evening.

"What's been going on?" Fernando asked after they had talked about Maribel's visit and his convalescence in general terms. Rumor had it that certain telephone lines were tapped.

"Not much," Gustavo said. "Why don't we meet at my house, then we'll go to Poets' Park and talk. How about tomorrow morning at ten?"

Fernando walked thirty minutes to Gustavo's neighborhood the next morning under a baking August sun. His friend lived in a racially mixed part of the city, in a humble but not run-down block of row houses. He had been to Gustavo's house once, when the meetings had first begun. During the walk, as the houses became smaller and fewer trees shaded the sidewalks, he knew that he would have to face the fact that he wasn't going to find a job in a law office without a degree. It was time he made a living and helped with the household expenses, especially since the only family income, his father's, had been reduced. But he didn't want to work at just anything—a waiter, a taxi driver, a sales clerk. The study of law was what he had devoted himself to, and with his whole heart he wanted to pursue it as a career.

On Gustavo's block, all the houses were painted in pastel colors. His friend's house was a sky blue, a detail Fernando remembered from his previous visit. The door was opened by Gustavo's mother, a heavyset Black woman, much darker even than her son.

"Come in, come in," the woman said, her smile as broad as her round face.

Fernando suddenly realized he didn't remember her name. "Thank you, Señora," he said, and followed her into the house, just as Gustavo appeared in the narrow entry hallway.

"Let's stay here," Gustavo said after he saw Fernando's face and hands. "Forget the park."

The two men sat in the minuscule backyard, the size of a child's bedroom, enclosed by seven-foot brick walls. Those barriers were festooned with multicolored broken glass embedded in a layer of cement, an indication of the lack of safety in the neighborhood. Two sturdy wooden chairs on the concrete deck were painted white. A thriving banana tree stood nearby in one corner of the yard, loaded with still-purple fruit. Gustavo's mother brought out two glasses of lemonade.

"So tell me," Gustavo said. "I heard from Maribel just how badly they beat you. But I want to know what they did."

"What did Maribel say?"

Gustavo shook his head. "She said it was bad. She knew right away it wasn't a car accident. The scars. Your fingernails." He shook his head again.

Fernando saw fear in his friend's eyes as he sketched out the ambush, the beating, the torture. He didn't go into too much detail when he saw Gustavo's forehead begin to scrunch, his eyes darting from the scar on Fernando's cheek to the mangled nail beds.

"We can't keep doing this," Gustavo said. "It hasn't done anything, like Maribel says. She's right."

"So what should we do?"

"Nothing for now. It's too dangerous. And I have to take care of my mom," Gustavo said, nodding his head toward the house. "She's getting old and is not in good health. She needs my salary."

"You found a job?"

Gustavo nodded, a small smile breaking through the worry on his face. "Just two months ago," he said. "What a relief."

"How lucky you are. I can't find anything."

Gustavo, in the same year as Fernando in the university's law school, was working at an American-owned casino as an administrator, preparing legal documents for the corporation's lawyers in the US.

"The company is expanding and opening up a new nightclub and casino in Marianao," he said. "They'll need somebody there to do the same work I'm doing at the Club Riviera."

Gustavo gave him the name of the man he needed to call. "I'll phone him Monday to let him know about you," he said as he put his hand on his friend's shoulder and gave it a squeeze.

22

The small, unimpressive hotel was not exactly dilapidated, but it needed painting outside and a good cleaning inside. Still, the sheets and towels were clean and the saggy mattress was good enough for two people to embrace, cuddle, and be completely intimate before breaking away and resuming their lives.

Elena parked the Ford two blocks away near a shopping district. She knew the car was distinctive and didn't want it seen near the hotel by someone she knew, because the place was a well-known love nest. As she walked to the hotel, she could feel the silky talcum powder she had applied between her thighs. The sensation always felt erotic and whetted her appetite for the encounter with Ramon. She and Antonio hardly ever had sex anymore. Her sexual hunger was fed mostly by Ramon now, the husband of her friend Betty, at whose house she played canasta with two other women every week.

Ramon was stocky, dark, and had a round, hard belly. Elena was amazed at how strong his arms were when he held her, as if he was afraid that she would try to get away.

As was their biweekly habit, she registered at the hotel desk, went up one flight of stairs, and waited for Ramon, who arrived after fifteen minutes. But it was he who paid the room charges when they left two hours later.

When Ramon first entered the room, they embraced, kissed, and went to bed quickly, without much being said. "Do we really need this?" he said when she put the condom on him.

"I haven't gone through menopause yet," she responded. "Things happen."

They talked afterwards, caressed. It wasn't just about the sex. There was a certain affinity, a connection, because emotional intimacy with their spouses was perhaps not as deep as it might have been. Specifically for Elena, Antonio was a dutiful, responsible husband, but formal, even distant. And there was a familiarity that had developed with Ramon because of the small talk that flowed between them after sex, a result of their interest in each other's lives.

Ramon seemed to care about what she was feeling physically during the act. Often, after they finished and he rolled away, he asked her if what he had done pleased her, and would she like him to do this or that specific trick with his tongue again next time. He seemed to take an interest in the pleasure he was giving her, whereas Antonio did what he had to do, and when it was over, there was no tenderness or discussion afterwards, as if he regretted having engaged in the act with her.

They talked about their lives at home. Ramon knew that Luis had left and that Fernando was worried about his future. She had felt comfortable talking to him about these things, and about Antonio not being in a position to help his sons find jobs. Of course, she had not told him about Fernando's abduction and torture, because she was not ready to identify her son as a subversive anti-Batista activist, even to this man she trusted with other matters. They did not talk politics, and she wasn't sure what his opinion of the current government was. There were all the other elements in their conversations. Elena, for example, knew that he was Jewish and that his daughter wanted to go to Spain to study the history of the Jews there before the Inquisition.

Today, Elena noticed a certain distance from him, a lack of total commitment to the lovemaking. She hid her disappointment as it was happening, but afterwards, while still in bed, she said, "Is something wrong?"

Ramon's eyes were on the ceiling and he glanced at her. "I'm just having some problems," he said.

"At work?" She knew he was an accountant, but in the two years that they had been involved she had never seen him distracted, had never heard him talk about work.

"Not really work. Sort of," he said.

"How is that, sort of at work?"

He delayed answering, as if considering whether to talk or not. "The thing is," he said finally, "I've been doing some work for the police. Business has been terrible lately. The past year."

"What do you do for the police?" she asked.

He took a deep breath. "I try to identify troublemakers for them, especially student activists who want to bring down the government." He paused. "The thing is, they're saying I haven't given them enough names, that I'm not doing enough."

Elena froze. She felt her face flush, and was glad they were facing the water-stained ceiling and not each other. "How did you get involved with that?" she asked finally. She hoped her uneven voice wouldn't arouse suspicion that she was dismayed by his revelation.

"My brother is in the police department. He knows my business is not doing well and he asked me if I was interested."

Elena said nothing. She was relieved no response was required or expected by Ramon, who was clearly upset by the discussion. A cold sweat had sprouted on her forehead and upper lip, and her dry mouth made her tongue stick to the roof of her mouth. When she finally found her voice, she said, "I have to get going."

"It's early," Ramon said. "We still have time to talk."

She avoided looking at him as she reached for her clothes, which she had draped over the only chair in the room. Ramon had hung his suit and shirt in the narrow closet, where there was only one wire hanger.

"I have an appointment with the dentist," she said.

After she was dressed, she forced herself to go to the bed, kissed him lightly on the lips, and left.

23

Luis had left suddenly, one could almost say, two weeks after he announced his plans to the family. He had secured a position at a small sugar refinery in Florida owned by a Cuban family. A cousin, Aunt Isabel's son, worked for them, and Luis had been in touch with him after years of little contact.

Fernando's position in the new casino and nightclub paid well. The gambling and alcohol were so lucrative, and the management staff was so well-paid, his hopeless prospects from just a month ago seemed remote. He bought suits that he wore to the office. Everyone in administration dressed well, a uniform of prosperity that served as a daily reminder of the privilege it was to work for this American organization.

Fernando communicated with the casino's attorneys daily about all sorts of issues: employees, accounting reports, leases and permits for expansion. His day was leisurely, not having enough to do to fill it. He walked the ample grounds, which included landscaped gardens and a terrace with a view of the ocean. The expansive terrace became an outdoor nightclub after dark, with elegant glass lamps hung from crisscrossing wires ten feet above. A large multilevel stage occupied one end of the terrace. He had seen the cabaret show in rehearsal, the voluptuous women in leotards and the handsome, hair-slicked men who partnered them. They all danced with ballet-like grace and suggestive sensuality. Many of the performers were light-skinned Blacks, which the American owners of the club thought would appeal to the tourists from New York and Florida.

He hadn't seen Maribel since her visit in July, four months ago. Although he had experienced a change in his feelings for her, something akin to tenderness, he couldn't help connecting her to the political activities that had resulted in his assault and his injuries. Still, he forced himself to call her, not allow the memory of the trauma to ruin what might turn into a warmer relationship, maybe romantic, maybe not.

They met at La Girafa, a popular ice-cream parlor in the Parque Central with numerous outdoor tables. They sat in the shade, under the canopy of a huge breadfruit tree, the ground around them littered with the ripe green globes. After a few minutes of chitchat, Maribel asked him whether he was working, and after he told her a bit about his new job, he asked, "And you? Have you found anything?"

Maribel's face turned serious and she looked down at her bowl of chocolate ice cream. "No," she said. "But I'm in training." She kept her eyes down.

"Training for what?" Fernando asked. He thought she might be clerking at a law office, as he had hoped to do.

Maribel pursed her lips. She glanced around them, making sure no one was listening. "For military practice," she said.

Fernando's eyes narrowed. Was she serious, or was this a joke? "I don't understand," he said.

Maribel shrugged and looked away. "It's exactly how it sounds." She looked around again, over her shoulder. "Anyway, I don't want to talk about it."

Fernando had planned to broach the possibility of their dating, start by maybe just going out for a walk in a park, but now he abandoned the idea. Her manner, which earlier in the afternoon had been mellow, the look in her eyes soft, suddenly was not just unromantic; it was back to being brisk, matter-of-fact. The glimpse of caring he had seen that day on the porch soon after the attack, and the gentleness of just a few minutes ago, were replaced by the return of a grim expression. Worse, it sounded as if she was involved in some kind of armed activity now.

They parted after they finished their ice cream, a quick and impassive goodbye, with no mention of seeing each other again. Neither of them made any attempt at a kiss on the cheek, nor even a handshake. He remembered those tentative fingertips she had placed on his arm once that might have been interpreted as affection. He watched her walk away until he could no longer see her in the crowd.

24

1958

Dear family,

I hope that on receipt of these few lines you all find yourselves well. I am fine but worried about Fernando. In your last letter Mamá you wrote that he had been badly injured and was recovering at home without more details and when I called last week and I asked none of you wanted to tell me what happened. I feel that you are hiding something from me like I'm not part of the family now because I left. I hope this is not the case. As I told you a month before I left I needed to have some chance for a better life than what I had there. I know that maybe you feel like I chose prosperity over my family but my frustration and the lack of opportunities for the future were ruining my life.

Things aren't easy here in West Palm Beach. It gets very cold at night 15 degrees but they call it 60 in Fahrenheit. We have to use electric heat. I'm sharing an apartment with another man who also works for Sunshine Sugar. Cousin Roberto's house isn't big enough for me to stay there but with my salary I am able to pay the rent in my apartment with no problem and I hope to get my own place in the summer. The chief of finance at the company promised me a promotion maybe in the spring. Mamá I haven't been able to visit your cousin Myriam in Tampa. Florida is huge and Tampa is very far away by car.

There is talk around the company that they will be selling their refineries in Cuba and expand here. The rumor around the company is that the Revolution in the mountains in Oriente is gaining support from the peasants and is moving west towards Havana and the refineries may suffer damage. I know we had heard that before I left but this makes it more likely to be true. If everything goes well and things in Cuba change I'll go back. The English I learned in the university is barely enough to do my work. I'm lucky that most of the people I work with are Cuban but when I go shopping or do anything outside of work it's very difficult.

I've made this too long. I wish calling wasn't so expensive because I'd like to hear your voices again. Please let me know in your next letter how Fernando is.

With all my affection,

Luis

25

The university had been closed for a year and a half. What a different life this was from what Fernando had envisioned. Luis gone, his parents anxious about their income. Instead of doing less as she got older, his mother was now doing more housework, since Ines's hours had been cut back. And he was working in a casino as a liaison for a law firm, closer to a clerk than an attorney. But at least now he was earning a salary.

He saw Gustavo regularly, his only friend now that he had no contact with any of the other students. The two of them went once or twice a month to the beach or to a bar. But today Fernando was going to meet Gustavo at Cristina's house, where a party had been planned for her birthday. He was looking forward to seeing some of the students he had lost touch with. Surely Maribel would be there, maybe even Enrique, skittish and elusive but loyal.

When he got to Cristina's house, Gustavo was already there. Fernando didn't see Maribel. He kissed Cristina on the cheek and wished her a happy birthday, and then immediately asked, "Have you heard from Maribel?"

"When I called her house to invite her, her mother said she wasn't living with them anymore," Cristina said, turning her palms up in helpless ignorance. "But she wouldn't say where she was, or why she had left."

After a drink and some brief conversations with people he had known at university, Fernando left the party without saying goodbye to anyone, even Gustavo, who was talking to a large-breasted woman in a snug dress, the only other Black person there.

Fernando drove home in his mother's Ford. He was making enough money to buy his own car, and although he had decided to do so weeks ago, he felt a sort of inertia. He was giving money to his mother now to help with expenses, but he had little interest in spending anything on himself.

He wondered why he wasn't happier. The job was good and his injuries had healed, although the scar on his left cheek was deep and coursed from his cheekbone halfway to his jaw. And his left hand was deformed and would never be the same. But he was healthy overall, fit, strong. Women looked at him. And yet he felt an emptiness, a disquieting lack of certainty that what he was doing with his life, if this was all there would be, was significant enough. The assault had been a price he had paid for caring about his country, wanting a better nation. But he had gotten nothing in return for that payment, except perhaps the sense that his activist efforts had been futile. The dictatorship was as oppressive as ever. The reports circulating in the underground estimated that political assassinations by the government had exceeded 20,000. Maybe Luis had it right. Abandon the sinking ship. Or maybe it was already underwater.

He had never visited the US with his parents, had always turned down their offers to accompany them on vacation. Luis had gone once, years ago, before he left for good. He hadn't loved it, he said, but there were parts of it he liked. The informality, the lack of pretense, the friendliness of Americans. But Fernando was wary of a country so huge, with so many people. Cuba was just a little larger than Florida, which was just one state out of what? Forty-eight? Forty-nine? He wasn't sure. And Florida wasn't even close to being the largest of them.

He had read about the lynching of Black people in the southern part of the United States, the laws that made it legal to treat them as inferiors. There was marked racism in Cuba. Blacks didn't have the same opportunities as whites when it came to employment or education, Gustavo being an exception. But discrimination wasn't as stark as it was in the US. Fernando had never seen a sign "Negroes Not Allowed" at soda fountains, or in shops, or restaurants like he had seen in photographs from the North. Here, Blacks didn't have to sit in the back of the bus or risk being arrested, or have to drink from separate water fountains. The United States didn't seem like such a decent, honorable country, and he wasn't sure he wanted to witness it firsthand.

26

First her little girl, two months old, had died, and now, less than a month later, her husband Pedro had spells during which he could hardly breathe. Ines watched as Pedro's eyes bulged, his chest trying to expand. His face turned purple, and then darker and darker. Ines took a piece of cardboard or anything else she could find, even a banana leaf, and fanned him. This had worked sometimes, but other times the attack continued and went away on its own after a few terrifying minutes. Pedro would be exhausted and sleep for several hours, right in the middle of the day. On those days, most of the sugarcane he was expected to cut still stood at dusk, and the overseer of the fields refused to pay him anything for the meager cartful he had managed to gather.

Only Ines and her mother were healthy now, her father dead a few weeks before the little girl Jasmin was born. Her father had lost weight for a few months, coughing, his skin pale, the color of newsprint. They had no money for a proper doctor in Havana, of course, and the local *curandero* had demanded a laying hen before giving her father a potion that did nothing. One of the old women from the village had said, "Cancer from smoking. No cure."

Ines and Pedro had moved in with her mother, saving on the rent for the small shack they had lived in. Ines was still working for the Leal family just five days, not the six she had worked months ago. It was difficult, the three of them in a one-room bungalow, no privacy for anyone. But it was the best arrangement for now, and Pedro was not very amorous these days anyway.

Her life had turned into a series of painful events. The loss of her baby daughter completely eclipsed the loss of her father. It was like a tear in her heart that had left her breathless and numb. She found it difficult to care about anything or anyone. It took the greatest effort to care for Pedro when he got ill, to get on the bus and go to the Leal household to work. Even getting out of bed seemed like an impossible task. And now all she had left was a very sick husband, an aging mother, and a struggle to pay for rent and food and electricity.

On the bus going into Havana, if Ines saw a newspaper left behind on a seat, she picked it up. She could read faster now, thanks to Margo, the teacher for whom she still cooked on weekends. Ines read the front page first with all the important political news, then the gossip about TV and movie stars. But it was the news about the rebels in Oriente Province, usually on page two or three, that drew her attention most. Pedro had talked about it months ago, and Señora Elena had said those stories were just rumors. And yet, here it was, in the paper. Pedro had been right.

Ines went into the living room when she knew Señora Elena would be watching TV. Señor Fernando was working and had bought a car, a strange-looking blue one. Ines hoped that meant the family had more money now.

"Señora, excuse me," Ines said.

Her employer looked at her, still smiling from whatever was on the TV screen. "Yes, Ines?"

Suddenly she felt too shy to ask, but she found her words and said, "Do you still want me to come only Monday to Friday, not on Saturdays?"

The señora looked surprised at the question. "Well," she said. "Do you want to come on Saturdays again?" Her tone was surprisingly soft. There had been a change in how she spoke to Ines since the death of the baby. Her manner was no longer quite so business-like.

Ines nodded. "My husband is sick and can't work much," she said.

The woman shook her head slowly, in a way that signaled sympathy, not rejection of Ines's request, and said, "Yes, please. Come on Saturdays again from now on."

Ines was able to say "Thank you" and turn away before her eyes watered and her mouth contorted.

27

The nightclub part of the casino had expanded its show. Profits had doubled since the opening six months ago. Club Maxime was now an essential nightspot along with the fabled Tropicana and the Club Riviera, for the Americans who visited and for the *Habaneros* who were financially comfortable. Fernando saw the weekly numbers in the documents he mailed to the American accountants and lawyers. He also saw the actual numbers that were only for his and the owners' eyes, and the difference was staggering. The income reported to the US was a third of what was actually being collected, and therefore subject to a fraction of American taxes.

But there was another, more disturbing matter. The accountant's figures included a thirty percent deduction from the real net profits that went into a special account. It was widely known in the administration that these funds went directly to Batista and the military, a whopping monthly fee for being allowed to do business. And so Fernando saw himself as part of a machine that fed the monster dictator and kept him in power. For the first time in his life, he was waking up at three or four in the morning, tortured by the immorality of what he was doing, the irony of having been a victim and now a facilitator of a corrupt government. He didn't know whom to talk to. Of course, his parents were out of the question because he was sworn to secrecy at work, and who knew where his mother would go with the information. He trusted Gustavo, but there was no point talking to him about it because he surely already knew, being his counterpart at the other casino under the same ownership. Fernando wished he were religious, could consult with some spiritual guide, perhaps a priest.

He needed fresh air and left his office for the nightclub's terrace. It was midafternoon and he would take a short break before finishing the day's documents and then filing them. He enjoyed sitting on the terrace, where the dancers rehearsed in the afternoons and performed for customers at night. They were there now, resting between sessions, drinking coffee or soda. Fernando saw Tony, the dance captain, and went to sit with him.

Months ago, before they had known each other, Tony had gone to where Fernando was sitting, watching the rehearsal, and introduced himself. He was an easygoing man approaching middle age, not only the oldest but the shortest of all the dancers, and yet he was the most athletic. Eventually, Tony introduced Fernando to the rest of the performers.

Fernando had become friendly with the dancers after weeks of watching them rehearse, sometimes for a half hour if his workload was light. No one supervised his comings and goings. So long as the work got done, the chief administrator left him alone.

Sitting with Tony, Fernando noticed there were now eight couples in the dance team, up from seven. The new dancing couple were not sitting with each other during this break in rehearsal. The woman was unusual for the club in that she was beautiful, yes, but not at all fleshy like the others. She was lithe and distinctly graceful and delicate in her movements. She was also by far the darkest of all the dancers, with skin so deeply pigmented she seemed to disappear when she was in the shade. But when the spotlights rested on her face, the sight was breathtaking, even during rehearsals when she wore no makeup.

Fernando didn't want to seem too obviously interested in the new female dancer. "You have some new people on the team," he said to Tony as casually as he could.

"Yes. The show is getting bigger, more elaborate, and the choreography is more complicated," Tony said.

"I'll meet the new dancers at some point." Fernando kept his eyes on the group. Some were stretched out on chairs, some sat on the ceramic tile floor.

Tony stood up. "Come on, I'll introduce you right now."

Julia was her name. She was tall, almost his height, even though he was taller than most of the men he knew. Up close her cheeks were lightly scarred from acne. But her smile, when Tony introduced them and she said *"Encantada,"* was irresistible. And her heart-shaped face, except for the flawed skin, was perfect, the eyes a translucent jade.

"Encantado," Fernando said, and he was utterly and completely enchanted. And suddenly he wanted to know everything about her. He had an endless number of questions in his head. Where did she live? Did she have a boyfriend? Was she from Havana? What did she … Why had she … When did she … Who was she,

in all her various aspects? But he focused and said, "Where have you danced before?"

She cocked her head to one side, a charming gesture of shyness, and said, "This is my first job. I just graduated from the dance academy."

Fernando was mesmerized, could have gone on talking to her all day. He had to suppress an urge to put his hands around her waist and kiss her. Tony turned, clapped his hands, and said to the group, "We have to get back to work. There's a lot to do."

As the dance team made its way to the stage, Julia looked back over her shoulder at Fernando. He wanted to follow her, not let her out of his sight, but he only nodded, as if in approval, and she smiled, as if she understood.

28

The family didn't talk about Señor Luis much, at least not in Ines's presence. She wondered how he was doing in the North. She couldn't imagine living in a new country, with a different language, strange foods, new ways of behaving. It didn't matter how difficult life was for her here. She was poor, she had lost her little girl, and Pedro was too ill to support them. They wanted to have another baby, but so far, despite their trying, she had not become pregnant. Still, no matter how difficult things were, she would be afraid to live anywhere else. She wouldn't even know how to begin, what was involved. Luis was a brave man.

Señor Fernando came into the kitchen.

"How are you, Ines?" he said. She had noticed that his whole manner had become much more relaxed lately. He reached for the electric blender in a far corner of the counter and plugged it in.

"I'm fine, thank you," Ines said. "Can I help you with something?"

"I'm going to make a papaya shake," Fernando said. He got the milk out of the refrigerator, took a papaya from the basket of fruit, and began to peel it.

Ines watched him work. She stirred the black beans, added olive oil to the pot but kept her eyes on what he was doing, glancing at his face to see if he knew she was watching him. His eyes were the darkest blue she had ever seen, like the ocean on a cloudy day. She was afraid of the ocean, didn't know how to swim. Maybe that's why she had always kept her distance from this man, hadn't felt anything like the interest she had felt for Señor Luis. But something else besides the reduced tension had changed in Señor Fernando recently. He stood up straighter, didn't have the constant furrow of worry between his eyebrows. She was becoming intrigued by him, although not attracted as she had been with Señor Luis.

Señor Fernando was making a mess. Half the papaya juice was dripping from the blender onto the floor, the scooped-out seeds covering the counter instead of going in the garbage.

"Let me make it for you," Ines said. "Where should I bring it to you?"

"I'll be on the porch," he said with a small chuckle, and went outside.

She found Señor Fernando in his usual red rocking chair that was old and in need of paint. He was reading a newspaper that looked different than the ones she had seen. It was much smaller, and the newsprint was pink, not the usual grayish white. And she didn't recognize the name of the paper, *La Libertad*.

Ines placed the glass with the amber liquid on the small metal table. He smiled in gratitude when she put the glass down. No one else in the family smiled at her much. She felt comfortable enough to ask, "That's a different newspaper than usual?"

He nodded. "Yes. It's American, but in Spanish. Luis mailed it to us. It's all news about Cuba, but it's printed there, in Florida."

Later that afternoon, Ines saw the newspaper in the living room on the pile to be discarded. She took the newspaper to the kitchen and put it in the tote bag she carried daily back and forth on the bus.

29

The change that is coming
   La Libertad staff writers

3 October 1958

The abuses of power of Batista's government may soon be coming to an end. Reports from journalists in the eastern part of Cuba point to an ever-growing movement of common citizens rising up against the government's military. Batista's response has been to dispatch his own secret terrorist forces, which are led primarily by Rolando Masferrer in Oriente, where most of the anti-government uprisings have occurred. Los Tigres, as Masferrer's gang is called, have been leaving no doubt in the minds of citizens that insurgencies will be dealt with ruthlessly.

A few months ago, four adolescents suspected of revolutionary activity were arrested in Santiago and turned over to Los Tigres. Subsequently, the four youths were found dead in an abandoned building. The bodies showed evidence of brutal torture. One of the victims, Carlos Perez Saenz, was fourteen years old.

Days after the discovery, over five hundred women dressed in black marched through the streets of Santiago, led by Perez Saenz's mother. Many of the women had lost sons to Batista's terrorists. They carried a sign that read "Stop the Assassination of Our Sons."

This resistance against government brutality has grown and moved west, toward Havana, and is gaining support and momentum. In retaliation, Los Tigres now hang the cadavers of their victims from telephone poles in Santiago.

Despite the brutality of Batista's henchmen, Fidel Castro, the leader of the uprising, has established a liberated zone in the Sierra Maestra, the mountains of Oriente Province. From this sanctuary he is directing the Havana-bound insurgency, by all accounts moving quickly and with great support from the population, most of them poor farmers working the fields of the island's land barons.

30

Lately it was Elena, not Fernando, who was the last to come to the dinner table, bringing the food in from the kitchen. Antonio hadn't failed to notice the change. It wasn't because Elena was sitting down later, but because Fernando was now appearing promptly when she called the two men in from the dining room.

There was something else Antonio had noticed. Fernando no longer sat at the opposite end of the table for six. He now sat close to his parents, the three of them at one end, Antonio still at the head, of course. Fernando was also more conversational, engaging his parents, making comments. For years he had been mostly silent during meals, absorbed in some internal process that had sombered his expression. Antonio had forgotten how outgoing and good-natured his younger son had been before starting university, and he attributed the recent positive change to Fernando turning away from political activity now that he had a job he seemed to enjoy. He was also wearing better clothes, his grooming was more meticulous, and he had bought a new car, a peculiar French contraption he researched and had been going on about.

It had been too many years since Antonio had felt good about his life. The political situation under Batista's grip produced constant tension. The corruption had hurt businesses, including his own employer's; his two sons had their plans upended; and activists were tortured or killed. Now, with Luis apparently safe in the US, and Fernando turned away from politicking, Antonio felt a lightening of the worry.

"There's a birthday party Sunday afternoon," Elena said to Fernando. She squeezed lemon juice on the fried hake on her plate. "It's for Rita, my friend Nina's daughter. You're invited."

Fernando frowned. "How is it I'm invited? I hardly know her."

"Nina wants you to come. Rita is about your age, and there'll be several of her friends there."

"I can't go," Fernando said. "I have plans."

"Plans for what? What are you doing?"

"I'm meeting someone. I have a date."

Elena hesitated, but she said, "You're seeing someone? You have a girlfriend?"

Fernando nodded, finished chewing, and said, "Yes. I've been seeing her now for about two months."

"What's her name?" Elena asked.

"Julia."

Elena looked at Antonio, whose mouth had curved into a smile, although his eyes were on his food.

"I'd like to meet her," Elena said. "Bring her here on Sunday."

"I can't. We're going to Santa Maria del Mar."

"How did you meet her?" asked Elena. She hadn't taken a bite of the hake, the fork in her hand still spotless.

Antonio didn't like to chide his wife in front of anyone, even his own sons, but he turned to her and said, "Elena."

"You'll meet her," Fernando said. "I'll introduce you one of these days."

After dinner, Fernando ambled out to the porch, stopping to look at a magazine in the living room. Outside, the sky was dimming, and on the porch he turned on the overhead light to read. He had changed the lighting to a new fluorescent bulb that would attract fewer mosquitoes. The book he had brought from his bedroom was a translation of Hemingway's *To Have and Have Not*. After a few minutes, his father joined him.

"How's the book?" Antonio asked.

"Very good. If my English were better, I'd read the original."

"Your English is pretty good. As good as Luis's."

"But not good enough to read a book like this," Fernando said.

Antonio nodded and looked out at the trees in the park across the street, fast becoming dark silhouettes in the vanishing light.

"I'm glad you found work. You like the job?"

Fernando hesitated. "It's not what I had planned, but it's okay for now. The money's good."

"It makes me happy that you're working. You're in a better mood."

"For the time being, this is okay," Fernando said.

Antonio paused, wondering how much to say. He didn't want to make his son uncomfortable, nor did he want to project neediness or inadequacy. He finally said, "I'm glad you're contributing to our budget. It makes everything easier."

Fernando shrugged. "You cared for Luis and me for so many years. It was time for me to be on the other side of it." He paused, then said, "I wonder how Luis is doing. I can't tell from his letters whether he's happy or not."

Antonio shook his head. "It sounds like it's difficult living there. I don't know if the money he makes is enough for him. He hasn't offered to send any. Not that we need it. But he doesn't even ask."

Fernando nodded, then said, "Maybe after expenses he doesn't have much left over. Although the salary he mentioned in his letter was very good."

Antonio knew what Fernando was thinking, that Luis would probably be oblivious to his parents' needs. His tendency toward self-centeredness was tacitly acknowledged in the family.

There were a few moments of silence. The crickets and the frogs had begun their chanting, and the trees had been swallowed up entirely by the twilight. The visible world was only as large as the porch. Fernando kept his book closed, an index finger marking his place.

"Are you thinking of leaving also?" Antonio asked. He had wanted to avoid the issue, but some uncertainty, or even outright fear that Fernando would be gone soon, brought it out of him.

"No. Never. And if I did, I would send you money."

"No. That's not what I mean. I'm not worried about the money part. I just want as many of us together as possible." Antonio felt a surge of emotion that might have turned into a sob if he hadn't cleared his throat. He was immensely grateful to God that Fernando had survived the attack by Batista's henchmen. Losing him was unimaginable. And now Luis was gone, who knew for how long, and there wasn't enough money nowadays for a quick trip to Florida to visit him. He lamented having taken for granted the complete family he had enjoyed for many years, regretted his stern demeanor, his unexpressed affection. He realized that in the past he had not felt the same degree of love for his family that he did now.

"I'm here, *Papá*, and this is where I'm going to stay," Fernando said.

Antonio nodded, got up from the green rocking chair, and raised his hand in a silent *Good night*.

31

For the past month, there had been strange food shortages. Eggs might be scarce one week, ham the next, then flour. The men behind the counters at the bodegas spoke of problems with distribution and interruptions of supply chains as trucks on their way to Havana were hijacked and the contents confiscated. Restaurants had to change their menus constantly. But nobody knew who these hijackers were, and if they did, they didn't talk about it openly.

There were also frequent power and telephone outages. The utility disruptions affected homes and businesses, including restaurants and nightclubs. Fernando had heard rumors that the peasant unrest in the east was moving toward Havana and was causing all the upheaval. Bombs were going off all over the city in parks, private businesses, and government offices.

Business in the casino had plummeted because of the brewing turmoil, now half of what it had been just a month ago, and attendance at the nightclub was also declining. The numbers translated into a huge drop in profits, and Fernando's reports to the American owners and their lawyers and accountants triggered phone calls and questions. There were audits, and one of the American owners, known to be a member of the Mafia, visited the casino with his bodyguards and an auditor.

Gustavo called Fernando. "Let's meet this weekend," he said. "We have to talk." His voice was strained and he kept the conversation brief.

When Fernando asked if there was a problem, Gustavo said, "Let's talk on Saturday."

Fernando saw Julia on Sunday, the day after his meeting with Gustavo. There was no show at the club on Sundays and Mondays, and they usually saw each other both days, when she didn't have to dance late into the night. The best part of his time with Julia on Sundays was their walk along the Malecón, that ancient seawall that went on for miles, a promenade for lovers, families, and solitary, sometimes pensive, individuals. They walked for over an hour, arms around each other's waists, passersby glancing at them and smiling, apparently charmed by their looks or by their evident love for each other. The ocean sprayed their faces, warmed by the sun. Afterwards they had dinner at their favorite Chinese restaurant, and went to Julia's apartment for a few hours of lovemaking.

Despite the problems at the casino with the unpredictable scarcities and power outages, Fernando had never been happier. On the day he had met Julia, he wished with all his heart he would get to know her, spend long hours with her. Although he was not religious, he had prayed that someday he would be one with her. His prayers had been answered.

Julia shared an apartment in Old Havana with another performer, a singer in a band. It was a small two-bedroom walk-up on the third floor with a view of the Capitol and the Parque Central. Being in the apartment with Julia felt like a joyful event, like Christmas or the amusement park when he was a boy. He had never stayed the night because the bedroom was just big enough for a single narrow bed. Still, they had already spent many happy hours there, Fernando usually dozing off for a few minutes after sex. Those naps, during which he was vaguely aware of her proximity, were blissful.

"Is something the matter?" Julia asked him after dinner on Monday evening, walking on the way to the movie theater.

Fernando hadn't been aware that the creeping darkness he was feeling was noticeable. He was surprised by her question, and for a moment had to look inside himself to remember what was weighing so heavily on him.

"Nothing too serious, I don't think," he said. "There are problems with finances at work. The owners are auditing the books, and they've been asking me questions."

"Are they doubting you?"

"No. I don't think so. They're just trying to go through everything in order to be thorough."

"I know business has been slow," Julia said. "But everyone is saying that there is a revolutionary movement, and that the peasants in the east are joining the armed groups that are getting closer to Havana. We haven't seen as many tourists, and the locals are worried about what's going on, all the bombs."

"I know," Fernando said. He put his arm around her waist, and the feel of her body made his troubled mood recede. "It's going to be okay."

"Let's hope," Julia said.

She made him feel confident that the future would be fine with just her way of being, and he leaned over and kissed her cheek, although he wanted to do more. He wished they were in her apartment. Her smile when he kissed her allowed the happiness that had receded to bloom again.

Fernando didn't tell her about the conversation he'd had with Gustavo two days ago. He didn't want to ruin the mood. The armed militia coming from the east was highly organized, Gustavo had said. They had been supplied with firearms by the US companies, as well as by some Latin American countries that wanted Batista out. They saw his corrupt government as untenable, and they wanted to curry favor with Fidel Castro, whom they saw as the inevitable next president of the island. The interruptions in food supplies were the result of the systematic hijacking of transport trucks, and the sporadic electrical and telephone failures were from wires being cut by the ramshackle troops as they neared Havana. The Revolution, Gustavo had said enthusiastically, was highly organized. Things were going to change.

As Fernando listened to his friend, he silently hoped there wasn't going to be a catastrophic bloody war right in the streets of Havana, or a new regime as bad as his parents were predicting. "People who knew Fidel Castro in the university say he was a Marxist," Elena had said only last week. "And it sounds like he's doing some awful things in the east on his way to Havana. Taking private land away, executing property owners who resist him."

Antonio had nodded and said, "We may be going from bad to worse if Castro's uprising succeeds."

Fernando thought his parents were exaggerating. How could the Revolution be Marxist? They were being supplied with weapons and other equipment by American corporations with the approval of the US government.

32

1959

There was a radio in the living room, a Grundig as big as a transoceanic trunk and made of fine burled wood. It stood on one side of the sofa as if it were an end table. Whoever wanted to listen to it would sit next to it and fine-tune the periodically drifting radio signal.

It was January 1st, New Year's, but everyone was up early because there had been only muted celebrations the night before. Bombs had exploded throughout the city for weeks and almost no one had gone out to ring in the new year. Antonio, Elena, and Fernando hugged after consuming the traditional twelve grapes and a glass of Spanish cider at midnight, and then went right to bed. Elena came close to crying because Luis was so far away; the first time, she said, the four of them hadn't been together for New Year's. She was glad that at least Fernando had been with them. He couldn't be with his girlfriend Julia, he had said, because she was working New Year's Eve.

Elena sat down by the radio at eight in the morning with a cup of café con leche. Just before midnight she had heard news of the rebel attacks on the government's strongholds in Matanzas, halfway between Havana and Oriente. The revolutionary forces, the radio announcer had reported the prior night, overwhelmed the military headquarters three hours from Havana, and were headed west toward the capital.

Elena gasped and almost dropped her cup and saucer when she heard the morning news on the Grundig. She got up from the sofa and looked out the window at the park and the trees across the street to see if the world still looked the same. Then she went into the kitchen, where Fernando was making coffee.

"Batista's gone," she said to her son.

Fernando's eyes were still bleary from sleep. "What?" he said.

"He's gone. He took a plane to the Dominican Republic right after midnight." Her voice was loud for so early in the morning.

Fernando had just put ground coffee in the pot and was about to put it on the stove, but he left it on the counter. "Are you sure?" he said, incredulous, and when she nodded, he hugged her. Elena didn't hug him back, and her eyes narrowed with annoyance.

Antonio came in, wearing his fine burgundy satin robe. "What's the matter?" he asked, and when he heard the news his face turned dark. "My God," he said, and went back to the bedroom.

"What's the matter with *Papá?*" Fernando said. "This is what we've been praying for."

Elena shook her head. She wanted to scold her son, but she tensed her lips instead. She remembered what she had heard listening to the Voice of America on the Grundig most nights, confirming the stories from the eastern part of the island. "Those revolutionaries are not good people," she said. "They've confiscated private lands and shot any owners who resisted. They divided the farms up and gave the land to the peasants. They've even killed ordinary citizens who defied them." She put the coffeepot on the stove and turned the burner on. "These are not the people you want in charge. It's not going to be any better than it was with Batista. Maybe worse."

Elena ignored the unhappy look on Fernando's face at first, watching as he turned down the flame under the coffeepot. On her way out of the kitchen, she stopped and said, "Your enemy's enemy is not necessarily your friend. Stay neutral. Don't let your enthusiasm for something new blind you."

She wished her twenty-two-year-old son were more cagey. She remembered him as a gullible child, more naïve than most of the other children in the neighborhood, and she wasn't seeing that much of a difference now. The angry tone in his voice surprised her when he said, "Well, I'm celebrating, because that son of a bitch is gone."

She held back from slapping him for using that tone and language with her. Her lips thinned in annoyance as she headed to the bedroom.

It wasn't until much later in the day, after she had talked to Nina, her friend and canasta partner, that she thought about Ramon. The news from the radio and from her conversation with Nina was that the police had disbanded. They had all disappeared into their homes in terror. Some had been beaten, and some of them, along with informants, had been killed. The military police were on stand-by in their barracks, but because the top generals had fled with Batista, no one was in charge yet.

She wondered if anything had happened, or would happen, to Ramon. Had he been found out as an informant and collaborator with the old regime?

Elena tried to sort out her emotions. Her imperfect love for Antonio intruded and she pushed it aside for the moment. She had truly cared for Ramon, then been repelled by his connection to the Batista government. It was possible that a man just like him had identified her son as an activist. A man like Ramon had caused her son to be permanently maimed. He might have been killed. She didn't know what to feel about the man, what to wish for.

33

Antonio loved to walk. On his way to work every day he took the bus, then walked a mile from the bus stop to his office, and made the identical trip in reverse in the evenings. Today, New Year's Day, he would miss that invigorating walk. Most businesses were closed, except for some bodegas, so for now there wasn't even an excuse to go to any kind of store. Instead, early in the morning he went to church by himself, as he did every Sunday. He assumed that today's Mass would be scantily attended and quiet. In the afternoon he would go to the local bodega, four long blocks away. He knew it would open at noon, Sunday hours. The men would gather around the domino tables on the sidewalk outside the shop, filling each other in on the momentous events of the day.

Elena sat by the Grundig most of the morning, listening to the news about looters breaking storefronts in Old Havana, of fires being set, parking meters destroyed because it was rumored that all their revenue had gone directly into Batista's pockets. When Antonio got home from church, she filled him in. Later, Elena rushed from the living room every few minutes to find Antonio and Fernando and give them an update on the news.

"Wait for me, I'll go with you after I finish this," Fernando said when Antonio mentioned he was leaving for the bodega. Fernando had just now taken the Peugeot's carburetor apart and was cleaning it. He didn't want his father to go alone. Things might not be safe on the streets, even in their usually quiet neighborhood.

"No," Antonio said. "I want to go right now. If there is trouble starting near us, I want to know about it."

Fernando planned to call Julia later. She had mentioned that she would be working late, the New Year's Eve show longer and more elaborate than usual. She probably had danced until midnight and most likely wouldn't have gone to bed before two. Their plan was to have dinner today, a day off despite it being Thursday, because Club Maxime would be closed.

When Antonio got back from the bodega, his face had changed; the skin pale, the eyes startled. "The news on the radio was not an exaggeration," he said. "Justino's hardware store was broken into, and looters took everything they could. And the bodega has its metal shutters closed and won't open today at all."

Elena closed the front window and made sure the Ford and the Peugeot in the driveway were locked. To no one in particular, she said, "I wish we had a garage." Fernando checked the phone line to make sure there was a dial tone, in case there was trouble. But what was the point? Who would they call if vandals tried to break in or steal their cars? The police themselves were in hiding.

Fernando didn't want to submit to a feeling of helplessness that was threatening to creep in. He went to the kitchen and found the biggest knife, a ten-inch chef's tool, and found his father's old baseball bat in the rear closet near the kitchen. He took both to the living room, where his mother was still sitting, and left them on the coffee table in front of the sofa.

"What have we come to?" Elena said, in a voice so high-pitched it sounded like a wail.

Fernando called Julia. The one telephone in the house was in the central hallway that ran from the living room to the kitchen in the back. There was no such thing as a private conversation here.

Julia had heard the news on the radio. "I hear gunfire, but I don't see anything out the window. The streets are deserted," she said.

"Please don't go out. If you need anything, I'll get it for you," Fernando said.

"Look, I don't need anything. And neither one of us should go outside."

"I'm going to miss seeing you today," Fernando said. He was dismayed that she might venture out and get hurt. He felt helpless and angry, and didn't want to hang up. "I'm worried about you. Is your roommate there?"

"No. She went to visit her family in Cienfuegos for New Year's. I'm hoping she'll be back tomorrow. Who knows now, with all this commotion."

"I don't want you to be by yourself. I'll come stay with you." His heart was racing at the thought of her being alone, although the idea of driving through turmoil and riots also worried him.

"Look, don't do that," Julia said. "Nobody's going to bother with this plain little apartment building. I'm fine." There was a tone of finality to her voice.

He went to sit with his parents in the living room. His father was somehow calm enough to be reading a novel by a classic Cuban writer, Cabrera Infante. Fernando had tried to read him once and had given up; the story went from realistic to fantastical without warning. Elena was staring into space, her head tilted toward the Grundig, which she would glance at with alarm periodically, as if it were a visitor describing some horror.

He didn't want to be here. He felt he should be with Julia, but perhaps she was right.

Or was she?

Why wasn't she in need of his company as much as he was of hers? She was affectionate, solicitous of his caresses, responsive in bed. And yet there was that independence, a limit she had begun to set to the time he spent with her. All these months, it seemed he was always the one to initiate their seeing each other. He remembered Maribel, her lack of receptivity, actually more like a hostility to his interest in her. What was it with the women he was attracted to? Was he that expendable a person, that unappealing, that they could take him or leave him? Or was he just too dependent on women's approval and affection?

"Everything's going to be fine, Fernando," his mother was saying. "This will pass. Don't take it so hard."

He opened his eyes and realized he was bent over in his chair, holding his head in his hands.

The phone rang and Elena rushed to answer it. "Fernando," she called out, and his heart stopped for two beats. He was certain it was bad news. "It's Gustavo for you."

The rioters had attacked most of the nightclubs, Gustavo said. Club Maxime's doors had been battered and the windows smashed. Most of the cash was gone and the gaming tables had their felt tops slashed. A fire had caused some damage.

"But why attack the clubs?" Fernando asked.

"Because they're owned by the American Mafia," Gustavo said. "And they were a big source of income for Batista."

"I'll go there tomorrow to check it out if things have calmed down," Fernando said.

"There's no point. I'll let you know when to go back," Gustavo said. "Be careful, my friend."

34

The leaders of the Revolution—Fidel Castro, his brother Raúl, and Che Guevara—would be at the head of the parade that would arrive in Havana on January 8th. A grand military convoy would make its way on the Malecón and continue along the main thoroughfares through the center of the city to the presidential palace.

Antonio wished he could just feel the relief of a cruel dictatorship ending, and not the dread of a suspect government taking over. That these new leaders had forged a ruthless, violent war against the landowners and confiscated their property was not just a rumor Elena had heard, or propaganda from the Voice of America; it was common knowledge now on the streets. People in Havana with relatives in the eastern part of the country confirmed it. Was that the best the country could do to replace a dictator? Antonio wanted to see for himself what these men looked like, how they behaved, and, most importantly, how the crowd would react. Would these revolutionaries be well-received and supported by the population despite their brutal reputation?

"The military parade will pass right by my office at the Cargo Cuba headquarters," Antonio said to Elena.

She nodded. "Yes. So what?" She was short-tempered lately, more so when she had to do chores. She was just now sweeping the hallway, pushing a pile of dust toward the kitchen. Ines hadn't come to work for three days, since the fall of the old regime. Elena knew that the buses weren't running properly. Ines wouldn't just quit, but Elena hadn't heard from her. She wished Ines had a phone.

"We should go and watch the military convoy from my office on the second floor," Antonio said.

Elena's broom stopped in mid-sweep. Her hair was disheveled, the housedress damp from sweat. "Leave me out of it," she said.

"I want to see what we've got coming and how the people react," Antonio said.

"I've heard on the radio and read in the papers what we have coming," she said, and resumed sweeping, but after two strokes she stopped again. "And you know,

Nina's brother was beaten in Matanzas because he resisted when these gangsters took most of his farm and gave it to the workers."

Fernando came out of his bedroom. He stepped carefully over the pile of dust near his door. "What's the discussion?" he said.

"The discussion is that your father wants to go celebrate the rebels' arrival in Havana."

"Who said celebrate?" Antonio's voice was uncharacteristically loud now. "I want to see what we've got on our hands."

"I'm not going," Elena brayed. She threw the broom on the floor and stormed into the kitchen in the rear.

Antonio regretted raising his voice. It was not something he thought of as becoming for gentleman, especially to his own wife and in front of his son.

"Why is *Mamá* so against the rebels? I would think she'd be glad to be rid of the tyrant."

"They're probably communists and have been stripping landowners of their property, giving it to the poor farmhands," Antonio said. "And they've even been cruel to the middle-class citizens."

"Yes, she told me, and I've heard about it elsewhere. But that's not so bad, is it? There's so much poverty in this country, so much injustice."

Antonio shook his head. "Fernando, there are ways of doing things properly, with order. The constitutional law you were studying—wouldn't you want those concepts to be respected? You think communists respect constitutional law?" He was sorry he sounded so testy.

Fernando said nothing and went into the kitchen.

Cargo Cuba stood on the wide avenue on which the convoy was to travel. But he was uneasy about the prospect of watching by himself, just in the company of coworkers. He thought that the sight of the arriving revolutionaries would be like taking a bandage off a wound to look at badly damaged skin, and didn't know how he would react, what his face would look like at the sight of these ruffians who were now in command. Who knew what his coworkers thought of the new regime. Based on what he had overheard in the office since Batista's departure, the employees were mostly in favor of the Revolution. It was possible that even the owners of Cargo Cuba, who had seen their profits dwindle when they refused to pay bribes to Batista's gang, would be in support. He wanted the comfort of Elena or Fernando with him. But he didn't want to ask Fernando outright to accompany him. He wanted to set an example for the family and appear strong and remain calm. If Elena was right and things were going to be even more problematic than they had been, they all needed to keep level heads.

Antonio found Fernando in the kitchen and said, "My office will be a good place to watch the parade, if you want to come."

"Good idea. I'll meet you there," Fernando said. "The nightclub is still closed for repairs for another few days, so I can't go to work anyway."

"Do you want to bring Julia?" Antonio asked. He was eager to meet his son's girlfriend, with whom the young man had spent so much time since Batista's departure and the ensuing riots.

Fernando shook his head. "No. I'll be seeing her this afternoon, so probably not tomorrow."

Antonio wondered why Fernando couldn't see his girlfriend two days in a row, but he saw a haze of sadness pass over his son's face, and he didn't pursue it.

The next morning, Antonio got to his office before the crowds started assembling on the street. By two o'clock, people lined the wide avenue two and three deep, waving the red and black banner of the Revolution as well as the Cuban flag. Fernando navigated the crowded sidewalk and finally made it to the Cargo Cuba building. Upstairs, on the second floor, he found his father. Several employees and their families stood at the windows. There was an air of excitement and anticipation in the spacious waiting room that Antonio found unsettling. How could all these employees—shipping agents, secretaries, clerks—display this childish enthusiasm over an incoming government that already had a questionable reputation? "Come into my office," Antonio said to Fernando. "We'll be more comfortable there."

The private office had a large picture window. Antonio closed the door. Soon, the first of the olive-green military trucks rolled past, bearded men sitting on top wielding rifles like celebrants in a festive parade. Except they were not smiling and did not resemble good-natured participants in a motorcade. On their faces was a look of arrogance, even hostility, and they held their rifles looking at the cheering crowds as if ready to point the barrels at them. Even at this distance Antonio could see that they were dirty, their hair and beards long and ungroomed, the olive-green uniforms filthy. To Antonio they looked like street criminals triumphant after a gang war. He exchanged looks with Fernando. Even in the privacy of this office, they said nothing, and neither one smiled.

35

Luis called the day after the new government had arrived in Havana and officially taken over. As usual, Elena was the one who spent the most time on the phone with him. The calls were expensive, and they could talk for only a few minutes.

"Don't even think about coming home," Fernando heard his mother say into the mouthpiece. "It's all uncertain now. Things are still in transition."

After the call, she said, "He's thinking about coming home. I didn't want to be too specific about what's going on. There's no reason to think this new government isn't tapping international calls, just like the old one did."

The club and casino were still closed and Fernando spent a lot of time at home. He had expressed some skepticism about the new government to Julia yesterday, Sunday, when he went to see her. He had confirmed from eyewitness accounts what he heard on the radio and read in the newspapers about property being confiscated and citizens who resisted being beaten or killed, and he told her. Julia had become angry when she heard his misgivings. "This is a change for the better," she said, and stayed morose the rest of their time together. No amount of explanation had softened her emotional withdrawal, and she had ended their date early, before dinner. He wouldn't see her again until tomorrow; that is, if she didn't cancel altogether.

The phone rang. Ines had returned to work but she was in the back, catching up on the laundry that had piled up. Fernando answered. His mother was at a neighbor's house for afternoon coffee.

"Is Elena there?" a man's slurred voice said.

"No. She's out. Who's calling?"

"It's Ramon Safran. A friend." The man had been drinking heavily, although it was only four in the afternoon.

"I'll let her know you called," Fernando said, wanting to hang up yet curious as to who this was. Suddenly he realized that this was Betty Safran's husband. His mother would have met him during one of the canasta games Betty hosted.

"Tell her that I'm worried about everything that's going on, and that I miss her very much. Tell her to call me at the office." The man hung up.

It took a moment for all this information to fall into place, and with that clarity came waves of nausea and lightheadedness. The condoms in his mother's car now had a more concrete and sickening meaning. Not that he had ever believed that his parents used condoms with each other. Antonio was deeply religious and refused to use contraception, had been clear and vocal about his beliefs. "Abstention is your best option," his father had advised him years ago when he entered puberty.

Fernando stood immobile by the phone a few seconds, stunned, then began to fidget around, restless with the distressing confirmation of what he had suspected. He paced the house, went into his bedroom and opened the dresser drawers and closed them again, not knowing what he was looking for. He finally settled down on the porch with a book he was just starting, a biography of José Martí, the great revolutionary who had led Cuba's revolt against Spain. How had one person, a poet who wrote such delicate verse, been so instrumental in the freedom of an entire country? But even Martí's rhyme and disciplined poetic structure couldn't distract him from rehashing the telephone conversation.

He saw his mother on the sidewalk coming from the neighbor's house next door, approaching the gate into the garden. He waited until she had climbed the last step onto the porch. "Ramon called you," he said, and watched her shoulders freeze in midstride, her neck stiffen, but when she looked at him he had turned his eyes back to the book on his lap. "He's Betty's husband, right?"

"Yes. What did he want?" Her voice was as thin as a girl's.

"He didn't say." Fernando turned the page without looking up. "He said you should call him at the office."

He watched his mother's back as she walked into the house, her shoulders slumped now.

Fernando couldn't concentrate on his book, reading the same page twice and closing the cover. He decided to walk to the bodega, four long blocks away, and buy some chewing gum. It was five-thirty, and the January sun was just above the trees.

At the bodega, things were as usual. There were men playing dominoes, groups of two or three talking and gesturing about the new government, no doubt. He bought a pack of peppermint Chiclets and popped two in his mouth. He didn't want to go home, but he knew none of the bodega congregants, was still too young for the know-it-all political discussions. The self-proclaimed sages were all in their forties and older.

He walked around the neighborhood, waving occasionally at someone he knew sitting on their porch. He tried to shape all the bits of information that had gathered in his head. His mother had been playing canasta at Betty's house and sleeping with her husband. Or could he have misheard or misinterpreted his telephone conversation with Ramon? But no, Ramon's words still resonated in his head, and his mother's reaction on the porch confirmed the suspicion.

He walked past Betty and Ramon's house. It was now near six, and Ramon's car was in the driveway. Fernando knew Betty didn't drive. Elena drove her sometimes for appointments if Betty couldn't get her daughter to do so.

The car in the driveway was new, a splendid 1958 Chevrolet Impala, turquoise, with exuberantly flaring tailfins. Fernando knew it had a powerful engine, a V8 with a four-barrel carburetor, and likely had air conditioning and electric windows. He had considered buying one before opting for the Peugeot, which was a more sensible, less flashy choice.

It was six o'clock when he walked in the door and Ines was just leaving.

"Have you heard from Señor Luis?" Ines asked. She had become less withdrawn the last few months, more self-confident. He had seen her reading the newspapers the family discarded.

"Yes. He called yesterday."

"How is he?" she said with a shy smile.

"He's fine. Wondering whether to come home."

The smile was now a full one. "Oh," she said. "When?"

"No one knows yet. Depends how things here go."

Ines nodded. "Until tomorrow," she said, and closed the door behind her.

Is attraction between two people always imbalanced, Fernando wondered, with one of the two always in greater need and the other maybe even oblivious? He didn't care. He couldn't wait to see Julia tomorrow evening.

36

Gustavo called Fernando on Saturday morning. "Can you meet me at Cristina's house at four this afternoon?" he asked.

"Sure," Fernando said. "What's going on?" It was eight in the morning and he hadn't even had coffee yet.

"I think there are things left to be done," Gustavo said, in his customary cryptic way. His caution was usually justified, but Fernando wondered why his friend seemed worried now.

"Who's going to be there? Just the three of us?" Sonya had dropped out long ago, and no one had heard from Maribel or Enrique.

"That's all. See you later." Gustavo hung up abruptly.

Fernando went into the kitchen and asked Ines to bring him some coffee in the dining room. He usually made it himself, but he was in a fog, hadn't slept well, had been awake since four in the morning. The certainty that Ramon was his mother's lover had opened a painful ulcer in his core he couldn't ignore now, the way he had minimized the discovery of the condoms. That finding had presented an abstract scenario that his mother was possibly, but not necessarily, having an affair. But now there was a name, the means his mother had used to commit adultery. He felt deep sympathy for his father, and a distinct distaste for his mother that had the potential to turn into emotional distance from her. And yet, when he looked deep inside and asked himself *Has anything really changed in what you feel for her?* the answer was that his love for her was undiminished, although now illuminated with different lights that cast deep shadows.

His sluggishness persisted throughout the day, and he considered skipping the meeting at Cristina's. He finally decided to go, but procrastinated his departure and was the last to arrive.

"Any news from Maribel?" Fernando asked after taking a seat on a divan next to Gustavo.

"Sonya thinks she's part of the new government," Cristina said. "She said she saw Maribel in a photograph in the paper with some rebels, organizing land distribution in Havana."

"Land distribution," Fernando said. "What land? There are no farms here."

"There's talk of landlords being stripped of their property and tenants being given ownership," Gustavo said. "They're calling it urban reform."

"Well," Cristina said, a look of chagrin on her face, "we always heard rumors that the Revolution might have a communist leaning, but I guess this confirms it."

Fernando indeed remembered his parents' comments about the new government having a connection with communism. There were some rumors, his mother had said, that the Soviet Union was involved in the Revolution, and Fidel Castro himself was said to still harbor the Marxist ideology he had adopted as a university student.

Gustavo said, "If it's communism, so be it. It has to be better than what we had." He waved the file folder. "Let's see if there's anything we want to do with this," he said. From the folder he took out two typewritten sheets and gave them to Cristina and Fernando.

"What is this?" Cristina said.

"A list of informants who worked with Batista's police to identify student activists," Gustavo said. "We need to decide whether to make these names public. The new government hasn't decided what to do about these people, because they were only part-time informants."

Cristina cocked her head. "Where did you get this?" she asked.

"Police headquarters. This list was for their payroll under Batista. I went there and explained that I had been part of an activist group, and they loaned me this carbon copy. But I have to give it back."

"There were police there?" Cristina said. "I thought they were all in hiding."

"No police. The barracks are being manned by the new military. They're recruiting officers, but for now the militia is keeping order."

Cristina said, "What made you go look for the list of names? Why even bother?"

"It's a loop that needs to be closed, Cristina," Gustavo said. "They hunted our fellow students down for torture and assassination. All those people need to be brought to justice." He gestured toward Fernando and said, "Don't forget what they did to one of us."

Cristina gave her list to Fernando as she said, "A lot of people would go after these informers in revenge. Maybe they deserve it, but what's the point?"

Fernando nodded. "I'm not sure what it would accomplish now," he said. "They might be prosecuted by the new government anyway. If this list is made public, they might also be attacked by citizens." He looked at the papers in his hand. His fingernails had not grown back normally. "It would just be revenge."

He glanced down the list of names, and his eyes froze on one that jumped out as if it had been written in red ink. Ramon Safran. An uncommon last name.

Gustavo was incredulous. "So we do nothing?" he said.

Cristina shrugged. "Like Fernando said, it would just be revenge. I don't see the point."

Fernando was still trying to process all the information spinning in his head. He forced himself to come back to the present moment. "No," he said. "There's no point."

Gustavo didn't look happy. "These men caused a great deal of pain, and maybe even death. They hurt you, Fernando. You could have been killed. The point is justice. They have to be made accountable."

"So what do you want to do, Gustavo?" Fernando asked. His voice was a soft croak, like a tired old man's. He didn't want to talk. He prayed his mother hadn't known that Ramon was an informant. That would be more than he could handle, more than he could live with.

"Give the list to the newspapers. Let them publish the names of these bastards."

Gustavo's face was full of venom, nothing Fernando had ever seen in him. "I just want the three of us to be in agreement," he added.

Fernando nodded, licked his dry lips.

"I guess it's fine to do that. They'll be found out eventually. Anything else we should be doing?" Cristina asked.

Gustavo gathered the papers from Fernando and put them back in the folder. "Yes. We should all organize neighborhood vigilance committees. The government wants them set up to report anti-revolutionary activity," Gustavo said, and glared at his friends. "We want this Revolution to succeed. I'm going to start one in my neighborhood. You should each start your own."

37

1951

The first recollection Gustavo had of his mother stressing the value of education was from elementary school. No illness was severe enough—no cold, or sore throat, or bellyache—to stay home. "You're not going to learn anything staying home," was her refrain.

By the time he was fifteen and in secondary school, he had internalized that concept and was an excellent student. After school he worked for a dry cleaner, making deliveries on a bicycle, steering with one hand while the other held the hangers on which hung dresses and suits and shirts.

When one of the girls behind the counter got married and left, Gustavo asked to take her place dealing with customers in the store. "Not you," the owner said. She was a large white woman with hair that was too black and too long for her age. "Customers don't like to see people like you behind the counter." He knew the "like you" meant his skin color, and he turned away in silence.

He took care to always use the same streets on his bicycle, as much as the various destinations allowed, because he wanted to be a familiar figure in the white neighborhoods and avoid suspicion and harassment. Still, there were times when people sitting on their porches or coming and going on the sidewalks looked at him with hostility or shouted a racial epithet, "What are you doing here, you Black shit," was one he heard often. But he persisted. He needed the money to buy books for school and help his mother with the groceries. His father was long gone, shot by the police in a case of mistaken identity when Gustavo was four. His mother, Obdulia, worked as a dishwasher in the kitchen of a restaurant.

On a cool, sunny afternoon Gustavo was cycling back to the cleaners after a delivery when he heard a shot being fired nearby. He looked in the direction of the sound and saw a man standing in his front yard aiming a rifle at him. Two young children stood near the man. Gustavo heard another shot and felt the bicycle shake and jerk to a stop, which threw him off onto the asphalt. When he looked up, he saw that the bicycle chain had been hit and now hung uselessly. He saw the man take aim again and he ran into an empty lot behind him, next to a small apartment house across the narrow street from the shooter. He crouched behind some weedy shrubbery. "Help!" he yelled out. "Help! They're killing a Black man!" Another shot was fired, and the bullet came close enough to Gustavo that he saw the tall weeds quiver.

People from the apartment building came out to look. One of them, a gray-haired old woman in a sleeveless housedress, walked unsteadily across the street to where the shooter was standing and gestured at him. She pointed at the two children, who were witnessing what the two adults were doing and saying.

Gustavo saw the man put the rifle down, the butt of the firearm now on the ground. The old woman hobbled to the bicycle and lifted it off the asphalt. Gustavo slowly stood up straight, ready to hit the ground again if the man picked up the rifle. He walked with hesitant steps to the woman holding up his bicycle. "You'd better find another route to do your deliveries," she told him.

"Thank you, Señora," Gustavo said. "May God reward you."

His father was not the only man who had been unjustly killed by the authorities. He knew of others, fathers of some of the dark-skinned boys and girls at school, killed not just by police but by ordinary citizens who had suspected their victims were criminals just for being in a white neighborhood. The killers always went unpunished, and the rage Gustavo felt at these wanton deaths came and went. More often than not, he was able to replace his anger with an ambition to succeed, have a professional future.

Still, something was wrong, Gustavo thought, with a country in which racially-motivated deaths occurred without legal consequences. He wondered whether something in the government could change in the future, or if he would be forever a target because of his skin color. He wished all white people were like Fernando, the young man with whom he played baseball in the park.

38

1959

For the first time since they had met, Julia wasn't excited about the prospect of spending time with Fernando. Up until now, all their times together had been not just fun, but charged with energy, the connection between them like electricity that made her muscles and her skin scintillate. She adored him, and until recently there had been no question in her mind that they would continue to be a couple. But the possibility of marriage had stayed in a nebulous background, undefined.

Fernando was the first white man she had ever been with, not that she had been with many men, just two really, and a third for a short time. This feeling she had now about seeing him, bordering on indifference, was new. But the fact was, she was annoyed with him. It wasn't a deep resentment, more like a frustration because of his doubts about the new government.

She was thrilled about the change in the country. She was nineteen and had lived most of her life under Batista's dictatorship. Like most of the island's people of color, her family was poor, with little or no education. Her grandparents had been slaves. Her mother, Clara, had never gone to school and had worked as a domestic alongside her own mother since childhood. Julia's life had been encumbered by poverty since birth. There hadn't always been enough to eat, and as a child she wore used, sometimes ragged, clothes. Her father had been a trumpet player with a band and disappeared when she was born.

Her mother still lived in the same tenement in a rundown neighborhood in Havana and depended on Julia's income as a dancer. Everyone she knew intimately—her family, the Black friends she had grown up with—were poor and struggling, unable to enjoy equal footing in this society because of their skin color. She was the only one with a good job and a decent income, thanks to her talent. Julia was convinced the new government, with their promise of economic and social reform, would bring equality to dark-skinned people. Didn't Fernando see that?

Julia had excelled in school, especially gifted in learning languages. And she had always loved to dance. Her English was decent. When she went to American movies, she tried not to read the Spanish subtitles. But her passion was dance. Her mother, working as a domestic in a wealthy household, couldn't afford the dance lessons Julia wanted, of course. On a hunch, and hoping for nothing more than a small increase in her salary, she took Julia to work one day, as her own mother had done. Julia had been ten, and Clara knew her daughter could charm anybody. "Let's see if they can help us with your dance lessons," Clara said to Julia on their way to her employer's house.

That day, the lady of the house commented on Julia's beauty and graceful, nymph-like movements. "I want to dance," Julia blurted out, "but *Mamá* can't pay for lessons." Even at that young age, Julia understood that this white woman in her huge house filled with marble and bronze and mahogany might be moved by her looks and her poise to help her. She already knew that people responded to her appearance and her manner. "Look! Look!" Julia said. She raised her arms and stood on tiptoe on one foot while the other leg did a pirouette. And, in fact, that day the lady of the house did offer to pay for dance lessons, and continued doing so until Julia was accepted with a scholarship, at age fifteen, into the Pro-Arte Academia de Ballet. After all these years, Julia still kept in touch with her benefactor and occasionally went to the family's house with her mother, who still cooked for them.

Only a handful of students at the ballet academy had skin as dark as Julia's. There were constant reminders from her light-skinned peers as well as teachers. "Don't arch your back so much," a dour ex-prima donna had said to her once, "it's not an African dance."

Fernando arrived at her apartment a few minutes early. She let him in, kissed him briefly, and went back to the bedroom to finish dressing, letting him wait in the small living room instead of inviting him to keep her company. Afterwards, walking to the car, she took his arm. She had to believe this suspension of her ardor would be transient and could be bridged by an honest discussion. All during dinner at a fine Spanish restaurant she worked at it so they would talk as they always did; no awkward pauses, no crossed signals.

They walked along the Malecón afterwards. There was a crescent moon over the ocean playing hide-and-seek with the silvery clouds. The background sound of the waves made the silent intervals comfortable.

"You know I come from a very poor family," Julia said after a quiet moment.

"Yes, I know." Fernando sounded hesitant.

"Black people like me have had it very difficult in this country. For many years. Forever."

"I know, my love." His arm tightened around her waist, drawing her closer. She felt a need for him deep in her pelvis, and she almost abandoned the line of conversation she wanted to pursue.

She said, "This new situation, with Batista gone, gives me hope that there will be a change for us."

Fernando held silent a moment. "I understand," he said, and paused. "But there are some signs that this new government may not be good for the country. For anybody. They've appointed an old Marxist politician to be president, although the power is still with Fidel only. If we become like the Soviet Union, there will be even less freedom than we had before."

Fernando told her how the new government was executing members of the old guard without a trial. The brief hearings, usually presided over by Che Guevara, were televised and sometimes took less than ten minutes. The handcuffed men were dragged away on camera after a list of their actions in Batista's government was read without an attorney present, and without an opportunity to respond or explain. They were usually executed by a firing squad the same day. The executions were televised, a warning to any citizen who might be contemplating anti-Revolutionary activities.

"I know," Julia said. "I've seen those trials on TV. But these men deserved it. They were killers, most of them, monsters."

Fernando didn't want an argument, but he said, "Yes, but they deserve a proper trial and justice, not certain execution."

Julia said nothing. She wasn't angry, but discouraged that what was so important to her seemed not to matter much to him, this man whom she loved in a different way than she had the others. And yet those men had been brown-skinned, like her, and surely would have understood what Fernando could not. She wished Fernando wasn't so considerate, so measured, so kind. Then she could leave him easily and let herself fully enjoy the future's promise. But for now she would stay the course and try to avoid any talk of politics.

39

Another sleepless night, up at three in the morning. He'd be going back to work in a few days. The club and casino repairs of the damage caused by the riots were almost finished and they'd be reopening to the public soon. He couldn't be functional with the little sleep he was getting now.

He was obsessed with the name on the list, his mother's lover. Ramon had been an instrument of misery and torture and maybe death for countless peaceful political activists. Fernando was certain Ramon had seduced his mother. Why would a man with sinister tendencies have any scruples? His mother had been receptive, of course—one could not say she was totally blameless—but Fernando could not believe she would have initiated the affair. Ramon was her friend Betty's husband, for God's sake. How much pain and suffering was one man capable of inflicting upon others, acting against the code of decency that people aspire to live by? Or was Ramon in that class of men, like Batista and his henchmen, who coalesced into teams and convinced each other that the atrocities they committed were justified?

Fernando looked at the clock again. Four in the morning now. Two hours until sunrise. He looked out the window from the twisted entanglement of sheets that felt like pythons ready to squeeze the life out of him. There was no moon, and the stars were hidden behind opaque clouds. He didn't feel he had any choice. Without specifically planning his actions or thinking about the steps he had to take, he got out of bed. The room was dark, but the vision of what he had to do became clear, illuminated by the flame of his rage. Some force pulled the strings that made him move, a silent but wrathful marionette.

He got dressed, went to the kitchen, and found the boning knife, the sharpest blade in any household. He got a flashlight from the broom closet and tiptoed in his stockings to the front door. He didn't want to alert his parents with footsteps if they were awake. On the porch, he put on his shoes, got into his car, and drove to the bodega.

Fernando parked his Peugeot and walked a block to his destination. The turquoise Impala was in the driveway. He made sure that there were no lights showing through the house's windows. He hoped the Impala's hood could be released from the outside and not from a handle under the dash like in some of the newer models. In the dark, he felt for the latch under the edge of the hood, just above the grille. When he pulled, the hood sprung open, and he propped it up with the rod.

He held the flashlight close to the engine so that the light wouldn't be seen by any neighbors who might be awake. The brake fluid reservoir was always easy to find. He had replenished the one in his mother's Ford when the brakes had leaked. Now, with his head over the Impala's engine, he found the hose that delivered the fluid from the reservoir to the brakes. He brought the edge of the boning knife to the hose and stopped. Something held his hand. He wondered whether he should consider the possible repercussions, realizing he hadn't really thought fully about the consequences of his actions. By the light of the flashlight he saw his mangled fingertips and remembered the agonizing pain of the pliers pulling out his nails. His hand was released then, free to move again, and the edge of the blade made firm, slicing contact with the hose. It took a second swipe for the fluid to ooze out in a slow but steady drip. He lowered the hood and squeezed the latch to close it without slamming it.

As he got back to the bodega, he noted with relief that the midnight-blue Peugeot was barely visible. He had parked it well away from any streetlamps.

When he got home, it was just after five. He undressed and put on his pajamas, returned the flashlight and the knife to the kitchen, and found that he was famished. He turned the light on. It didn't matter now if his parents saw a light on or heard noise. He sliced some bread, toasted it, and slathered it with gobs of good Danish butter, precious as myrrh. He wolfed it all down before going back to bed to wait for sunrise.

40

It was Nina who called Elena with the news in the early afternoon. There was no chair by the small telephone table in the center hallway. Conversations were therefore kept brief, and in the event of bad news, there was only the wall for support. And anyone having an emotional reaction to terrible news from the other end of the line would be overheard from anywhere in the house. Fortunately, when Elena answered the phone, Antonio was at work and Fernando was on his way to meet his girlfriend. She allowed herself, therefore, an involuntary yelp when Nina told her that Ramon—"Betty's husband, you know…" as if Elena needed the clarification—had been killed in a car accident.

"They say the brakes failed as he was going down that steep hill in El Cerro," Nina said, and Elena tried to formulate a response, although all she managed to say was a whispered "My God."

"He couldn't stop at a light and was hit by a bus," Nina added.

Elena found it difficult to move her mouth, as if it too had died. "When did this happen?" she said finally, and leaned against the wall. She considered sitting on the floor but kneeled and sat on her heels instead.

"This morning, on his way to work. They wouldn't let Betty see him because his face was damaged. Their son Samuel had to identify the body."

Elena went into the bedroom and sat on an upholstered armchair by the window. If she had been religious, like Antonio, she would have prayed. But for what, really? For Ramon's soul? For her own? She hadn't wished him ill in any specific way, but she had in a general sense by cursing him, because she had come to believe he had a debt to pay to his innocent victims. In fact, she had imagined a scenario in which Ramon was identified as a collaborator with the corrupt police and was beaten, or worse. Within the context of Fernando's injuries, that had been a reasonable outcome in her mind. Although not the only one. In another version, the importance of Fernando's attack would recede over time, Ramon would survive the political turmoil, and society and life in general would become stable again, even better, less oppressive. She and Ramon might even reconnect in the old way. It wasn't as if there had been nothing there other than the sex. After a year of furtive meetings, something like affection had developed, their time together an interval she had looked forward to regularly.

In the late afternoon, Elena changed from her housedress to a simple navy-blue dress, combed her hair, and put on a pale-orange shade of lipstick. She drove to Betty's house, where she had gone so many times to play canasta. Now it was a different game she was going to play, a sort of charade or farce, but not a calculating, unemotional one. Fortunately, the large house was full of people. Betty, like Ramon, was Jewish and would be sitting shiva. The grieving tradition meant there would be frequent visitors. Alongside the weeping Betty was Fefa, the fourth canasta player. Nina was not there yet, or perhaps had been and left. Betty's son, Samuel, sat with friends and with his sister, Rebeca, home from her studies in Spain for the holiday season.

Elena hugged Betty and struggled to express her shock and sorrow in terms that would sound heartfelt but not extreme, grappling with the swell of emotions—grief, guilt, remorse. She kept the depth of her wound disguised and didn't stay long, because she didn't trust herself not to blurt something out or show some inappropriate intensity of heartache that would make Betty suspicious. Elena knew that Betty would be sitting shiva for a week and promised her that she would be back, knowing full well that she would not.

Back home, Elena heard Fernando's car in the driveway. She went to the door to meet him, desperate for interaction with someone who would bring her emotional comfort. She vaguely remembered Fernando's conversation with Ramon on the telephone, which had filled her with so much uncertainty and distress at the time, but which seemed unimportant now.

"I'm glad you're home. Where were you?" she asked her son.

"I drove to the club to see what's happening with the repairs. They're almost finished."

"I'm glad," she said.

"Is something the matter? You look upset," Fernando said.

Elena brought her hands to her hair and smoothed it. She almost covered her face but caught herself. She said, "You remember the man who called? Ramon? Betty's husband."

Fernando's face displayed a livid alertness suddenly, which troubled her. "Yes," he said. "I remember."

"He died in a car crash this morning."

Fernando's face changed again. She saw his eyes widen in alarm, just for a second, and his jaw relaxed from what had seemed to her an angry tightness. "He did?" he said, and there was incredulity in his tone. Or was there something else?

"I went to see Betty this afternoon. You can imagine how bereft she is, crying constantly." She paused. "That's why I look like this."

Fernando nodded without looking at her and started for his room.

"Do you want some coffee?" she asked his back. She didn't usually offer to make anything for her family, other than a weekend meal, but she wanted to prolong this encounter with Fernando. Something in his face concerned her, as if something had been left unsaid that needed to be discussed.

"Maybe later," he said without turning around.

Elena sat in the living room and tried to watch TV. But Fernando's reaction still disturbed her. She had the distinct feeling that because of Ramon's telephone call, Fernando knew more than just the fact that the man was Betty's husband. There had been that glint in his eyes when she first mentioned his name, and then the change to surprise and unease. Had he read her face well enough today and on the day of the phone call to figure it all out? She swept that possibility away. This was more than she could deal with now.

Her *novelas* seemed childish and unimportant, and she turned the TV off. She tried reading a magazine but could not concentrate. She went out to the porch and watched the people in the park across the street, trying to sort out whether the couples she saw were in love or just casually connected. It was the only thing she could do until the sun had sunk to the treetops.

When Antonio came home and saw her face, he said, "What's happened?" with so much concern that her off-kilter emotional state almost skidded out into panic that Antonio would learn about her relationship with Ramon. But somehow she managed to focus on the facts.

"Betty's husband, Ramon, was killed. I went to see her this afternoon."

Antonio frowned. "What a pity."

He had never met Ramon, Elena was sure. She wasn't even sure he had met Betty.

He continued. "From the look on your face, I thought something bad had happened to you. How did he die?"

"A car accident this morning. Betty's a good friend," Elena said, and she hated herself for overstating the relationship to justify her distraught expression. They were just canasta friends, not like Nina, with whom she was close. "You can imagine the state she's in." She realized she was parroting what she had said to Fernando, like a prepared speech.

Antonio nodded and started for the bedroom to change. "I'm sorry it seems to have affected you so much," he said.

Elena struggled to get through dinner. The swordfish Ines had prepared was perfectly cooked in a sauce of garlic, capers, and lemon, but she could barely eat. She tried not to think of Ramon.

"That girl's cooking just keeps getting better," Antonio said.

Elena was grateful for the distracting conversation. "Yes," she said. "We're lucky to have found her." But the grim look on Fernando's face kept her on edge and didn't let her forget the events of the day, and she avoided looking at him.

After dinner, Elena and Antonio watched TV, while Fernando read on the porch. At nine, much earlier than usual, Elena went to bed. Antonio followed soon after, and she was still wide awake, trying unsuccessfully to read a translation of a Perry Mason novel.

When her husband got into bed she reached across and put her arm on his chest. She wasn't intending to arouse him, merely wanted physical closeness from an unexciting but kind man, despite his emotional limitations. A terrible feeling of loneliness and vulnerability had been enveloping her since she had spoken to Nina, as if the same loss could happen to her that had happened to Betty, guileless and withering with loss.

Antonio turned to her and began foreplay in his methodical, predictable way. By the time he had lowered his pajama bottoms and raised her nightgown, she was ready. She clasped herself to him, holding on tight as if they were in a fierce wind tunnel.

41

Ines and Pedro paid a small sum for the rent of the modest wooden shack where they lived with her mother. Still, with Pedro not working much, the salary Ines received from the Leal household was barely enough to pay for food, electricity, and the rent. Her mother and Pedro worked the small plot of land they leased and sold the harvested mangoes, coffee, and root vegetables in the central market. That income was meager, a third or less of their monthly budget.

"Someone from the government was here today," Pedro said to Ines when she got home in the evening. "They told me we didn't need to pay rent anymore."

"How is that?"

"It's a new law. They call it urban reform. We're going to pay less to the government for five years, and the house is ours afterwards."

"How much less?"

"He said about half. They'll let us know when we go to the urban housing office."

"But how about Señor Dominguez? What did he say?" Ines couldn't believe the owner of their house would agree to that.

"I asked the man from the government about that. He said not to pay him. We go to the government office and pay there. If Señor Dominguez complains or threatens us, we report him and they take care of it."

Ines hadn't heard of this. She read the paper almost every day but knew nothing about this urban reform. She would ask Señor Fernando or Señora Elena in the morning, since they had more free time than she did and listened to the radio and watched TV. She wouldn't approach Señor Antonio. He smiled, said good morning to her, and occasionally complimented her cooking, but he was a serious man who didn't say much, even to his family.

"Are you sure this man was from the government?" Ines asked Pedro. He was peeling potatoes for a stew her mother was making outside. The old woman had already browned the pork over an open fire, and Ines had smelled the aroma as she approached the house from the bus stop.

"Yes. He was dressed in a military uniform and was carrying a clipboard, and he had an ID card around his neck."

"It doesn't seem possible," Ines said.

After dinner, instead of listening to the radio with her mother, Ines wanted to take a walk in the neighborhood. She normally would have been too tired to do anything but sit after she and her mother washed the pots and the dishes, but today she felt a boost of energy. She wondered if it was the prospect of paying less for their home and the idea that the house, humble as it was, would someday be theirs. Pedro agreed to go with her. The sun had set and there was no moon yet.

There were no sidewalks on the narrow cobblestone streets, and the lampposts were far apart, their light dim. They made their way in silence by the lights of the homes they passed slowly, avoiding the ruts and gaps where the stones in the road were missing. The houses were made mostly of wood like theirs was, and sometimes cinder blocks, some painted, some not. Ines could see through the windows that, like their own home, the lighting consisted of a single bare lightbulb hanging from the ceiling. She understood she was poor and would never live like her employers, but she was filled with hope that the new government would make their lives better. At least, she thought, somebody was aware of their difficulties and needs. Perhaps people like her and Pedro and her mother, and all the people whose houses they passed, would no longer be ignored, as if they didn't exist.

"You'd better go see Señor Dominguez tomorrow," she said to Pedro.

"Why?" Pedro said. "The rent isn't due for another two weeks, and anyway, he won't be getting it anymore."

"We should let him know what the man from the government said. We don't want problems with him."

"If he threatens us we'll report him, like the man said."

"I don't want to do that. I don't want to get him into trouble."

"All right. I'll go tomorrow," Pedro said.

Before she married Pedro, when Señor Dominguez came to the house once a month to collect the rent, it was her father, then her mother after he died, who dealt with the landlord. He was not always very nice. In fact, he was a stern, unsmiling man with a brown mane and a bristling mustache. And she had overheard her parents speak anxiously about how they were going to handle him and what they would say, because sometimes they were short of cash and didn't have the full rent. He had threatened them with eviction at the hands of the local police officer, a pale, oily, overweight man. Still, she thought that it was understandable that he would want his money, what was fairly his. She didn't have to like him, but she understood him, and she had no interest in harm coming to him if he did something that was now illegal, like trying to evict them. It wasn't his fault the laws had changed.

42

When her period was a week late, Julia didn't think much of it. They had been irregular all her life. But when her breasts became sensitive two days later, and still no menstruation, she suspected she was pregnant. Not that she had been careless with Fernando. She had used a diaphragm, as she had before, mostly successfully. But she knew from experience it was no guarantee.

When she next saw Fernando a week later, she said nothing. She wasn't sure she wanted the baby, and was annoyed with herself that she was again in this situation. While still in dance school she had become pregnant, and was sent by another dancer to a woman who knew how to end pregnancies. She had not had any problems, only tolerable pain as the woman inserted a metal rod she had wiped with alcohol. But there was another issue weighing heavily on her mind that was impacting her feelings about the pregnancy.

Her cousin Susana was light-skinned. Her father had been a white man whom Aunt Tita, as dark as Julia's mother, had fallen in love with, and the man disappeared after learning of the pregnancy. Fair Susana and Julia lived near each other and saw each other regularly because their mothers were sisters as well as neighbors. But even as a child, Susana didn't like to play with Julia and would seek out lighter-skinned, sometimes white, children in the neighborhood. Once, when Julia asked her to come to her house to play checkers, Susana said, "No, I don't want to go to your dirty house."

"Look, my house isn't dirty," Julia said.

"Yes, it is," Susana said. "You and your mother are dark, and you have frizzy hair. My hair is just wavy, and my skin is light."

The sting of that exchange had receded only slightly through the years. Julia was observant enough even as a child to see that having lighter skin meant better jobs and nicer clothes than people with her own skin color.

Not that long ago, Julia had gone to see her mother and found her Aunt Tita visiting. Her aunt's eyes were swollen, the face still disfigured from crying, and she didn't stay long. Afterwards, Julia asked her mother what was upsetting Aunt Tita.

"Susana went to see her to tell her she was getting married, and that Tita could come to the church as a guest but not as her mother, and not to the reception at all." As Julia's mother said this, her voice was unsteady, as if she might begin to weep, but she only shook her head in disbelief.

And now, the memory of what Susana had said to Julia and done to her own mother gave her an added reason not to have this baby, who might be light-skinned enough to be emotionally distant, or even shun her. Julia also had terrible memories of things that had happened to her in Susana's house, and just thinking of her cousin made her shudder.

Baby or no baby, Julia wasn't sure she wanted to marry Fernando, even if he asked. He was acting as if the relationship were serious, hinting at meeting his parents and he meeting her mother, but she didn't trust the idea of an interracial marriage. Very few people did it, and she knew that the ones who did suffered social snubbing, especially by the white side of the family. She wasn't sure she wanted to expose herself to that. What if Fernando's parents disapproved? Did she want to be the outcast daughter-in-law? If she wasn't willing to put herself in that position, take that risk, maybe she just didn't love Fernando enough. Besides, there was that horrible soilage she had sustained at Susana's house that she would carry with her forever and which had damaged her. Didn't he deserve better? And what about his skepticism about the Revolution, a political change that had to signal a better future for people with her skin color? No, there were too many barriers; the gap between them was just too wide. The baby would be a bond with him she didn't want.

Two days later, during rehearsals at the club, she had a sudden strong urge to urinate. She was able to wait, just barely, for a break in the practice of a new and challenging routine that required repeated high kicks. When she finally got to sit on the toilet, along with the urine came blood and a large, complicated clot the size of a lime. She looked at what she had passed into the bowl and was flooded with a shocking sense of loss, and along with it, recrimination. Had the procedure ending her previous pregnancy caused this? She knew it was possible, although other women had babies after an abortion. Or were her insides damaged because of what her aunt's boyfriend had done to her at Susana's house? She closed her eyes and stilled her vocal cords before she flushed the toilet.

She was late getting back to rehearsal because she had spent several minutes splashing water on her eyes and cheeks. When they saw her, the look on the other dancers' faces was one of concern and inquisitiveness, not resentment for being late.

43

On Saturday afternoon Elena called out from the living room to Antonio, who was on the porch. The window was open. "Did you hear that?" she said. When she didn't get a response, she went out to him.

He was sitting on the green rocking chair reading a novel by Alejo Carpentier, and he was so immersed in it that he took his time looking up.

"What did you say?" The book stayed open on his lap.

"The news I just heard. They're ordering churches to limit the number of Masses on Sundays."

"That's absurd," Antonio said. "Why would they do that?"

Elena said, "Because many priests are critical of some of the government measures, like the Marxist indoctrination going on in schools. And they're warning in their sermons about the government making abortions legal."

"I haven't heard anything about priests speaking out." He paused. "Although the priests are right. Brainwashing children in Marxism, and abortions…God help us," he said.

"You spend your life in your books, Antonio. They're posting militia outside every church on Sundays to enforce the new rules," she said. She sat down on the small wooden table that was usually ignored. "Fidel is calling the Church the enemy of the people. This is unbelievable."

"They're not going to control the Church. That they cannot do."

"Maybe you shouldn't go to Mass tomorrow."

Antonio's face flushed as he snapped the book closed. "How am I not going to go to church tomorrow?" he said with an agitated voice. "Tomorrow is Sunday."

Elena stood up. "Then I'll get Fernando to go with you. You can't go alone."

"Don't be ridiculous, Elena," he said. "Fernando has no interest in going to church. And I don't need a bodyguard." He was irked with himself for sounding annoyed, and he opened his book.

Antonio was secretly relieved when he saw Fernando getting ready to go to church with him the next day. Still, as they left the house, he said, "You don't need to go with me. It's not necessary."

Fernando said, "I'm going for Mom's peace of mind. I'm sure nothing will happen."

There were unusual gatherings outside Our Lady of Charity, several groups of four or five people scattered on the wide steps that led from the sidewalk up to the church doors. These people were clearly not dressed to attend Mass, but carelessly, as if to do household chores, wash a car, go to the bodega. They were shouting at the faithful going up the stairs, taunting them. More troubling was the presence of two military men dressed in standard green fatigues who did nothing but stand and talk to one another. They ignored the protesters who shoved and punched the shoulders and backs of the men and women trying to reach the church doors. Under the watchful eye of the military men, the worshippers did what they could to avoid the attacks without fighting back.

"Let's go around to the side entrance," Fernando said. But when they rounded the corner, they saw a scattering of citizens loitering near that door as well.

"This is ridiculous," Antonio said. With quick, angry steps he approached the two soldiers, both of whom were wielding rifles. "Why don't you protect the people trying to go into the church?" he said to them.

One of the men looked away, as if he hadn't heard. The other gave Antonio a hard look and said, "We're not here to protect counterrevolutionaries."

Antonio turned away and joined Fernando on the stairs. As they went up to the door, they were shouted at by three women, one of them holding a broom. "Filth!" they screamed. "Worms!"

Perhaps it was Fernando's height or his glowering eyes that discouraged the women from hitting them, as they had some of the other parishioners. Still, Antonio was rattled, and he trembled as he and Fernando took their places in a pew near the altar.

Antonio was so outraged he could barely concentrate on the Mass. The sermon disturbed him even more because it focused on understanding differences of opinion and loving one another. What if someone who didn't believe in God resorted to violence, like the people he had just seen outside? What love and understanding could there be then?

It was customary at the end of Mass for one priest to stand just outside the church doors and a second one at the bottom of the stairs, near the sidewalk. Today, the clergyman on the steps near the sidewalk was being taunted by the crowd. Antonio saw the priest being grabbed from behind by a man, while another ripped off the white cord that served as a belt around the brown cassock. Once the rope was off and the garment was flapping open, the priest was released and two women ripped the robe off. The man was left wearing only a threadbare undershirt so tattered his chest hair was plainly visible. There were holes in the knees of his black trousers from frequent kneeling. The soldiers stood by and smiled, and the other priest came down the steps and shouted and waved his arms at the attackers.

The victim's face had turned chalky and he stood immobile, with his arms clasped across his chest trying to cover up his undershirt, or perhaps just embracing himself for comfort. The other priest talked and gestured to the soldiers, who bared their teeth in a snarl at him as they answered back. Antonio picked up the rope and the cassock that had been thrown on the sidewalk by the mob and helped the shaken clergyman get dressed. The brother's hands shook so much he couldn't tie the rope around his waist, and Antonio did it for him, while Fernando stood between them and the jeering citizens.

44

When Fernando turned twenty-two he became suddenly and urgently aware that his brother, two years older, had been born when Antonio was twenty-three and Elena twenty-seven. This was roughly the timeframe he had long imagined for himself, the ideal age at which a man should start a family. He didn't want to be elderly or middle-aged and be a father to a teen. In short, he thought that it was time to marry and have a first child, with maybe more to follow.

There was no question that Julia made him happy, much more so than any other woman he had known and dated. He wanted to be one entity with her, a concept he had never experienced before. Sex was more than just physically pleasurable. It became a spiritual experience of melding with another person who seemed indispensable.

There hadn't been many women before Julia. He had always found them too passive, too willing to do his bidding, accommodate his wishes without challenge or opinion. He didn't trust that. How could anyone be honest in a relationship and not express an opinion about what food to eat at a restaurant, what movie to see, what to do on a Sunday afternoon? Julia had no problem voicing a preference or rescheduling a date with him if she was tired; apologetically, of course. But she showed a certain mettle he liked. The time they spent together never seemed to be enough for him, but her work schedule and the presence of her roommate made it difficult to see her more than he did.

The rift between them about the virtues and sins of the new, revolutionary government had been bridged, or so Fernando thought. And yet, there was an apparent reluctance on her part to let the relationship grow. Every time he mentioned introducing her to his parents she tipped her head sideways, not a yes, not a no. The last time he had brought it up and she remained silent, he asked, "Don't you want to meet them at some point?"

"Look, I do," she had said. "But when the time comes."

In his mind, the time had come. But did she think so too? Did she love him? He had said to her "I love you" more than once, and her response was always, without fail, "And I you," the word "love" glaringly absent from her replies. She seemed to be comfortable with the repetitive awkwardness of the phrase, so long as she didn't have to say the simple word.

Or maybe love was always asymmetrical, and here was that imbalance again, like he had experienced with Maribel. The unreturned attraction of one person for another. But had any women shown interest in him that he had not returned? He didn't remember any. Or were they just better at disguising their feelings?

On Sunday, Julia's day off, they went to their favorite restaurant, an elegant Spanish café. When he suggested over dessert that they go to his house so she could meet his parents, she demurred. "Not today," she said. "Another day."

Fernando stayed silent. A feeling of vexed frustration surged up in him. He said, "Would you like to marry me?" in an annoyed, almost hostile tone, but his irritation was suddenly replaced by a swell of love by the words he spoke, as if of their own accord they had transformed his emotional state.

Julia looked down at her empty dessert plate. "Are you sure that's what you want?" she said.

"More than anything," he said.

"Look, let's go outside and talk," she said. "I don't think you really know me."

Fernando refrained from asking her what she meant. He wanted to give her some space, not be persistent to the point of becoming a nuisance. They walked to the Parque Central and strolled the various brick paths for close to an hour. Julia did most of the talking.

Starting at the age of twelve, she had stayed with her older cousin Susana every afternoon after school while her mother and Aunt Tita were at work. Martín, Aunt Tita's boyfriend, was always at the house and watched TV while the girls did their homework. Once a week, Martín would send thirteen-year-old Susana to the bodega on an errand. At first, he just lowered his pants and underwear and showed Julia his genitals. Soon he was forcing her to touch them. "I'll tell Aunt Tita you showed me your breasts if you tell," he said to her. Eventually, he started lowering her panties and putting his fingers between her thighs while he rubbed his crotch, and after some weeks he put his finger inside her, and soon after that his tongue.

Julia paused and seemed to be short of breath, and Fernando stopped walking and tightened his arm around her waist. She resisted being pulled in closer and instead broke away from his arm and continued walking. Fernando took long strides to catch up.

Aunt Tita kept an open box of rat poison pellets under the kitchen sink, little green ones. One afternoon, after Martín had finished with her in the living room, Julia organized the ideas that had come into her brain while the man molested her. She went to the kitchen and made a batch of chocolate milkshakes in the blender, a snack she often prepared for the three of them and which Susana loved. Julia poured two glasses, and in the remaining mix in the blender, she added the green pellets and turned the blender on again. She walked into the living room just as Susana was coming in from the bodega and handed a portion of the shake in a green glass to Martín, the blue glass to Susana, and went back in the kitchen for her own portion in a clear glass.

This time, it was Fernando who stopped walking and let go of Julia's waist. She stood still and didn't look at him.

"And what happened?" he asked.

"He died that night. He didn't even make it to the hospital. Aunt Tita told us the next morning that he started vomiting blood that evening and died in the ambulance." She paused. "And that they blamed the bleeding on all the alcohol he drank."

Her back was to him, and she didn't move.

Fernando saw many options, some contradicting, conflicting. Believe her, not believe her, pull back, stay the course, tell her about Ramon, not tell her. But what he chose to do was go to her and look into her face, which she was turning away from. "Let's keep walking," he said, and for the first time he didn't put his arm around her, because he felt she needed her own space now. He also chose not to confess what he had done to his mother's lover. Nothing would be remedied by telling her, not either of the two deaths, not her obvious remorse, and not his lack of it. He considered that by telling her about Ramon he might lessen her distress, but he didn't trust that common history to be a desirable bond between them.

They didn't speak much the rest of their time together that afternoon, Fernando deep in thought, Julia's skin drained of its rich color. They walked side by side, not touching. "Nothing's changed," he said some time later when he dropped her off at her place. "I still want you to marry me."

45

Business at the nightclub was a third of what it had been at its peak. The scant tourists were now mostly European and not as interested in nightclubs as the Americans had been, and the locals who could afford the evening were too unsure of the new government. And bombs were still going off throughout the city.

Gustavo called Fernando at work in the morning. "Meet me for lunch," he said. They hadn't seen each other in weeks, an unusual span of time for them.

They caught each other up. Fernando told Gustavo about Julia, but underplayed it, not sure how upper management would view a relationship between him and a dancer. Gustavo told him about Tania, the woman he had met at Cristina's party.

"Is it serious?" Fernando asked.

Gustavo shrugged and tilted his head. "Not so serious. We'll see. But there's something I have to talk to you about." He paused. "Remember at Cristina's I said we should each start a neighborhood vigilance committee?"

Fernando nodded. He knew one had been started in his own neighborhood, three doors away from his house. A sign had been hung on the door with "CDR" in bold red letters, and below that, in smaller print, "Committee for the Defense of the Revolution."

"Your parents' names appear on a list of people not participating in their meetings and not sympathetic to the government. Yours too, of course."

"That's right," Fernando said. "We didn't sign up to be part of it."

"This is a problem," Gustavo said. "I asked you and Cristina and Enrique to start one so that you'd be seen as friendly toward the Revolution. None of you are even participating in the meetings, and you're being seen as potential enemies of the government."

There was an urgency in Gustavo's voice that Fernando interpreted as either concern for his friends or a warning. Either way, Gustavo's zeal for this government was crystal clear.

"You know, Gustavo," Fernando said, "we just don't want to be spying on neighbors and reporting them if they have a gathering without permission, or if they have a party. Or if they buy a new car and don't have a government permit to do so. That's like being in Soviet Russia. It's worse than the dictatorship we just got out of."

Gustavo rolled his eyes. He said, "But don't you see? The government needs to know about these things to detect counterrevolutionary activities. A lot of people are eager to have this government fail. The CDRs have the power to see proof and issue permits for the sake of the Revolution."

Fernando shrugged, although he was anything but indifferent to his friend's commitment to repressive tactics. "I just don't think that monitoring our neighbors is anything we want to be doing," he said. He didn't elaborate further about the parallels between these new tactics and the Soviet Union.

"But we have to safeguard the Revolution," Gustavo insisted. He was leaning forward, elbows on the table where the empty lunch plates remained.

"We're just not political," Fernando said, then quickly added, "now that Batista is gone." He hated himself for saying that. He should have been able to trust his friend with his skepticism of this new government.

Gustavo shook his head. "I can't protect you if anything happens. If there's any protest or unrest, the military is going to interrogate you and your parents, maybe even detain you."

"I understand," Fernando said. "We'll see what happens."

46

During dinner, a seafood paella heavy with shrimp, mussels, and bonito, Antonio said, "This is delicious. Ines is so young, but she cooks like a professional chef. It's incredible."

Elena said, "Yes. I taught her some simple recipes and some techniques, but she's gotten really good in the kitchen."

"She is absolutely excellent," Fernando said.

With the mention of Ines, Fernando's mind went back to his conversation with Gustavo. As his parents turned to other topics, he pondered what the lower classes, including Ines, were feeling about this new government, with the confiscation of private property, such as apartment buildings and large farms, for the sake of favoring the poor. He had not broached the subject with Ines, didn't want to seem like he was interrogating her. But he hoped that the government's methods, which seemed radical and repressive, might prove to be good for the country at large, including for people like Ines. He knew a Soviet-style totalitarian system would be catastrophic, but perhaps this new government would implement merely a socialist democracy. Gustavo, Cristina, and Maribel were all in support of the new leadership despite its faults, less mistrustful of what seemed to be a communist regime. And of course Julia was too because, like Gustavo, she had been a victim of racism in the previous system, and was enthusiastic for the new one, no matter its obvious flaws.

"What's for dessert?" Antonio asked.

"Flan," Elena said.

"Wonderful. She makes great flans."

And the flan was perfect as always, silky, just sweet enough, with a hint of bitterness from the lemon and the caramelized sugar. Its complexity on the tongue was entrancing, and Fernando watched as his father closed his eyes in gustatorial rapture. He realized that a great deal of the joy he felt at home during meals came from his father's enthusiasm for the food, his lavish praise of Ines's cooking. And it struck him also that due to shyness, or formality, or misplaced respect, his father had never, as far as Fernando knew, complimented Ines directly. In fact, Fernando couldn't remember his father ever talking to the young woman at all.

Antonio's generosity of spirit, the benevolence that was hidden behind a formal and at times stern exterior was becoming more evident to him. Fernando had experienced mostly the drier aspects of his father's personality, but there had been moments of connection, particularly those evenings on the porch after dinner. His father's routine to sit with a book, the overhead porch light on, had become a comfort, a symbol of civility and grace. And that his mother sat a few feet away in the living room watching TV, between them a large open casement window for easy communication, was evidence of their bond. It was something he hoped to have someday.

"What are you reading?" Fernando asked his father that evening. He sat down in the old red rocking chair. Antonio showed him the cover of the book he held, a novel by Lezama Lima. Like the other Cuban novelists Fernando had tried to read, he found this one too dense to understand. "Too difficult for me," he said.

"You're not old enough yet."

Fernando laughed. "I'm twenty-two."

"Not old enough. I wouldn't have understood him either at your age."

"You married Mom at my age," Fernando said. He wanted to tell his father about Julia, about his wanting to get married and start a family.

"Yes," Antonio said. The syllable was low and drawn out, as if he had doubts about its complete accuracy even as he spoke it.

There were crickets, or maybe tree frogs, singing in the darkness; Fernando could never be sure which. He sensed a receptivity on his father's part, an easy mood that was rare in this usually dour man. Still, he wondered how far his father would allow the conversation to go. But he knew so little about his father's youth, and was so curious, that he pressed on. "And between university and marrying Mom, you worked? You had a good job?"

Antonio hesitated. "Sort of," he said.

Fernando was disturbed by the evasion. "Sort of? In shipping also?"

"Not exactly." His father looked out at the darkness.

Fernando ignored the gesture that signaled a reluctance to continue the conversation. He asked, "What did you do, then?"

A pause, and then in a soft voice his father said, "I spent time away. Away from society."

Fernando's skin prickled. This sounded ominous, not like good news to him, and he considered ending the exchange, never mind talking about Julia. But no. This was his father. This man could never have been in prison or done anything to be ashamed of.

"So where were you?" Fernando said finally. His voice was small, as if he didn't want to offend Antonio with the question.

Antonio lowered his lids briefly, as if he were looking inside himself for an answer. He then looked at Fernando with a distance he had never seen in his father's eyes.

"I was in a Jesuit seminary."

Fernando replayed those words in his head as he moved his lips, almost speaking them out loud, because a seminary was as surprising an answer as a prison would have been.

In the few seconds of silence, Antonio's face changed from reflection to one of remote but profound sadness. Fernando felt a pang, a surge of compassion, and he resolved not to talk of Julia tonight. His father's whole being—the devoted church-going, the pristine language, the measured behavior—was suddenly all of a piece. Antonio's expression communicated nostalgia, and maybe also regret. But regret about what? About the path he had chosen?

The memory of his mother's affair intruded. Now it seemed more beastly than just merely abhorrent, the change spurred by a more complete understanding that his father was a spiritually complicated person. Within the constraints of a limited budget, Antonio had provided for his family well and done very little for himself, had unstintingly paid for his sons' education through preparatory school and university. He had bought his wife a fine car and indulged her wishes to vacation in Miami. There was something saintly about him.

"How long were you in the seminary?" Fernando asked. He spoke gently, not wanting it to sound like an interrogation.

"A year. But let's not talk any more about this."

Fernando nodded, stood up and went to him. He might have hugged him if the man had been standing, although hugging did not come naturally in this family. He cupped a hand around his father's shoulder and went out into the darkness to walk and digest the conversation, maybe around the block, or the park across the street with its dim yellow lamps and nature's night songs. It didn't matter. He needed to be alone now and not set eyes upon his mother for the rest of this evening.

47

The neighborhood where Gustavo lived was in the same municipal district as Fernando's, and as leader of his defense committee he had access to the roster of other members in the city. Fernando's name was still not on the list for his neighborhood. Gustavo called him. There was going to be a meeting on Saturday at Cristina's house, and he wanted to make sure that Fernando was planning to attend. After he hung up, his girlfriend Tania, who was helping to take care of his sick mother, said, "Why are you so grumpy?"

Gustavo said, "I'm not grumpy. I'm worried that Fernando is going to get into trouble."

"Why?"

"He won't join the CDR in his neighborhood."

Tania folded the freshly laundered sheets she had taken off the clothesline in the backyard. She told Gustavo she didn't think everyone needed to join a CDR, and that it seemed absurd that he was taking it so hard.

"You don't know," Gustavo said. "If there's any trouble, a protest, people who aren't members can be questioned or detained and who knows what else."

"That's an exaggeration," she said.

He shook his head. "Trust me. I know. There's been talk in the district."

On Saturday, Gustavo, Maribel, and Enrique all arrived at Cristina's at around three o'clock. Fernando was late, and Gustavo was afraid he wasn't going to show up at all. Eventually, he appeared in the backyard, where everyone was sitting under the large, multicolored umbrellas that provided shade.

Fernando hadn't seen Maribel in over a year and he walked up to where she was sitting. He was expecting a hug, or at least a handshake, but she didn't get up and merely said, "Hello, Fernando" without smiling.

"Before we begin, I have some bad news," Cristina said. "My parents have asked me not to have any more meetings here. And they want me to keep this one short."

"Why?" Maribel asked. She was dressed in a brown shirt and trousers, the uniform worn by the adjunct government staff.

Cristina shrugged. "They aren't political people. They don't want this activity here."

"Let me tell you, Cristina," Maribel said. "In this Revolution, you're either a friend or an enemy." Cristina's eyes opened wide, but she said nothing. Enrique looked at his feet.

Gustavo looked at Fernando, who glanced back briefly before saying, "Not being political doesn't mean anti-government."

Maribel shot him a look and said, "You either support us or you don't. And if you don't, you're under suspicion."

Fernando stood up. Cristina had always been the compliant and cooperative one, and gracious enough to offer her parents' house for all the meetings. He found Maribel's attack unacceptable. He said, "I don't believe it's the government saying this, Maribel. I think it's you saying it. You haven't changed."

Maribel shouted back, "For your information, you've already been named as a possible counterrevolutionary."

Fernando ignored the threat. He had had enough and turned to leave the way he had come in, through the house, at the very moment that Cristina's father came in to see what the commotion was about.

The gentleman was impeccably dressed in black trousers and a white linen shirt. He said to Cristina, "This has to end now," and then looked at the others. Fernando continued his exit through the house, and the rest of them stood up, except Cristina. Gustavo apologized, the only one in the group to do so.

Outside on the sidewalk, Fernando was nowhere to be seen. Gustavo said to Maribel, "You know Fernando is a good person. He was the only one of us to be tortured by Batista's henchmen, and he supports the Revolution. But you can't force people to participate. He needs time."

"We can't take chances, Gustavo," she said. "We can't risk losing what we've achieved."

48

1924

Thousands upon thousands of Jews fleeing virulent anti-Semitism left Eastern Europe for Cuba in the years before World War II. Although for most of them Cuba was not their final destination, they chose it because of its proximity to the US, and because the standard of living for the middle and upper classes was better than anywhere else in Latin America. However, because of the restrictions the American government imposed on Jewish immigration, many thousands of Jews made Cuba their permanent home.

Fourteen-year-old Elena and her older sister Isabel were enrolled in an all-girls Catholic school in Havana. They were driven there every day by a chauffeur in the family sedan, a 1923 Packard. Their father was vice president of the family business, the manufacture of chocolate. The company was the largest candymaker in Cuba and one of the biggest in all of Latin America. Their mother painted terrible oils in a studio that had been one of the house's eight bedrooms.

Isabel was sixteen and already had a boyfriend. Most middle- and upper-class women got married between the ages of eighteen and twenty, and poor country girls even earlier. Twenty-five was considered mature, and by thirty an unmarried woman would be casually referred to as a *solterona*, which meant "spinster" and derived from *sola*, the feminine form of "alone."

Like Isabel, Elena also had a boy she liked and, like all the other young ladies, matrimony was her ultimate goal. She didn't think that at fourteen she was too young to be planning her adult life. Most of her sister's older friends had married men they had dated as teenagers. Of course, dating per se, which even the older Isabel could do only with a chaperone, was still out of the question for Elena. Get-togethers at friends' homes, supervised by the adults of the house, was the most common form of interaction with the opposite sex.

Elena met Jaime at his parents' small general store, right in the neighborhood. He spoke with a slight accent, a rather clipped cadence. Elena knew he had been born in Germany and had arrived in Cuba with his parents just a few years prior.

She had liked his looks immediately—the ginger curly hair, the full curved lips, the freckles on his nose.

Elena visited the store at least twice a week in the late afternoon, when she knew Jaime would be working behind the counter after his school day. Sometimes she didn't really need to buy anything, but she would get something from the paper goods section—pencils, a notebook, a ruler—and ask Jaime to help her decide what color, how large, how many.

"Can you walk with me part of the way home?" she would say to him as she paid at the counter, and Jaime asked Raquel, his corpulent mother, who would nod permission and then shake her head in resigned disapproval.

There was just one time they were allowed to go to the movies with Isabel as chaperone, but his mother ultimately was not happy with the date, and it never happened again. Still, they could go to the park by themselves, walk, sit on a bench. They didn't hold hands, lest a passerby take note, recognize one of them, and tell their parents. The time she spent with Jaime brought Elena great happiness.

"Do you think we could be a couple in a year?" Elena asked Jaime impetuously. "Or are you in love with someone else?"

"You want to be my girlfriend?" Jaime asked, and Elena nodded. He was a year older than she was. "I like you, and I don't have another girlfriend. But I don't know if we could get married."

"Why not? I don't mean right away, but when we're older."

"I know what you mean. But I'm Jewish. I don't know how that would work."

"It doesn't matter if you're Jewish," Elena said. "If we love each other."

"I'm not sure getting married is possible, but I'd like to be your boyfriend someday, yes."

Elena was ecstatic. Jaime walked her home and she invited him inside the massive wrought-iron gates.

"I can't," he said. "I have to get back to the store. And I have homework."

"Come with me into the garden just a moment," Elena said. "I want to show you something."

She led the way to the side of the house where there was a large garden shed. They stood on the side of the structure that was not visible from the house. She looked into his eyes, the color of honey, and she kissed him. It was the first time she had kissed anyone on the lips, and she kept her mouth closed tight. The kiss felt terribly significant. She imagined that they were like lovers in a movie, and her mind flashed back to countless scenes she had seen at the local cinema and on TV.

Elena couldn't wait to tell Isabel about her boyfriend and their plans to get married someday. That afternoon Isabel got home from a friend's house in the neighborhood, close enough so that she had walked the tree-lined streets along the stately manses alone.

"Jaime?" Isabel said. "But isn't he Jewish?"

"Yes, he is. He told me."

"He can be your boyfriend, but you can't get married," Isabel said.

"Why not? We love each other."

Isabel said, "First of all, you're too young to be thinking of this. And second, even when you're older you can't marry him if he's not baptized."

"I'm not that young. I'm fourteen," Elena said. "You've had your boyfriend for a year. I'm almost as old as you were last year."

"That's true. But there's still the problem that he's Jewish and not baptized," Isabel said. "Anyway, let's not worry about this now. If things get serious, we'll talk to Father Carlos and see what he thinks. But I think *Mami* and *Papi* are going to be very upset."

When Elena turned fifteen a few months later, a lavish outdoor party was planned. By tradition, a young lady's fifteenth birthday was a landmark, a girl's official entry into womanhood, and the celebration was always as lavish as a family could afford. For Elena's celebration, the expansive gardens were festooned with colorful overhead lanterns hanging from wires strung between the trees. Uniformed waiters carried trays of drinks and canapés while a musical combo played boleros. The singer was an internationally celebrated Black American woman who lived in Paris.

Of course Jaime attended the party, but he had no friends there, since most of the guests were young women from Elena's school and the sons and daughters of her father's business associates. Elena introduced him to her friends, but she saw that Jaime stayed by himself most of the afternoon. She danced with him and sat nearby as much as she could.

"I'm a woman now," Elena said to him at sunset, standing close.

Jaime smiled and lowered his eyes. "I know. And you look beautiful in that dress."

He had never complimented her before, his interest in her always communicated with soft looks, smiles, a tender manner. Elena was overtaken by desire. "Come with me," she said. She took him by the hand, drawing bemused looks from her friends, and led him from the well-lit part of the garden to the shed, now in twilight. Hidden from view she kissed him, this time with parted lips, and he held her while his thumbs caressed her breasts through the silk of the bodice. He pressed in close, and she felt his arousal on her thighs through the ruffled skirt.

"We'd better go back," she said. She was afraid that she would give in to him, if not here and now, then at some point in the very near future. This was something Elena knew she could not do without being married first. Marriage all of a sudden seemed urgent.

"So you're still serious," Isabel said when Elena told her what had happened behind the shed. "Well then, he has to get baptized."

"Does it matter if he already had a bar mitzvah?" Elena said.

"What is that?"

"It's like a ceremony to become a man if you're Jewish."

Isabel said, "You mean like your fifteen party?"

Elena shook her head at her sister's ignorance, even though she herself had not known anything about the significance of a bar mitzvah until Jaime explained it to her. She said, "No, Isabel. It's a serious religious ceremony so that boys become men."

"It doesn't matter if he's had the whatever it's called. Anybody can get baptized."

Elena thought a moment. "How do we get him baptized? Father Carlos will tell *Papi* and *Mami*, and they'll be furious, and who knows what they'll do because he's not Catholic."

"We don't need Father Carlos to do it," Isabel said. "If you're sure it's what you want, I can baptize him."

Elena opened her mouth in surprise. "You?' she said.

Isabel nodded. "It doesn't have to be a priest. You just need to know the right prayer and have some holy water."

The three of them went to the nearby Chapel of Santa Margarita on Tuesday afternoon, when it was likely to be empty. They stood by the font of holy water just inside the thick mahogany doors. Isabel dipped her fingers in the water and said a two-minute prayer out loud as she made the sign of the cross on Jaime's forehead three times with her thumb. "Jaime Stern," she said. "You are hereby baptized into the arms of Christ."

It was the last time Elena would see Jaime for many years, when they happened to run into each other in that same neighborhood, because on the evening of the baptism Raquel called Elena's mother and narrated her son's account of the afternoon. "This cannot be," Raquel said. "We have different faiths, and they cannot marry."

At the dinner table, after the dessert plates had been cleared by a servant, the girls' mother told them to go to the parlor. "Your father and I need to talk to you," she said.

The girls' father shook his head. "This is for you to handle," he said, and left the dinner table for his study.

Within a week, Elena was matriculated in an all-girls Catholic boarding school from which she was driven home in the Packard one weekend a month. The school was twenty minutes from the house.

49

1932

It was of course something he couldn't even think about for long, and acting on it was out of the question. Antonio had heard of men doing this, but he also knew it was against the laws of the land and of God. Men were ostracized, marginalized by society, jailed when they were caught in the act in a car or a movie theater or a bar.

He had tried once. Two years before, at the age of fifteen, when it was said you left childhood and entered adulthood, he had fixed his attention on Raul, an effeminate classmate. He thought it was time he explored sex. Many of his friends at school boasted of having already done it with one of the girls from the poorer neighborhoods. Antonio had been careful approaching Raul in school, because the thin, beautiful boy was tormented by the others, who called him names, ridiculed him. Even the girls snickered when he walked past them. Raul's only friend in school was a boy with thick glasses who was in one of the remedial classes.

After school one day, Antonio walked away slowly from the school's gates. He knew that, for safety, Raul waited on the school grounds until the other boys had left the neighborhood. He waited at the corner and saw Raul's elongated figure carrying his books like girls did, tight against his chest. He saw Raul exit the gates and turn, walking away from where Antonio stood. With long strides, he hurried to catch up and looked around to confirm that none of their classmates would see him talking to the boy.

"Hello," Antonio said when he was alongside him.

Raul flinched as if Antonio had thrown a punch. "What do you want?" he said. His voice was high and tremulous, like he was being shaken. But worse was the look of terror in his eyes, the mouth gaping with fear.

"I just wanted to say hello," Antonio said, but he was deflated in his attempt by the young man's panic, and he stopped. He watched as Raul hurried on, looking over his shoulder to make sure Antonio was letting him go on his way without harassment.

For days, perhaps weeks, the encounter soured him from pursuing his plan, and even his deep yearning to make a connection with someone who was like him was suppressed. A certain peace-tinged dejection enveloped him, and he focused on his studies. He declined his friends' invitations to play stickball in the park, which he usually did every Saturday. None of those boys were like him—it seemed nobody was, except Raul.

A magazine rescued him from his feeling of alienation. He needed a textbook for school that was sold only at a small but well-known bookstore on a narrow street in Old Havana. The shop was cramped and poorly lit, but he finally found the book he needed. With the textbook in hand, he saw at the rear of the store a curtained-off area with a sign that read "Adults Only." Because he was tall, and the clerk behind the counter wasn't paying any attention to him, he felt confident enough to go in.

There were scantily dressed women on the covers of the magazines displayed on the racks, some with their breasts exposed, and a few with a grinning man in a bathing suit. At the far end, in the most secluded part of the Adult section, there were two magazines with photos of half-naked muscular men with prominent genitals bulging inside their underwear. He was alone in this separate part of the shop, and he opened one of the magazines with only men on the covers and saw photographs of acts he had only imagined and some he had not. His ears burned, and along with the excitement he felt short of breath. He put the magazine back on the rack and left.

As he walked to the bus stop he felt detached from his surroundings, kept his sight from resting on anything for very long. There was a new relationship he had now with the world around him, the people on the sidewalk, the vehicles on the street. Nothing would ever be the same because he knew now that there were others like him who wanted to see these muscled men engaging in intimate acts with each other. They might be all around. Maybe that man wearing a blue suit, maybe the younger one waiting for a bus.

On a Friday afternoon during recess at school, he heard Lito, one of the boys he played stickball with, say to Raul in a mocking tone, "So, you're going to the zarzuela Sunday afternoon?" Raul pretended he hadn't heard and walked away.

"There's a zarzuela playing in Havana?" Antonio asked. He had never seen a Spanish operetta.

"Don't you know anything?" Lito said. "The zarzuela is the northern end of the Parque Martí, where on Sunday afternoons all the *maricones* go to meet each other."

Antonio thought about it all day Saturday. He considered going to the park to play stickball because he was now feeling less alienated from a society that included men with the same desires he had. Perhaps some of the boys he played ball with had the same tendencies and kept them hidden. He would just have to keep things discreet. But instead of going to play with his friends, he stayed home and read and thought about going to the zarzuela.

On Sunday afternoon, Antonio took the bus to the park. He walked through the landscaped southern end, where families and couples strolled, sat on benches, bought pink cotton candy from a vendor with a cart painted bright blue. When he got to the northern end, with overgrown shrubs, vines, and trees that were gnarled and needed attention, he saw only men standing around or sitting on benches, no women or children. A few men seemed to be alone, a few in pairs. He stood and watched. Some of the men who had paired off walked away from the open area into the thick shrubbery.

So here it was, the oasis he had hoped to find, with the opportunity to bring that side of him to the surface, quench the thirst he had for skin-to-skin contact with another man. It was something he thought about alone in his room at night. He ambled about, unsure of how to act or where to stand or sit, and then he saw a man in a suit who had been sitting on a bench walk in his direction. Antonio stopped his slow walk and turned toward the man.

"Are you enjoying the afternoon?" the man inquired.

Antonio's mouth was so dry with nerves he could only nod his assent, and the man laughed. "I think you need something to drink," he said.

He was much older than Antonio, maybe in his thirties, with a thick black mustache and a tan fedora perched on his head. He said, "Would you like to come to my place? I don't live far."

The stranger turned and began to walk away, looking at Antonio over his shoulder, smiling his invitation. Antonio took a few steps toward the man but could not continue. He was afraid of taking the lid off that jar. He turned and walked in the other direction, out of the park and to the bus stop for the return home.

And now here he was two years later, seventeen, a year from finishing secondary school. It was time to lay out the plan for his life as an adult. Enrolling in university was the next step most of his friends would be taking, and the default plan he had all along. By now all his friends were sexually active, or so they boasted. He still played stickball in the park with them, but unlike them he didn't talk about his conquests, nor did he chat with girls at school, a necessary first step to find a girlfriend and be like the other boys. And he did not respond to the girls' flirtations or suggestive comments about going to the movies or parties or any other social events.

During a stickball game he sat on the bench with his team, waiting to go to bat. Next to him sat Mateo, one of the team's best players, a husky boy with bad teeth who always wore tattered shorts. Antonio saw a familiar figure walking not far from where he sat with Mateo, and he eventually recognized the man as one of the priests from the church he went to every Sunday with his parents. The man was dressed in a plain blue shirt and black trousers.

"Good morning, Father," Mateo said to the priest as he walked past, and the man waved and smiled. "He's a good person," Mateo said. "He's the only one I'll let hear my confession."

Antonio thought nothing more of the exchange until the next morning. During Mass, he saw the same priest in his brown robes and overlying vestments as an exception in society. Celibacy and remaining single were not just expected, but necessary. For the rest of the day he thought about his future and began to see that religious life was a retreat that would require him to remain celibate. As he considered this avenue over the next few weeks, he became convinced that the priesthood would prevent him from the temptation to engage in acts that were considered immoral, criminal, an aberration.

His parents were devout Catholics and yet they were restrained in their response when he announced his intention to enter the priesthood. His father's expression communicated something like sadness, his mother's more skepticism. Was it doubt that she felt about his commitment? Still, neither one said anything to discourage him, although the mood of the household over the next few days was more subdued than usual. Whenever the subject came up again, their words amounted to quiet support without much enthusiasm, and the wheels to enter a Jesuit seminary, in the absence of any real impediment, were set in motion.

The remainder of his last year in secondary school was atypically untroubled because of the psychological comfort of having found a path to an acceptable role in society. The pressure to lose his virginity disappeared. He would be a respected citizen, and his unsettling desires could easily be repressed by the righteousness of his new role.

On the first day of his new life, his parents accompanied him in a taxi to the monastery on the outskirts of Havana. There would be years of study and prayer. He carried a small brown leather suitcase with a few necessities—toiletries, books, undergarments. He stood with his parents on the circular driveway in front of the massive colonial building, its heavy wooden doors already open for him and the other seminarians who would be arriving. His parents hugged him when it was time for them to leave after all the useless chitchat had been exhausted, and he watched with deep uncertainty and a sense of abandonment as they climbed into the taxi.

There were twenty first-year seminarians, and they prayed and studied together in groups of four. One of the men in his group, Leonardo, immediately caught his attention. Here it was again, that unmistakable hijacking of his focus. The man was an older version of Raul, although more masculine, and they exchanged looks that Antonio, with some dismay, interpreted as interest.

The same devil was back for another battle. Antonio had hoped to submerge that part of himself, but it was rising to the surface like scum in a pond. He found himself thinking about visiting Leonardo's room every night after bedtime was announced by two tolls of the campanile. An irresistible force in every cell of his body made Antonio sit as close as possible to Leonardo during study groups and turn his head slightly in his direction as he knelt next to him in chapel. Leonardo didn't seem to notice, but Antonio was sure he had and was simply ignoring him.

After lunch one afternoon, during the hour of private meditation, Antonio spotted Leonardo in the areca garden near the chapel. They had exchanged glances loaded with suggestion that morning, and Antonio thought the tension had come to its apogee. In the garden, Leonardo was sitting on a stone bench leaning forward, his elbows on his knees, and Antonio sat next to him. "Can I be of help?" Antonio said as softly as he could, unsure of whether to intrude. After a moment, Leonardo looked up, and Antonio saw that his eyes were red.

"You're making this very difficult. I'm struggling," Leonardo said.

Antonio felt stymied, but also happy that Leonardo, on some level that could not be allowed to surface, had responded to his interest. He walked away and prayed, but there seemed to be no help coming from God, no source of willpower to change his behavior.

After a few days of self-reproach, regret, and repressed desire, Antonio decided he could not do this alone. The road he had chosen was his salvation, and he needed to get help to follow it without wavering. He would go see the seminarians' spiritual adviser, an ancient monk with a badly curved spine that made him wobble when he walked.

Brother Francisco had a bushy, unkempt gray beard and yellow teeth. "What do you want?" the old man barked when he opened his office door. Without waiting for an answer, he turned around and walked back to his desk with steps so unsteady that Antonio was sure he would topple.

Sitting across the desk from the hostile man, Antonio said, "I'm having thoughts and desires that are getting in the way of my purpose here."

The monk narrowed his black eyes. "What sort of thoughts and desires?"

Antonio wasn't sure how explicit he should be. He paused, trying to collect his thoughts, but he saw the monk tapping his fingers impatiently on the desk and said, "I'm trying to form a close bond with one of my fellow seminarians."

Brother Francisco's face resembled a stone carving. "You're supposed to bond equally in fraternity with all your fellow seminarians."

When Antonio said nothing, put off by the monk's reaction, the old man said, "This man is aware of your intentions?"

"Yes, but he's rejected my interest."

The monk closed his eyes and nodded. "You're not the first. Self-denial is a virtue you must develop and nurture like a seedling." When he opened his eyes, the look was hard.

Antonio said, "I have tried. But it's very difficult. It's distracting me from God, pulling me away."

After a moment, during which Brother Francisco seemed deep in thought, he said, "What was this other seminarian's reaction to your interest?"

"He was very distressed," Antonio said. "He looked anguished, actually, and he said I was making it difficult for him."

Brother Francisco brought his bony hands together as in prayer in front of his mouth. "Why are you here?" he said.

"I'm hoping you can help me," Antonio said.

The monk bared his teeth like a vicious dog. "No," he growled. "Why are you in this community?"

Antonio didn't hesitate. "I want to save my soul."

Francisco tilted his head back and released a guffaw, then he shook his head and said, "So you've caused this man spiritual distress and put his soul at risk, but you're just interested in saving yourself." He paused. "You're self-centered and don't belong here. You should be trying to save other souls, not worrying about your own. Get out of my office and go pack your bags."

That same afternoon he was summoned to the rector's office, and the next morning he called his parents before he got in the taxi that took him home. During the ride, he was despondent, and the feeling that he was a complete failure overwhelmed him. He had no hope for a happy life.

50

1935

It was almost nine o'clock, and Antonio would have to hurry because he didn't want to keep his friend Alberto waiting. The baseball game started at ten and Alberto would stop by to pick him up. Like his parents, Antonio hadn't learned to drive. He could have taken the bus to these games on Saturday mornings, but in his baseball uniform he would draw attention, which would make him uncomfortable. And besides, he would risk getting the ivory-white uniform dirty before he even got to the field and assumed his shortstop position. He took pride in looking as good as possible for these cherished games.

Antonio wondered if Isabel, Alberto's wife, would be coming along today. She was a beautiful, outgoing woman, and in the year he had known Alberto he had met her several times when she accompanied him to the baseball games. But now that they had a daughter, Isabel didn't come to watch them play as often; only when she could get her sister, Elena, to watch the infant at home.

He heard Alberto honking the horn, picked up his glove, and went out to the front of the house. Antonio saw that he'd have to sit in the back seat today. Isabel sat next to Alberto in the front holding the baby, and in the back of the car sat a woman he had never seen before.

Elena was not as beautiful as Isabel, but she was attractive in a Mediterranean way, with large brown eyes and a prominent narrow nose. Her generous mouth broke into a smile in response to comments anyone in the car made, and she spoke frequently and with great energy. She glanced at Antonio often during the ride, and he felt that she appreciated his reserved demeanor.

After the game was over, on their way back to the car, Isabel said, "Let's go to our house for lunch."

Antonio balked. "I'm filthy," he said.

Isabel said, "It doesn't matter. We're all sweaty. It's been a hot day."

"Maybe it would be better on another day," Antonio said.

Elena, walking alongside him behind Alberto and Isabel, put her hand on Antonio's back. He could feel his sweat-soaked shirt between his shoulder blades and knew her hand was now moistened with it. "It doesn't matter if you're dirty," she said quietly, as if only to him, although he knew the others had heard. "Come have lunch with us."

He felt the warm comfort of someone he had just met liking him and offering an easy familiarity. He had never experienced such a smooth connection so quickly with anyone before. After lunch, instead of wanting to get home to clean up and help his father with the chores, he chose to linger at Alberto and Isabel's house. He had known Alberto since his days at the university, had played baseball with him countless times, and gone to the movies with him. He felt as if he was becoming part of this family, but at three o'clock he said, "I should be going home."

"I'll drive you," Elena said.

They saw each other again at Alberto and Isabel's for dinner, began to go out to movies and walks in the park. One evening, when Elena was going to care for the infant while Alberto and Isabel went to the movies, they asked him to keep Elena company. Alberto picked him up, and when Antonio got out of the car and Isabel climbed in, she said, "Have a good time," with such a wide smile that Antonio blushed.

And, in fact, Elena took charge that evening and Antonio lost his virginity. A chain of pleasurable events followed in the ensuing weeks—dinners, movies, more evenings alone. And when Elena announced that she was pregnant, he looked at her in stunned silence. Somehow it hadn't occurred to him that this might happen, enmeshed as he was in discovering a new side of himself. He hadn't even thought of precautions and assumed that Elena had. He knew women used diaphragms and men condoms, but he had not thought to use one and chided himself for laying all the responsibility for contraception on Elena.

"I thought I'd be safe at certain times of the month," she said, as if she were reading his mind. "Are you going to marry me?" she added, not in a demanding or petulant way, but softly, almost pleadingly. It was the first time he had heard that vulnerable tone of voice from her.

Antonio didn't know what he was supposed to feel in order to marry somebody. He imagined that you had to love the person, and he liked Elena, had found the sex physically satisfying, but no more. If being in love meant wanting to be with that person as much as possible, inhabit her world and have her inhabit yours, then he wasn't in love. He was happy to see her occasionally, as he was doing now. And yet he saw that this was his destiny, and probably had been all along, because he had no other options. Sexual and emotional intimacy with men was impossible, with the furtiveness, the guilt, the risk of legal repercussions. Elena was the only woman who had meant something special to him other than his mother, and he didn't want to live a lonely life. This was, he believed, what he was meant to do after the other alternative, the Church, had rejected him as one of their own. "Yes," he said. "Of course."

51

1960

When she heard the clanging of the vegetable cart's bell, Ines didn't waste time. She left the broom leaning on the wall of the hallway and rushed out to the street. For months the scarcity of food staples had been severe. Even potatoes, rice, and beans were scarce. All animal protein—chicken, beef, and pork—when available at all, was limited to what was specified on the ration card each household was issued, usually to half a pound per person per week.

There was already a line at the vendor's cart. No longer did the women congregate informally and take their turns more or less in order. The rationing made it imperative that no one cut ahead in line, lest the limited potatoes or onions or garlic sell out, which they often did. As she got near the front of the line, Ines could see that the old horse had lost weight, the ribs showing, and the vendor himself looked haggard, his clothes loose, the formerly ropy arms thin.

"What will it be today, Señorita?" the man said. This close, Ines could see he had lost a front tooth.

"Two pounds of potatoes," Ines said.

The man shook his head. "I can only sell you one pound."

"But potatoes aren't rationed this week," Ines said.

"The supplies are tight and I have to limit each customer," he said. "Otherwise, I'll run out before I've finished my route and people will get angry."

As she started back to the house, Ines looked for Caridad on the queue. She hadn't seen her at the vendor's in several weeks and missed their brief chats about which vegetables looked good, which didn't, what to do with wilted, yellowing greens so as not to waste them now that they were scarce.

Ines started to put away the produce she had bought. Señora Elena came into the kitchen and surveyed the purchases.

"Where are the tomatoes?" she asked.

"He didn't have any," Ines said.

"How could that be, no tomatoes?"

"And all I could get was one onion."

Señora Elena helped her put away the produce. Ines said, "Where is it all going? What's happened?"

"Because the large farms have been broken up and given to the peasant farmers, and they don't have the equipment or the manpower to produce as much." Señora Elena sounded annoyed, but Ines knew the anger was at the government and what they were calling agrarian reform.

"This is communism now," the woman said in a lower, calmer voice. "I don't see how it can last."

Later, Ines brought the *señora* coffee in the living room. "No cookie?" she said.

"The bodega didn't have any yesterday," Ines said. "I'm sorry."

"What can you do?" Señora Elena said in a resigned tone. She sipped her coffee and grimaced. "Did you put sugar in this?"

"Yes, but there isn't much left. I'm trying to stretch it out."

Ines started to go back to the kitchen, then turned and said, "Did the family in the big house on the corner move away?" She thought that was probably why Caridad hadn't been around.

"Oh, you mean the Nieto family? Yes, they left. They moved to Miami last month."

"To stay?"

"Yes, of course. Gone. The house is being converted into apartments." The woman shook her head.

Ines wondered what Caridad was doing now, where she was living. She saw that the price of the Revolution trying to improve the lives of the lower classes like herself was dismantling the lives of the upper classes. But there was more of a cost. The shortage of everything—the long lines at the bodega just to buy a pound of flour or half a pound of sugar, then standing on another two-hour line at the butcher's for a pound of ground beef- was taking its toll on the citizens, including her. Señora Elena had to stand on some of those lines also; otherwise, Ines wouldn't get any other work done around the house. Ines saw that life for everyone was harder, and she wondered whether what the government said was true, that the difficult times were temporary adjustments and that in the future the country would be the best it had ever been.

From the kitchen she heard loud voices, among them Señora Elena's shouts. There was no one else in the house, and Ines followed the sound of the ruckus to the living room.

Señora Elena was at the front door, and just beyond it Ines could see two women. She recognized one of them as a crude customer of the vegetable vendor, someone who wasn't a cook or a housekeeper but a housewife. And Ines knew that both women at the door arguing with the *señora* were from the neighborhood vigilance committee.

"You need to show us your ration book to make sure it's accurate," one of the women was saying. "We know only three people live here, because one of your sons left."

"I don't need to show you anything." Señora Elena's voice was the loudest.

"Then we'll send the military police to inspect. And if you refuse, they'll arrest you."

"Let them try," Señora Elena said and slammed the door shut.

Ines stood looking at her employer's red face. She didn't know what she should do to comfort her and could only worry her apron. "Let me bring you some lemonade," she said, "although I can't make it too sweet."

Señora Elena looked at her as if she had just become aware of her presence. "Yes, please," she said, and sat down on the sofa next to the Grundig. She looked at Ines and said, "Stop worrying, Ines. Nothing's going to happen."

52

When Gustavo called him at work asking to see him, Fernando thought it was to try to convince him yet again to participate in the vigilance committee. He was relieved when Gustavo suggested they go to the beach on Saturday.

"Will Julia come too?" Gustavo asked.

"No," Fernando said. "She works late Friday night and she has a show Saturday night, so she'll want to rest."

"She's a disciplined girl, then," Gustavo said. "I know most of the dancers enjoy their weekend days as if they had the nights off too."

Fernando hung up, relieved that Gustavo just wanted to socialize. "No politics," his friend had said on the phone. "Let's just have fun. Tania will go with us."

He wished Julia could go with them. These days he was continuously frustrated with the limits she set on their relationship. They were still seeing each other Sundays but on Mondays only occasionally now, and rarely and briefly another day of the week. And although they could exchange a few words at the club when she wasn't rehearsing or performing, they underplayed their relationship to avoid management's disapproval.

The day was mild, not too hot for May, the sun playing peek-a-boo behind fluffy clouds. Fernando drove and picked up his friends at Gustavo's house, really his mother's house. He still lived with her, and Tania spent time there as well, although she still lived with her own parents.

At the beach club gate, the guard checked membership cards for Gustavo and Fernando and allowed Tania in as a guest. He gave Fernando a disapproving look, as if to chide him for the company he kept. Fernando hardened his face at him as he took his membership card back.

The two men changed into bathing suits quickly in the locker room and opened their outsized umbrellas on the beach. They waved to Tania, who was on her way back from the women's changing rooms. She was wearing a green bathing suit that made her look like a plump, curvaceous avocado.

"Guess who I ran into in the locker room," Tania said to Gustavo. "Ariel, from work. She's with a friend who also works with us. I told them we'd meet them for lunch at the bar around one o'clock."

They took turns going into the water. Fernando stayed behind at their spot and kept an eye on the beach bag and valuables, while Gustavo and Tania swam and splashed. He loved how his friends laughed in the water, the sound bouncing off the liquid surface and reaching him in bright tones. Their teeth were brilliant in their dark faces.

When it was his turn to go into the water he felt odd, alone despite his nearby friends. What was the point of going in the water by himself? But he forced himself to swim out until he was winded, well beyond where he could touch bottom, treaded water to rest, and swam back in. He wanted to be engaged in the day despite his sadness about Julia not being with him.

"Let's you and I go for a walk," Gustavo said to Fernando later. "Okay, Tania?"

"Of course. I'll be here," Tania said, looking up from the romance novel she was reading.

The two men walked on the wet sand. The sun was behind benign white clouds.

"What do you think of Tania?" Gustavo said.

"I like her. She's smart and she's a lot of fun. And she's beautiful."

"And you should see how she helps take care of my mother," Gustavo said. "They get along so well."

"How long have you been together?" Fernando asked.

"About a year," Gustavo said, and looked down at his sandy feet.

Fernando looked at him and smiled. "It's time," he said. He thought it was time for him as well, and wished he could make it come true.

"I think so. I'm going to ask her."

Fernando put his arm around his friend's shoulders. "She's wonderful. And you look happy."

"I am," Gustavo said. "And you? How serious are you with Julia?"

Fernando wasn't sure he wanted to talk about Julia's lack of commitment to the relationship, as if keeping those perceptions unspoken would diminish their chances of being true. But if he couldn't trust his best friend, then who could he confide in? He spoke openly of his wish to marry Julia and of her reluctance to consider it, and beyond that, of the distance she seemed to need between them. Of course, he steered clear of any mention of the abuse she had suffered as a teenager and the murder, even though these events were apparently what was preventing Julia from agreeing to marry him. She had just about said as much, and even though he didn't understand the connection, he hadn't challenged her or explored it with her. She had seemed too pained to talk about it further. "I'm very confused," he said to Gustavo. "I really like her and I thought she liked me and I don't know what to do."

"What do you like about her? I mean, besides her looks," Gustavo said.

Fernando thought a moment. "Her tenderness," he said. "She's affectionate, so spontaneous. She'll kiss me on the cheek when I least expect it, like during a movie, or when she gets back to the table from the bathroom at a restaurant. But there's also a mystery to her. She seems to withdraw at times, lost in thought with a far-off look in her eyes." He considered making reference to Julia's troubled past, but decided against opening that door. He also wanted to explain the undefinable need he had for her, a thirst for her company that arose in every cell of his body, but he had no words for what he felt. Instead, he added, "I've never known anyone like her."

"You seem to have a magnet for Black people," Gustavo said, and smiled. "Or they have a magnet for you."

It was true. The two closest people in his life, besides his family, were two people of color.

Gustavo said, "Why do you think that is?"

"I'm not sure," Fernando said. "I think I trust Black people with my feelings. I think they're more honest with their own emotions than whites." And then he added, "And yet when I mention marriage to Julia, or even just her meeting my parents, or me meeting her mother, she's evasive. She tenses up and says it's too soon." As he said this, he was not unaware of his own evasion.

Gustavo was nodding, and after a moment said, "I'm not sure that Blacks are more up-front with their feelings. But in any case, don't waste your time with Julia if she's stringing you along and not committing. Think about moving on. I hate to say this, but I think she's going to leave you when she finds someone else."

A wave of nausea overtook Fernando and he stopped walking. These words had come from the most reliable person he knew.

Gustavo turned to him. The sun had come out from behind the clouds and was scorching them. He said, "I hope I'm wrong."

They started back, mostly in silence. Gustavo put his arm briefly around Fernando's shoulders as they got closer to their spot on the beach.

Tania said, "Let's go have lunch. We'll meet Ariel and her friend at the bar."

The thatch roof over the open-air bar was massive and extended several yards beyond the wooden floor. They chose a large round table, and immediately Tania stood up and waved at two tall women who were walking in from the sand.

Ariel was friendly and kissed not just Tania but Gustavo and Fernando also, as if they were already acquainted. Despite her bony, aquiline nose, she had a striking face. The eyes were large, gray, and surrounded by long dark lashes, the mouth small and round. Her light brown hair was tied back in a careless ponytail. Her friend was just as tall, her hair a thick black mane framing a round, smiling face.

"Hello," Ariel's friend said, and extended her hand toward Gustavo. "Rebeca Safran."

When the woman extended her hand to Fernando, he could barely manage to shake it and force a smile, and because no words came, he simply nodded. Her last name was extremely uncommon, and she had to be related to Ramon in some way. Could this be his daughter?

Lunch took two hours. The table was covered with plates of ham croquettes, potato omelets, and fried clams. Rounds of beer were brought out. Fernando didn't want to be rude to Rebeca, and forced himself to glance at her occasionally during the conversation, as he did the others when he spoke. But what he really wanted to do was pretend she wasn't there, while also having the opposite urge, which was to ask this outgoing, self-confident woman about her life, whether she was indeed Ramon's daughter, and if she was, how she was doing now after her father's death.

Sitting across the table from Fernando, Ariel made it easy for him to be distracted away from Rebeca, who was seated right next to him. He realized that his initial impression that Ariel had an interesting face was off the mark, because he saw now that she was extraordinary. Her fair skin was already sunburned despite the clownish white streaks of sunblock, the lips chapped, but the features were arranged in perfect balance. Those luminous gray eyes were windows into what she was thinking or about to say, and they animated her speech with a vivacity Fernando found entrancing.

The three women worked at the Spanish Cultural Institute—Ariel as administrator, Tania as her assistant, and Rebeca as the chief curator. Their connection to each other seemed strong and almost familial to Fernando.

After lunch, Ariel and Rebeca joined the three friends on the beach. During the rest of the afternoon Fernando continued to be mesmerized by Ariel's blend of energy and thoughtful conversation. At one point, his attention was drawn to a few strands of rich honey hair peeking out of the groin edge of her bathing suit, and he had to cover his hips with his towel to hide his arousal. The only shadow on the afternoon was Rebeca's presence, although she too was friendly and animated. He wondered how much of her affable personality was the product of her father, if she proved to be Ramon's daughter. Had he also been energetic and sociable, without apparent guile? It didn't matter. Ramon had caused lethal harm, not only to peaceful activists but to his mother's faithfulness to his father. And based on her good spirits, Fernando came to the conclusion that if Rebeca was Ramon's daughter, she had apparently recovered from her loss. Still, her presence was an ineluctable reminder that he might have played a damaging role in the life of this good, maybe wonderful, person, somebody he could easily be friends with. It was the closest he felt to remorse for what he had done. But this realization did not ruin the afternoon for him, and whenever he exchanged smiles with Ariel he became enthusiastic about his options.

53

The weekly canasta games resumed at Betty's house six months after Ramon's deadly car accident. Elena looked forward all week to Wednesday afternoons, when she could escape the terrible news and the food lines and the obstacles of planning even mediocre meals with the meager food allotments. How do you cook without oil, or flour, or salt? How could a family make do with the minuscule rations the government distributed?

Elena drove to Betty's house earlier than she needed to. For years, Elena had kept her friendship with Betty and her affair with Ramon in different compartments. Immediately after the car accident, Elena's grief for Ramon and her compassion for Betty had coalesced like a ghastly whirlpool. It had confused her. She had come to question whether the two components were equally valid. Had one been counterfeit? Which one? Betty's many months of withdrawal and grieving had given Elena time to refresh the boundaries that had been blurred right after Ramon's death. Her friendship with Betty and her extinct fondness for Ramon were equally genuine and lived in separate spaces now.

The card table was already open and set up with playing cards in the middle of the living room. Betty asked the housekeeper to make them coffee. The furniture had been grand once, but the yellow satin sofa sagged now, the fabric threadbare at the corners. The mint-green drapes had faded to a discouraged blue in the sun.

"How are Rebeca and Samuel?" Elena said.

Betty sipped her coffee. "Oh, they're fine." She paused, and in a lower voice said, "They're thinking of leaving the country." She glanced toward the open double doors that led to the kitchen to confirm that the housekeeper wasn't within earshot.

Elena said, "Your girl is Fidelista?"

Betty nodded sideways. "I'm not sure. I watch what I say. We have to be careful when she's around." She looked in the direction of the kitchen again. "My children and I can't discuss their wanting to leave in front of her. If she reports us, the vigilance committee will start trouble like they do with anyone who plans to leave."

"I've heard," Elena said. "What do they do?"

"They come to the house with an armed soldier when they find out you intend to emigrate, and they take inventory of everything, and I mean everything. They do that again when you apply for the exit permit, and again just before you leave. They count every fork, every dish, every towel, and nothing can be missing after the initial count or they cancel the permit and you have to start the whole process again."

Elena had heard about the difficulties of getting an exit permit. It took many months to apply and then have it granted. She shook her head. She and Antonio had discussed the possibility, but Fernando was completely uninterested. "I'm not going anywhere," he had said.

"Have Rebeca and Samuel started the application process?" Elena spoke in an even lower voice, almost a whisper.

Betty looked toward the kitchen and nodded. "We have family in New York. Rebeca and Samuel will go first, and after they're settled and have jobs, I may follow."

Elena said, "You're not sure?"

Betty shook her head. "Ramon is buried here. I'm not sure what I want to do."

Elena could only nod at the disturbing news. Several families in the neighborhood had left, and her older sister Isabel had mentioned that she and her husband had applied to leave. She didn't want to be left behind while her friends and family disappeared. She would talk to Antonio and Fernando again. But the idea that Betty would be stranded in an oppressive environment because of her devotion to Ramon, even in death, was the worst thing she had heard today. Since Ramon's death, Betty's stature for Elena had grown from pleasant canasta partner to friend and confidant. Elena missed Ramon, and she felt that Betty's loss, of necessity, had to be more devastating. She had developed a certain protectiveness and compassion for this woman.

Elena didn't feel like playing canasta now. She had hoped to escape the difficult day-to-day realities and instead she was struggling with a stressful discussion. She hated her life now and what she had done. She got up and, after inventing a headache, gave her friend a hug and went home.

54

They weren't talking much. They went to a movie matinée, then walked around Old Havana. It was Sunday, the stores were closed, and it was too early for dinner. They ambled about, mostly in silence. For Julia, the ostensible reason for her reticence was her continued faith in the Revolutionary government in the face of Fernando's disapproval of it. But she knew that more important for her was the racial difference, and this would be too complicated to discuss with him. And being white, it was not something he would likely understand. She was also tired of the litany of his grievances about the Revolution: imprisonment of dissident journalists, harassment for criticizing the government, closing down churches. These were just a few of his complaints. She tied his skepticism of the new regime to his skin color, another reason to distrust his lack of pigment.

"This is all temporary," Julia had said. "It's only necessary until the monster in the North isn't a threat."

"But we've become a satellite of the Soviet Union," Fernando said.

"I don't care," Julia said. "It's a better system for those of us who grew up poor, and for the peasant farmers in the countryside."

The aftershock of that conversation, similar to others they had, was coloring her mood with him now, at least on the surface.

"What do you want to do until dinnertime?" Fernando asked.

Julia shrugged. "I don't know."

They went to a quiet bar and took a table, ordered drinks. It had been several weeks since Fernando had once more suggested she meet his parents, and she had declined yet again. Her confession of what had occurred at Susana's house evidently hadn't derailed his desire to marry her. She was touched by this, but wasn't sure she could trust his acceptance of her crime to endure.

After the drinks were brought, he said, "What's the future for you and me?" He took a sip of his rum and cola. He hadn't said "Cuba Libre" to the waitress.

Julia looked down at her daiquiri. "Does it have to be different than what we have now?"

Fernando moved his eyes to the large window and the street beyond. She saw his expression harden, but he said nothing, and she put her hand on his. "Look, I don't think I'll ever be married," she said.

He stiffened and withdrew his hand from under hers. There was a look of bafflement in his face, as if he hadn't heard correctly. "All this time," he said. "All this time I thought we would be together forever. That I at least had a chance with you."

A wave of fresh affection came over her that temporarily diminished her doubts about the relationship. "Give me your hand," she said.

Fernando brought his hand out from under the table, and she took it.

She said, "Marriage is not for me. Not with you, not with anyone."

His face collapsed into an abyss of sadness Julia had never seen in him before. She hoped he wasn't going to weep, because she would feel compelled to put her arms around him and this was not what she wanted now, in this moment when she was trying to create a distance. She was relieved when he stroked her fingers with his thumb and nodded.

"So just this. We're not going to be a family," he said, and his voice was so small and tremulous it didn't sound like him at all.

Julia shrugged and looked down. She used her paper napkin to wipe the condensation off the table. "I think we'll always be like family," she said.

The words surprised her with their unplanned candor. She realized they had come from a deep, elemental place, and had escaped her as impulsively as her actions to poison her abuser. If that act still seemed justified and caused no regret, then her emotional commitment to Fernando had to be just as true. The political differences between them suddenly became superfluous, a convenient false note of an excuse. What was left for her to decipher was the real reason that she was so reluctant to marry Fernando, make their union legally binding. Was it really just about race, then?

She was convinced that at some point he would be horrified at the murder she had committed, because how could he not be? How many killers had he ever had contact with? His abhorrence for what she had done would almost certainly destroy his affection for her eventually, would rise like magma from an innocent-looking crevice. And, yes, the race issue was still there, because she was skeptical about an interracial marriage. The color difference between them always simmered in the background for her. She was convinced it was, in fact, the major factor in their different opinions about the Revolution.

But what disturbed her most today was that she had seen in his face, even as he caressed her hand, self-blame, as if he were defective in some way, not worthy of her. And she was convinced that because of her history of being abused, it was exactly the opposite.

55

Fernando got Ariel's work phone number from Gustavo. What good luck, Fernando thought, that Tania worked with her.

At first, their dates were brief, always during daytime, and sometimes just at her house. He wanted to enter this potential relationship slowly. Despite their last conversation, his focus was still on Julia, and in his mind daytime dates with Ariel did not carry the same weight as evenings out would have.

Ariel's parents were much older than his own, and were pleasant but reserved. Their house was large and well cared for, the paint immaculate inside and out, and it was about a mile from his parents' house.

Fernando saw Ariel primarily on Saturdays, when Julia was working. Eventually, he asked Ariel to go to the movies on a Friday night, and she agreed.

"Your parents won't mind if we have no chaperone?" Fernando asked her.

"Oh, no," she laughed. "I'm twenty-five. They want me out of the nest."

He liked Ariel. She was as pretty as any film actress, her manner relaxed, her mood light. And she was affectionate. She took his arm when they walked side by side in the park or along the Malecón. Fernando felt fortunate that this beautiful woman lavished affection on him, even more than Julia did, stroking his scarred left cheek spontaneously when he least expected it. The first time she had touched the deep scar she had asked about it. "An accident," he said, and left it there. He didn't want to ruin the sweetness of their dates with an account of the tortures he had suffered. "Magical" was the word that best described their time together.

Julia had been the only other woman he had dated extensively and, in comparison, Ariel was droll, light-hearted theater to Julia's serious drama. His time with Ariel bordered on joyful at times. He also felt a not inconsiderable attraction, because Ariel's body was voluptuous and drew glances and even outright stares from others on the street, both men and women. And yet he did not feel as captivated as he did with Julia despite her barriers. Even as he dated Ariel, Fernando tried to woo Julia again into deepening their relationship, but it was not to be. He knew that if he wanted his relationship with Ariel to turn more serious he'd have to give up Julia altogether, not only seeing her, but even the idea of her. It was not something he could envision, at least for now, and he wasn't sure how he'd be able to in the future.

He did not tell Ariel about Julia, of course. He made it a point of seeing Ariel on Fridays and Saturdays, then once more during the week. But Sundays and Mondays, when Julia was off from work, he made himself available to her, and she almost always agreed to see him one of the two days, but no more than that.

He did tell Julia about Ariel in an offhand way. He mentioned a movie he had seen, and Julia asked, "Who did you go with?" After a slight hesitation, Fernando said, "Ariel, a girl I met," and Julia nodded.

Fernando thought afterwards that he should have been more open as to who Ariel was. He and Julia had been dating over a year now, and she, like Maribel before her, simply put the reins on the relationship. He was resigned now not to ever marry Julia and to just get from her whatever she would allow him to have. "We'll always be like family," she had said.

Four months after seeing both women, Ariel said, "How do you see us a year from now?" They were walking back to her house from a movie theater in her neighborhood. She was not given to serious topics of conversation. Discussing the film they had just seen would have been more typical, so he was taken by surprise. Of more consequence was the fact that he really hadn't decided whether Ariel was the woman he wanted to marry. He had been floating along in this easy, pleasant relationship with no finite destination planned.

"It's all so uncertain," he said. "You said you're thinking about leaving the country."

"I think we have to," she said. "Don't you agree?"

They had talked about the political situation, the country's descent into a communist dictatorship. Ariel held no hope that there would be a lessening of the repression, and saw emigration as the only solution. Through it all Fernando had listened and nodded but without being convinced that leaving was the answer for him. It seemed like a drastic step, turning your back on your country if you believed that the oppression would be lifted once the economy was on sure footing. He didn't entirely discount the claim that censorship was justified because malcontents supported by the United States were waging a disinformation campaign.

"I don't know," Fernando said. "There are rumors that an invasion is being planned." This would be the best solution for him, an erasure of the totalitarian regime.

Ariel said, "I know. I've heard that too. But what if it's just a rumor?"

Nothing else was said about their future together until they were in front of her house. Fernando kissed her lightly on the lips, as far as they had gotten in the physicality of their relationship.

"Think about it, at least," Ariel said. "Our future. If we're going to stay together, it can be here if that's what you prefer, or in another country. But we should make plans. Decisions have to be made. If we decide we have to leave, which I'd like to do, it may be more difficult as time goes on."

Fernando felt somewhat pressured, and yet he saw her point. His own parents had a similar urgency about planning a possible departure. If they weren't going to be married, Ariel could start planning her own emigration. And she was right that life became more difficult each month, with the food shortages, the censorship, the menace of the vigilance committees. The oppression was multifactorial. He wished he didn't feel so rooted in this country, even with the dismal political history that had always plagued it and continued to do so.

56

All Christian religious services were banned completely now, not only Catholic ones. Jewish services weren't affected, because politics had not entered into their sermons, at least not so far as the government could detect. Churches were still open for private prayer, and baptisms and weddings were allowed. Antonio went to confession one Saturday a month despite Elena's objections. "The vigilance committee is bound to know," she said. "You can be sure they keep track of where you go on Saturdays, and you're being branded as a possible enemy of the Revolution." But Antonio felt the need to cleanse his soul periodically, even if he couldn't attend Mass and receive communion.

"What do you have to confess?" Father Belarmino said to Antonio through the grid of the confessional. Antonio trusted this elderly clergyman completely. He was already in his fifties when he had officiated over Antonio and Elena's wedding and had baptized both Fernando and Luis.

On his knees, Antonio's face was inches away from the sitting priest's, barely visible through the grid. He whispered, "I've been having impure thoughts again."

"What kinds of thoughts?"

Antonio tucked in his chin. "Immoral ideas about men," he said.

"You know those thoughts are against the teachings of Christ, and the acts are against the law."

"I wouldn't engage in any acts," Antonio said. "But the thoughts just enter my head."

Father Belarmino heard the rest of Antonio's confession and dispensed the prayers of penance. Before he left the confessional, Antonio said, "I feel so incomplete without communion. I wish there was a way."

After a moment the priest said, "Come to the rectory after you've said your prayers."

Antonio knelt on one of the front pews of the empty church and said his five Hail Marys, the Credo, and two Lord's Prayers. Still kneeling, he brought his fisted hands to his mouth and spoke not in a mere whisper but in a soft voice that he could plainly hear, because he hoped that listening to his own words would bring him strength and reassurance that he would not stray. "Help me with my struggle, dear Lord," he said. "Help me so that I never hurt Elena. She's a good wife, so sure of the right thing to do always. I need her. Help me so we can be together until my last day on this Earth."

Afterwards in the rectory Father Belarmino opened a wooden box that sat on his desk. He extracted a round wafer and made the sign of the cross over it while his lips moved in a silent blessing, then placed the host on Antonio's waiting tongue.

"Thank you, Father," Antonio said. "I'm so grateful. I miss going to Mass, the hymns, your sermons. I hope they will allow religious services again soon."

The priest shook his head. "I don't see that happening. And so many parishioners have left the country." He paused. "If people of faith continue to leave, I don't see how we can survive here," he said, waving his hand at the dark wood of the walls and ceiling.

Antonio nodded. "Elena and I have spoken of it also. But my son doesn't want to leave."

"Go with God," the priest said.

On his way home Antonio felt a lightness in his step, the weight of his sins lifted, even if only temporarily, until the thoughts came back. He was grateful for his faith and for Father Belarmino, with his nonjudgmental compassion. Even in the rectory after his confession, he had not felt the slightest awkwardness that his confessor had heard of his sins yet again. During the walk home he prayed that Elena, Fernando, and Luis, none of whom were devout believers, would find a source of peace, as he had.

57

It was already noon. Julia hadn't slept well, worried about the day ahead. She finished her café con leche and showered. She hadn't seen her mother in weeks and wanted to visit her before meeting Fernando at three. He had mentioned a movie and dinner, their usual Sunday date, but today she had other plans for them.

She put on a yellow sleeveless dress, radiant against her dark skin. Fernando had never seen her in it. She looked in the mirror. Her hair was longer now, straightened and softly waved. Although she wanted to look good for her mother, she did not want to look like this for Fernando. She changed into a plain white linen dress she had worn countless times and wrapped her head in a black silk scarf that made her look like a Santeria priestess.

Julia had thought carefully about Fernando, her vision of their future. A complex vortex was pushing her to break up with him completely. There was the feeling of unworthiness because of the sexual abuse, which consumed her self-esteem as a leech ingests its victim's blood. But then also there was the question of bearing children in the future, which she knew Fernando wanted and she wasn't sure was possible for her. And there was that remnant of pretty Susana's taunts, she of the straight hair and hazel eyes, because of Julia's dark skin. What would Fernando's family think of her? Would they look down on her? Blacks and whites just didn't marry or even cohabitate, at least not in this country. She had heard of it happening more often in the US and in Brazil, but not here. These thoughts buzzed around her like tenacious flies and undermined her belief that it could work out between them. There were too many uncertainties, and there was no point contemplating an ill-fated future.

When Julia saw her mother, she wondered whether she really had changed so much or whether she wasn't remembering accurately what the old woman had looked like the last time. She appeared much more frail and elderly now. Julia felt remorse at spreading herself too thin, seeing Fernando on Sundays, Reinaldo on Mondays and one other day during the week.

Reinaldo played the flute and the trombone in the club's orchestra. His grandparents had been slaves, as hers had been. "There is a rumor you're going out with that white guy from administration," he had said to her when they first met, "but I would really like for us to get together." He said this smirking and suggestively, and she thought he was somewhat slimy, but she started dating him. Two months later, she was juggling the two men. She hadn't told Fernando about Reinaldo yet, but it was time, even though the man was just a dispensable distraction, a caricature of the unreliable flaky musician who would not be in her future either.

"Are you okay?" Julia asked her mother after she kissed the crinkled cheek. She loved the jasmine fragrance of her mother's talcum powder.

"I'm tired. The work is getting to be too much," her mother said. They sat in the small, tidy living room of the apartment at the edge of a humble but safe neighborhood.

"Why don't you work five days instead of six?" Julia said.

"What? And who's going to cook for the family when I'm not there?"

"Who cooks for them on Sundays?" Julia asked.

"They go out on Sundays. And I don't want anybody else in that kitchen."

Julia made them coffee, her mother putting two heaping teaspoons of sugar into the small espresso cup of the rich foamy liquid.

"Are you still seeing that man you mentioned last time?" her mother said. "What was his name?"

"Fernando."

"That's right." The woman sipped her demitasse.

"Yes, I'm seeing him later today," Julia said.

Her mother sipped the last of her brew. "Make sure he's right for you," she said. "Don't rush into anything. Better alone than in bad company."

Later, as she kissed her mother goodbye, she told her she'd be back in a week and resolved to keep her promise. She didn't want to squander the chance of being with her quickly aging mother as much as possible.

Julia thought, on her way to meet Fernando, that it was time for some changes. It wasn't just that things with Fernando had to end. It was time she lived in her own place and had her mother live with her. The woman was fifty-four but looked and acted older. The years of hard labor in the tobacco fields before becoming a domestic had taken their toll.

Fernando was already sitting on their customary bench in the park when she arrived. He smiled broadly when he saw her, as he always did, stood up and kissed her, hands on her shoulders, pulling her in. She resisted with a certain stiffness, and he stepped back with a disturbed, quizzical look on his face. He looked at her intently but said nothing.

"Let's stay here and talk for a while," Julia said, and she saw his face drop into a mixture of apprehension and alarm.

They sat on the bench, Fernando facing her and she looking out at the shrubbery across the paved path.

"We're not going to have a future, you and I," she said after a tense few seconds of silence. When Fernando said nothing, she went on. "You've said you want children, and that's not what I want." She resisted the temptation to look at him.

"We don't have to marry or have children," he said.

She shook her head. "But it's more than that. I don't see myself attached to only one man. I've never been with anybody this long. I just haven't felt that spark with anyone."

"And not with me either?"

Julia shook her head again, said nothing, and stopped herself from biting her lower lip.

"What have I done to break us up?" Fernando asked.

"Look, it's not you. It's me," she said. "It's who I am."

Fernando sat in silence, hands between his knees. She wanted to take his hands in hers but sat still.

"It's not because of the political situation, is it?" Fernando asked, frowning.

"Of course not. I know you agree the situation is temporary."

Fernando nodded. After a moment he added, "So it's just that you don't want a long-term relationship. At least with me."

"I don't think with anyone," Julia said.

Fernando looked away, seemingly at the foliage of the trees dancing in the warm breeze. He said, "But we'll see each other? Go out like we have been doing?"

Julia shrugged. "Look, I've loved the time I've spent with you. But I think we should go our separate ways for a while."

They sat in silence. Out of the corner of her eye she saw Fernando cross his arms on his chest and look straight ahead. After a minute he stood up abruptly.

"This is very sudden. I think you're hiding something," he said. "You said we'd always be like family. There must be someone else in your life." Still standing, he looked at her a few seconds. Julia glanced at him and realized there was no need now to tell him about Reinaldo, but she nodded. He walked away.

Julia waited until he was out of view, lost behind the pedestrians on the wide avenue. Her hands were gripping the edge of the bench, and she let go so she could find a handkerchief in her purse to wipe her nose.

The Malecón was a few blocks away. She could take a long walk because there was no one else she was going to see today, and now she didn't want to see Reinaldo tomorrow as planned. The air was light and the sun strong along the sea, an occasional November breeze refreshing her, bringing with it the illusion of relief from her wretchedness. The people walking along the seawall were families and couples, some holding hands as they strolled, some just sitting on the concrete wall. Not one of the couples or families was biracial.

She had obsessed about Fernando, turned it over in her mind again and again: fear of rejection by his family, doubts about her ability to conceive, the stain of sexual abuse. And now there was a new understanding that brought it all together into a hand grenade that she could not lob but would carry with her forever, and which would destroy her if she moved too quickly and carelessly into happiness. For a long time, until not that long ago, she thought that what Martín had done had only ever happened to her, and that he had chosen her and not Susana because of her darker color. Susana, with her light skin, had escaped Martín's paws.

Does damage always annihilate happiness? Fernando deserved a less tortured woman. He might not fully understand all the implications of being a person of color, but he really was an extraordinary man.

58

It was over with Julia, long overdue. He should have known many months ago that it wasn't going to work out. Julia, pretending that the relationship meant more to her than it did, had used him as a pastime for over a year. Fernando wished he hadn't been so gullible, so inexperienced. Gustavo had been right that day on the beach, as if he had been clairvoyant and seen it in a crystal ball.

He was angry with himself for squandering his love on someone who didn't want it. But there was also an element of wounded self-esteem, and he used the idea that Ariel was now the most important woman in his life as a balm. He hoped that he would be able to generate some enthusiasm about the prospect of a life with her.

Fernando didn't want to wait until he saw Ariel again on Friday evening, and two days after his meeting with Julia he called her. He had chatted with her parents whenever he went to her house to pick her up for their dates, once or twice a week. The older couple were pleasant and low-key during these brief meetings, but he hadn't had much extended interaction with them because Ariel was usually ready to go soon after he arrived.

"*Hola*," Fernando heard on the phone, and knew it was Ariel's mother. Her dulcet voice was not unlike Ariel's.

"Good evening, Señora. It's Fernando."

"Ah, yes, Fernando. How are you?"

"I'm very well, thank you. And you?"

"Very well, thank you. Let me get Ariel for you. Excuse me."

Fernando pondered how he would broach the subject when Ariel got on the line. He and Ariel had spoken in only the vaguest terms about a life together, because whenever he was with her he felt that being married to her was an indistinct path that he might or might not choose to follow. And then suddenly she was on the phone, her voice like music, and after they exchanged greetings, he simply said, "I'd like you to meet my parents."

"I would love to. When?"

"How about Saturday afternoon? We'll go to my house and then later you and I can go to a movie and dinner."

"It'll be nice to meet your parents. And at some point, you'll come to my house for dinner so you can get to know my parents a little better."

"I would like that," he said, although he realized that his response had been automatic, and that becoming more acquainted with her parents was a necessary formality but that, in fact, he had no great desire to get to know them better.

On Saturday, on his way to pick up Ariel at her house, Fernando considered changing plans, skipping his parents' house altogether and going directly to the movies with Ariel. But, of course, his parents were expecting her, and they had talked about how eager they were to meet her. His mother and Ines had spent hours in the kitchen making finger food and flan for Ariel's visit.

The afternoon went perfectly well. Ariel charmed them, seemingly without effort, behaving the way she usually did, without false flattery or pretense. Antonio didn't say much, but he smiled, nodded, and occasionally chuckled at something that Ariel said. Elena was her usual talkative self, but atypically subdued. She refrained from any of her customary opinionated pronouncements.

After the four of them had been chatting a few hours, during which they consumed the better part of a tray of croquettes and ham sandwiches, Fernando said, "We should go, Ariel. We don't want to be late for the movie."

"So soon?" Elena said. "What movie are you going to see?"

"The new Doris Day movie," Ariel said. *"Please Don't Eat the Daisies."*

"Oh, yes. That's one of the last American movies they allowed into the country."

"I like all of her movies," Ariel said.

"She's funny and a wonderful singer," Elena said. "But you're much prettier than she is."

Ariel laughed and shook her head, and Antonio said, "It's true."

Afterwards, as they watched the movie, and then later during dinner, Fernando felt a sense of relief. He was relieved the meeting had gone so smoothly and glad that his parents seemed to like Ariel. He detected, however, more than a bit of apathy in himself about the deeper significance of the afternoon. It was as if an event that he was not entirely sure he wanted to occur, and which would usher in a new stage of his life he wasn't sure he wanted, was fast approaching with the inevitability of an avalanche.

59

How everything had changed. She could no longer spend the afternoons reading magazines or watching *novelas* on TV or listening to the Grundig. Some days she was out all day standing in queues for an hour or more just to buy soap, or toilet paper, or milk. She let Ines stand in the line for meats and chicken because the butcher knew her and gave her better cuts. Same for the vegetables. And Elena wasn't going to stand around the vegetable cart along with the trash from the vigilance committee Ines had warned her would be there.

Elena trusted Ines. She wasn't sure the young woman completely agreed with the family that the political situation was dire, but she nodded when any of them expressed frustration and shook her head in agreement if she heard them talking about a repressive new measure. Two popular magazines had been shut down by the government for reporting news that didn't adhere to the party line. And Ines had actually said "those people" when Elena told her of an encounter at the bodega with a vigilance committee member who demanded to check her ration card.

Many changes in her life, but not canasta. She still went to Betty's house on Wednesday afternoons. Nina and Fefa would be there too, of course. Nina was the one with whom Elena felt the most affinity, although she was now fond of Betty also. But with Betty, there was still the guilt that the memory of Ramon brought. It kept the friendship from becoming as full-fledged as it might have been. There was that withholding of spirit Elena was aware of in herself, that guard she kept up.

But with Nina, there was a chemistry, a connection. It was Nina who for years called Elena just to chat, or with whom Elena would go to a movie matinée. It was therefore disconcerting when Elena noticed Nina withdrawing from the group, not physically, but in demeanor. There was less joking now than there had been before the Revolution. Nina didn't call Elena anymore, or did so rarely.

Fefa, her improbably blond curls carefully set, was already sitting in Betty's living room when Elena arrived. The canasta table was open in the middle of the room and the cards arranged. It was nearly time for the game to start.

"Nina's late," Elena said. "Not the usual for her." She noticed Betty and Fefa exchanging looks.

Betty got up and closed the double doors that led to the hallway and the kitchen. "We have to be careful what we say around Nina," Betty said in a low voice. "With respect to the government, I mean."

Elena frowned. "Don't tell me she's a communist," she said in a loud, incredulous voice.

Betty brought an index finger to her lips and glanced at the door. "I think she did join the Party."

Elena wasn't sure she had heard correctly. "What?" she said. "How can that be?"

Fefa said, "A few weeks ago, when you weren't here, she defended the Revolution when I complained about the food lines."

Elena remembered now that subsequent to that afternoon, the day she had been overwhelmed by the memory of Ramon, whenever she made a negative remark about the government her three friends around the table kept silent. She had attributed their reaction to their concentrating on the game. Now she understood that Nina's presence had stifled the conversation, and she understood her friend's new distance from her.

There was a knock on the double doors. "Come in," Betty said. The housekeeper opened the doors and Nina walked in.

Elena got up and kissed Nina on the cheek, more than the casual greeting any of them usually exchanged, because she wanted to repair the friendship if at all possible. Elena detected not exactly a pullback from her friend, but there was a certain telltale stiffness. One more loss, she thought. One more loss among so many.

60

Instead of sitting on the porch after dinner for his evening reading, Antonio now sat in the living room. If Elena was watching TV, he'd go into the dining room or sit in the lumpy armchair in the bedroom. He no longer felt at ease sitting on the porch reading a work of literature that might be considered bourgeois and therefore subversive. One of the neighborhood watchdogs or a member of the Communist Party might walk by and report him if what he was reading was not approved by the government. Several of Cuba's most respected novelists—Lezama Lima, Carpentier—had left the country when their novels were banned from publication and from bookstores.

Antonio sat down to read in his usual spot at the head of the dining room table. Tonight Elena was watching a noisy comedy. Fernando appeared in the wide arched entry from the hallway. "Can I come in?" he asked. "I don't want to bother you."

Antonio closed his book, a complicated novel by Cabrera Infante that required close attention, and looked at his son. He was looking disheveled lately; hair uncombed, shirt untucked here and there, and his lower lids had darkened, making him look older than twenty-three. "You're not bothering me," Antonio said. He missed Luis as if a wheel were missing from the solid horse-drawn carriage that was the family, and he welcomed any interaction with his remaining son.

Fernando sat close to his father. "What do you think of Ariel?" he asked.

"She's very pretty. And smart. She seems like a wonderful young lady," Antonio said.

"I'm thinking about asking her to marry me."

Antonio nodded. "If you're sure that's what you want," he said.

After a moment Fernando said, "How can I be sure she's the one for me? How did you know *Mamá* was the woman for you?"

Antonio had left the closed book on the table near him, and now he pushed it further away. He wished he had a definitive answer for his son. "If you're happy being with her, and can imagine living with her the rest of your life, then you take that step. It's an important one."

"I know. So how were you sure *Mamá* was the right one for you?"

Antonio gave a small shrug, then regretted the gesture, which he thought implied that he hadn't been so sure about his decision. He remembered the agonizing options years ago in the monastery, and before, and after. "I don't think anybody can really be sure, one hundred percent," he said. "Things work out between two people, or they don't. And you don't ever know if that person was indeed the best possible option or if someone else would have made you happier. Life is not a predetermined fairy tale. It's a process and a game of chance."

When Fernando remained silent, looking down at the tablecloth in front of him, Antonio added, "You had mentioned someone named Julia a few months ago. What ever happened with her?"

Fernando shut his eyes tight, and when he opened them, they had reddened. "She doesn't want to marry me, or even see me anymore," he said, and his son's broken voice made Antonio's throat tighten.

Fernando covered his face and let out a small moan, and Antonio felt his heart contract forcefully in his chest, not in a beat but in a sustained, almost painful spasm. How do you protect an adult son from emotional suffering? He resisted the urge to pull Fernando up out of the chair to hug him. He stood up. "I'll bring us some brandy," he said.

61

1961

Club Maxime, like all the other foreign-owned nightclubs in the country, had been nationalized, and the casino part of the establishment was closed permanently. All employees, therefore, including Fernando, now worked for the government. He had been bypassed for the position of general manager because he did not belong to the Communist Party, and was named assistant director.

During his breaks, which were as often as he wished, he still strolled the landscaped grounds and gazed out at the sea from the club's raised terrace. If the dancers were using the space for rehearsal, he avoided it altogether, and hadn't seen Julia in almost two months.

On a Saturday afternoon he asked Ariel to marry him, presenting her with a black velvet box that contained a splendid diamond ring. They were sitting in the living room of her parents' house after a wonderful lunch of cold-pressed beef and salade niçoise. Ariel had cried soundlessly while she hugged him, her cheek on his shoulder.

"It's so beautiful," she said. "I've never seen anything like this."

He was pleased with the ring, and it had been a difficult find. Or, rather, Fernando had set himself a high bar for the jewel he wanted to present to Ariel. None of the first ten or twelve jewelry stores he visited had anything he liked, but he pressed on in his search. It was as if sorting through dozens of rings, spending weeks in his quest, and being thorough in his assessment of every detail, he was guaranteeing success in his future marriage.

Finally he had remembered Luis's friend Joaquin, whose family owned a wholesale jewelry business.

"We moved the business to Miami a few months ago," Joaquin said on the phone. "My parents are already there and I leave in a few weeks. But I can tell you that the best jewelry nowadays is imported from Czechoslovakia."

Joaquin gave Fernando the name and number of a friend with a wholesale jewelry business. The ring Fernando selected was a large blue diamond solitaire set in palladium, exceedingly expensive but stunning. Fernando had little outlet for the money he was making, other than helping his parents with the household expenses.

He wanted to tell Gustavo. His girlfriend, Tania, would hear about the engagement from Ariel at work, of course, but he wanted his friend to hear it directly from him. Over lunch on Monday, Gustavo clapped his hands, stood up, and hugged him when he heard the news. "The two times I've met her she's been wonderful, fun, and pleasant. And she's beautiful." He laughed in delight. "Let's celebrate," Gustavo said. He called the waiter over and ordered two glasses of champagne.

Fernando felt inadequate witnessing his friend's elation with the news. Why was he feeling lukewarm about the whole thing compared to Ariel and Gustavo? He had announced the engagement to his parents on Sunday with Ariel at his side, and his mother had yelped in delight. His father, smiling widely, had hugged him and then Ariel. Maybe that's just who I am, he thought. Maybe this is the best I can do and Julia was just an infatuation, not my durable true love. He had until May, still four months away, to fully process his engagement and muster some enthusiasm for his wedding day.

62

By March, the rumors about an imminent invasion by the US were so widespread in Havana and indeed throughout the entire country that for everyone it was a matter of when rather than if. People with relatives in the States were the main source of the news. The reports came from Cuban exiles training with the CIA in Central America, who constantly leaked information to the American press about their activities, as well as to their relatives.

"Betty spoke to her children in Miami," Elena said at dinner. "They think it's going to happen soon."

Antonio nodded. "Our office is putting a hold on most long-distance shipping," he said. "We don't know where the invasion is going to happen, and we don't want to risk losing merchandise."

Fernando looked at his parents. At the nightclub, now under the direction of the Communist Party, there was no such discussion. "We'll see what happens," he said, making himself sound skeptical.

"But it's everywhere, Fernando," Elena said. "Everyone with relatives in the North says they know someone training in Guatemala, getting ready for the invasion."

Fernando and Gustavo had talked about it, and they agreed it seemed certain. He just didn't want to get his parents' hopes up that they would be liberated from communism soon, in case the invasion didn't happen or somehow wasn't successful. He had expressed these doubts about the invasion to Gustavo. "How can you say that? We know for a fact it's coming," he had responded. "And how could an American invasion fail?" And then he added with a worried look, "We'll be going back to the corruption we had before."

During their conversations, it had become clear to Fernando that Gustavo was no longer as fanatically in support of the government as he had been, but he still accepted the abuses of human rights as the price to pay for what he saw as the greater good. Fernando believed that people of color, always the most downtrodden, would be willing to turn a blind eye to totalitarian measures if it led to racial equality, or at least the promise of it. It made perfect sense.

And that kept bringing him back to his failed relationship with Julia. Fernando was sure that she was indeed seeing someone else. Gustavo, as reliable as an oracle, had been right that she would drop him eventually. Had he brought it on himself? Had he shown sufficient understanding for her support of the Revolution? Or had she detected his strong and not fully expressed reservations pouring out uncontrollably like sweat? He had reconstructed their conversation a dozen times. It had been months since that final exchange in the park. Nowadays she looked his way and smiled if they both happened to be on the club's terrace at the same time, something he tried to avoid. On one occasion they passed each other on the grounds. Julia was in conversation with another dancer, and her eyes stayed on him and she gave him a small wave. He had just nodded at her and not been able to do much work the rest of the afternoon.

Fernando relaxed and read the newspaper on the terrace during his morning breaks, but the news was all the same, praising the government for this or that. They also printed fabrications about the advances of the Revolution that ignored the food shortages, the power outages, the jailing of protesters.

His afternoon breaks were another matter. They often coincided with the dancers' lengthy rehearsals, which unsettled him. But he forced himself to go anyway and didn't run away when the dancers appeared. He saw that Julia was aware of his gaze on her, and when she glanced at him as she worked, he was filled with an irrational hope. He fantasized that he could bridge the schism in their relationship, convince her that she was wrong and that they could have a future together. It might not be the future he had envisioned—a full family, or even cohabitation—but together in some form.

One afternoon, he waited until the rehearsal was over and the dancers would be free until showtime. Fernando knew Julia would probably be going to her apartment to rest, and he followed her to the stage door that led out to a side alley. Her stiff steps told him she was aware he was behind her. Once they were outside she stopped, turned to face him, and said nothing.

Fernando found himself tongue-tied for a few seconds. During rehearsals he had noticed that she had gained some weight, her figure fuller. And now, up close, the intense attraction ravished him and caused a yaw in his abdomen.

"Can I see you?" he asked.

She averted her eyes. "What for?"

"I just want to talk."

She said, "Look, Fernando, what's the point?" There was no unkindness in her voice, but rather a comforting tone, as if she were speaking to a child.

"I just need to understand something. Please," he said. "Let me see you Monday after I finish work."

"I can't Monday," she said.

"Sunday, then." He was supposed to be with Ariel on Sunday, but he ignored that.

Julia hesitated. "All right. Sunday, late afternoon. I'm having lunch with my mother."

On Sunday morning he called Ariel to cancel their date. "I have to help a friend replace a solenoid in his car," he said, thinking of Gustavo as a ghostly alibi, although his friend didn't even own a car.

"Whatever that is," Ariel said. "But why can't your friend get a mechanic?"

"He can't afford it. I promised I would help him."

"Oh, Fernando. You and your cars," she said, and then blew him a kiss.

63

When Ines got home, it was near seven. The buses were taking longer nowadays. She had heard stories from the bus drivers about breakdowns and parts not being available from the US now that Cuba had terminated trade with them.

Her mother was already inside with the food she had cooked on the fire pit, a few feet from the shack. The old woman was sitting at the badly marred table, made of the same knotty pine as the two chairs. "Where were you?" she said. "I've been so worried." Her normally flat tone sounded unsettled today.

"The bus was crowded and slow," Ines said. "Where's Pedro?"

"He's gone. I don't know where."

Ines said, "Gone? Since when?"

"This morning."

"He went to work?"

The woman shook her head. "He hasn't been to work all week. This morning he coughed up blood after he had a cigarette. When I got back from the field he was gone." She pulled the chain to turn the light bulb on over the table.

If Pedro went to work, he was always home before Ines, well before sundown. That certainty and the coughing of blood closed like a vise around her head.

"I have to go look for him," Ines said. She put her shoes back on.

"Have dinner first," her mother said. She was ladling a stew of chicken, corn, and yuca into earthenware bowls. "Where are you going to look for him?"

"I'll check the bodega and the *curandero*. Maybe they've seen him."

"The *curandero*?" her mother said. "That fake hasn't been there in months. The government closed him down and they started a clinic with real doctors."

"So maybe they saw him today," Ines said.

"You can go see, but they're almost always closed. I don't know why they got rid of the *curandero*. He was better than nothing."

There was no moon, the clouds fading in the growing darkness. She knew the cobblestone streets well enough to walk without the light from the lampposts, most of which were dark nowadays. The flashlight at home was for emergencies, when the electricity went out.

As her mother predicted, the clinic was closed, and the man shutting down the bodega for the night hadn't seen Pedro all day. As a last resort, Ines went to the part of town where Pedro's late mother had lived. He still had friends there, but no one was out on the street socializing the way men used to do in these parts.

Ines woke up several times during the night, startled by the empty place on the bed. She stepped outside into the darkness, the cool air refreshing her, and then tried to go back to sleep. She got up an hour earlier than customary and walked around again in the growing daylight, hoping to see Pedro sleeping under a tree near the house. He had been coughing more than usual the past few weeks, especially at night. Maybe he had spent the night outside so as not to disturb her sleep.

That evening when she got home from work she went to the clinic again, but it was still closed. She hadn't seen the village policeman since the Revolution, and, therefore, had no idea where to report him missing.

The days repeated themselves, her hope dimming. When Señora Elena asked what was wrong that she looked so sad and she heard the news, she shook her head and said, "Oh, Ines. How sorry I am to hear this." This was what Ines needed to allow herself to weep, quietly and alone in the kitchen, and by midafternoon her employer told her to go home and rest.

64

He was just about to call Gustavo when his secretary appeared at the door. "Gustavo Fornas is here to see you," she said.

"I was going to call you," Fernando said. He noticed the apprehension in his friend's eyes, the deep lines on the forehead.

"Let's go outside a few minutes," Gustavo said.

Out on the terrace Gustavo led the way to the rail that overlooked the ocean. "There's trouble coming," he said. "The invasion is going to happen very soon, like in a day or two. The government is going to detain all men suspected of being against the Revolution. You're going to be one of them." Gustavo spoke in a whisper, although there was no one else on the huge terrace.

"Are you sure? When?" Fernando said.

"Tomorrow night. They want to prevent any possible uprising once the invasion starts."

"But I'm not involved in anything," Fernando said.

"It doesn't matter. Listen to me. Tomorrow morning before coming to work pack some things, and at the end of the day, come to my house."

"You're going to hide me?" Fernando said. This seemed surreal to him, like a movie.

"Count on being in my house two or three days. I'll cover for you here. Tell the director you've got a death in the family outside Havana," Gustavo said.

"Is this really necessary?"

"I have to go back to the office," Gustavo said. "Don't tell your parents where you'll be."

"But what about my father? Will he be safe?"

"They only want to arrest the younger men. Your father is not on the list," Gustavo said, and left.

Fernando remained where he was as he watched his friend disappear into the casino. Through the large glass windows he could see a taxi waiting for him at the front of the building. He had wanted to tell Gustavo about his brief and disastrous meeting with Julia on Sunday, which had seemed so pressing, so important, even though the conversation with her had led to nothing but more rejection. He trusted Gustavo not to judge him for wanting to see Julia despite his engagement to Ariel. Of all his friends, he sensed an acceptance, an understanding from Gustavo that was unique. Now that conversation with Julia and the deflating outcome seemed trivial, and maybe it was in the wide overview of what was going on in the country, but it had crushed him. Julia's tone of voice had been so soothing, so compassionate, that it had only deepened his longing for her.

"I have to go on a business trip tomorrow," Fernando said to his parents at dinner.

"A business trip?" Elena said. "Where?"

"Las Villas. They're planning to open a new nightclub there."

"Las Villas? Why would anybody want to open a nightclub in Las Villas?"

He realized that he shouldn't have picked Las Villas at random. It was mostly a rural province with a few beach towns and a magnificent but socially conservative city, Cienfuegos. "I don't know," he said. "Maybe to increase tourism there."

"How long will you be gone?" Antonio asked.

"Two or three days."

"Be careful," his father said. "It's almost certain an invasion is coming. The newspapers are full of the warnings. We just don't know where it's going to happen."

At the end of the workday, Fernando picked Gustavo up at the Riviera Club and drove to his house. He had only been in the living room and the enclosed backyard of Gustavo's house previously. Now he saw that beyond the small kitchen and dining area there was only one bedroom with a single twin bed. He concluded that either his friend or his mother routinely slept in the living room, and wasn't sure what arrangements Gustavo had in mind for him.

Obdulia, Gustavo's mother, made a delicious dinner of red beans with ham hocks. At bedtime, Gustavo lowered the back of the sofa, turning it into a bed, and put sheets and a pillow on it. From the bedroom closet he brought out a cot and another pillow. Fernando could see Obdulia helping his friend find more bed linens.

"This is where I usually sleep," Gustavo said, pointing to the converted sofa, "but you take it. The sheets are clean."

"Absolutely not," Fernando said. "The cot will be fine."

Fernando was so unsettled by the sleeping arrangements he thought he'd never fall asleep, although the cot was comfortable. Gustavo made good money now, at least as much as he did, so why was he living like this? Where did he and Tania spend time alone? But nervous exhaustion eventually won out over his hyper alertness and he finally fell asleep.

In the morning they took turns in the bathroom off the tiny dining area. Obdulia made them café con leche and toast.

After Gustavo left for work, Fernando spent the morning reading, mostly in the backyard. He was grateful for the high walls enclosing the space that gave him complete privacy. He watched TV with Obdulia, who for lunch fixed him a masterful plate of black beans, redolent of cumin and olive oil, followed by creamy bread pudding.

Later, while he was once again reading in the backyard, he heard Obdulia shriek in the living room and he rushed in. Her eyes were bulging in alarm, and on the radio the announcer was reporting an invasion of US forces in the Bay of Pigs, a hundred miles east of Havana. The attack had started at dawn, and already Cuban forces had captured hundreds of invaders and killed dozens more. Insurrections had occurred throughout the island, but they had been quickly suppressed by the militia.

Gustavo came home early, in mid-afternoon. "Any more news?" he asked. Fernando and Obdulia were sitting on either side of the radio in the living room.

"They're reporting a lot of losses for the invaders," Fernando said. "You think that's possible?"

Gustavo said, "I hope so. Although I can't imagine the giant to the north won't win in the end. But I'm keeping my fingers crossed. And by the way," he added, "last night they rounded up over 1,200 men in Havana alone, and they're in detention."

"So you were right, and they must have known the invasion was going to happen this morning," Fernando said. "I hope my parents are okay."

"They should be fine. Like I told you, your father's name wasn't on the list," Gustavo said.

"Good," Fernando said. "Then I guess I can go home today."

"Better spend another night here," Gustavo said. "They'll probably go back tonight looking for the men they didn't get last night."

"Yes, spend another night, Fernando," Obdulia said. "I like having company during the day."

Fernando nodded, and although he missed the comfort of home, he saw that it was the safest thing to do. "Thank you," he said. "I'll stay another night, then. Although I'm worried about my parents, and I hate to inconvenience you," Fernando said. "When you offered me a place to stay, I thought you had your own room."

Gustavo chuckled. "I wish," he said. "My mom doesn't want to move. She loves this house and the neighborhood. And I'm not going to leave her."

"No, I'm not going anywhere," Obdulia said.

Later, when they were alone in the backyard, Fernando hesitated, but he asked Gustavo, "How do you spend time alone with Tania?"

"It's very difficult," Gustavo said. "We go to her house sometimes, although her parents are usually there. I don't know what we're going to do when we get married." His smile was full of anticipation.

Fernando nodded. He wished he could envision his life with Ariel with the same enthusiasm his friend had for his own future with Tania.

65

It was mid-April, and the night was much cooler than the day had been, unusually so for a tropical spring. Antonio could feel the fresh breeze through the open shutters in the bedroom. The armchair was close enough to the window so that he didn't need the noisy fan, and he heard some loud voices coming from the front of the house. He closed the book and got up to see what the origin of the commotion was. It didn't sound like the TV, which Elena was watching in the living room.

From the hallway he could see Elena at the front door. Was she arguing with someone? He saw that she was pushed aside by a man in a green military uniform carrying a rifle. He had a bushy brown beard. Behind him was another armed man in civilian clothes, whom Antonio recognized as one of the neighborhood vigilantes. Antonio heard Elena say, "I've already told you he's not here," as he darted to the confrontation.

"What do you want?" Antonio said, his voice loud with outrage.

"We're looking for Fernando Leal," the soldier said.

Despite his growing anger, Antonio registered a stench emanating from the man. "He's not here," he said.

Without another word, the two armed men walked into the hallway, opened the closets and bedroom doors, went into the kitchen, and finally behind the house where Ines did the laundry.

"Where is he?" the military man said.

"He's in Las Villas on a business trip," Antonio said.

"Oh, yeah, sure," the neighborhood watch said, sneering. "I'll bet he's hiding somewhere in the city."

"That's absurd," Antonio said. "How could he have known about this?" He knew he sounded indignant and too loud, but he wasn't expecting the soldier to hold his rifle up with both hands, as if ready to take aim.

"If he's not here, then you'll have to come with us," the soldier said, still holding the rifle up to his chest, finger on the trigger.

"But what has he done?" Elena said, her voice shrill and agitated.

"It's a security measure," the neighborhood watch said, and clasped handcuffs on Antonio. The soldier prodded him out the door onto the porch with the butt of his rifle.

Antonio could hear Elena's wails as he was dragged to a waiting van. He was pushed into the rear compartment, which held several men squeezed into two bench seats. There was no place to sit, one man already crouching between the knees of the others and the front bench. Antonio could only do the same, kneeling between another captive's knees and holding on to the back of the seat in front, lurching and toppling side to side as the van sped through the city.

When they came to a stop, he recognized the huge theater, a landmark which had recently been renamed the Karl Marx. It was the largest venue in Cuba, with over 5,000 seats. As he stepped out of the van, his legs, stiff from the prolonged kneeling, gave way and he toppled to the ground. In the darkness, the large man behind him stepped on his calf full weight, crushing it. The pain was excruciating. He managed to scramble up when he felt the barrel of a rifle prod his ribs. Groups of men from other vans were being escorted at gunpoint to the main entrance of the building.

For Antonio, the sight of hundreds and hundreds of men inside the theater, some in pajamas, some without shoes, reminded him of photographs of European war victims from the Second World War. Nothing like this had ever happened in Cuba. Some of the men around him had makeshift bloody bandages on their arms and legs—rags, torn shirts, handkerchiefs. The men milled around in the aisles or sat in the red velvet seats that would normally be occupied by an elegant audience.

Antonio looked at the men carefully. Almost all of them were younger than him. He didn't belong here. There was a section of the theater in the rear under the overhang of the balcony that was not as brightly lit, where just a few men sat. He chose a seat as remote as possible from the others and resolved to remain quiet and patient. He rubbed his calf, which was now throbbing.

For two days, he hardly ate any of the stale bread that was brought once a day by the guards. The only water that was available to drink was from the tap in the filthy bathroom sink, unfiltered and not considered potable. Like many of the other men, after twenty-four hours he was racked by vomiting and diarrhea.

On the morning of the third day, the men were released in random groups of fifty. Antonio had no way of contacting Elena. No transportation was provided, and he had no money for a bus. In the parking lot outside the theater, another detainee's wife, a total stranger, offered to drive him home. Suddenly he saw the pink Ford and Elena standing next to it craning her neck, looking for him. He didn't remember Elena ever hugging him that long or that hard. "How did you know I was coming out today?" he asked, with difficulty because his throat was like sandpaper and he was short of breath. "I didn't," she said. "I came every day to wait for you."

66

Obdulia had been extremely kind to him, and Fernando embraced her and kissed her on the cheek before he left in the late morning. He would miss her wide morning smiles and generous meals—Galician stew, Spanish potato omelets, chicken empanadas. Gustavo was at work and would be coming home, he had said, in the early afternoon and not at the usual time because of the invasion. All nightclub activities were suspended, of course.

One look at his father sitting in the living room told Fernando that Antonio not only had been arrested but mistreated. In the short span of time since he had last seen him, he had lost weight and his cheeks had become hollow, his eyes sunken. Worst of all, he seemed to be only mildly interested in the fact that Fernando had walked in after being gone for almost three days.

Fernando swallowed a surge of anger, his fists white and his jaw clenched. He could feel his heart pounding in his neck. It wasn't anything he had ever done as an adult, but he bent over and kissed his father on the cheek. He wanted to do more, hug him and hold him, try to restore him.

Antonio's face remained inert, and he looked at Fernando with a blank expression. "I'm glad you're home," he said, the voice unrecognizably ancient.

Fernando covered his face and let out a howl of frustration and rage. How could the country's government be subjecting this family to physical cruelty again, and worse now, to his father?

He went to find his mother. She was in what had been Luis's bedroom, rearranging his brother's old clothes in the closet. The drawers of the dresser were open and stacks of folded clothes lay on the bed. "Oh, Fernando," she said when she saw him, and dropped onto the bed. "I'm so glad you're home."

She filled him in on what had happened, her voice shaking at times. "How they treated him, like a criminal. And you saw what he looks like." She shook her head, got up, and continued making space in the closet.

Fernando wondered where she got her strength. "Has he seen a doctor?" he asked, his voice raspy with dread.

"The doctor was here yesterday and prescribed antibiotics for an infection in the intestines. He thinks your father has parasites."

"How did he get parasites?"

Elena said, "He had to drink tap water. They didn't give the prisoners anything to drink."

Fernando recoiled at the term "prisoner" referring to his father. It was inconceivable that this was happening. He pounded the wall with his fists.

"Stop that," Elena said. "Calm down. You're not going to accomplish anything doing that."

He took a deep breath and sat on the bed. In a calmer but hoarse voice he said, "What are you doing with Luis's clothes?"

"Making room for Ines. She's going to stay here until the invasion is over. There are very few buses running."

Fernando went back to the living room and sat on the sofa next to his father, who barely looked at him, his gaze on an empty wall.

Gustavo had meant well, but his suggestion had resulted in Antonio being placed in serious danger. Fernando would have been more resilient to the mistreatment and outright abuse his father had suffered. He redirected his anger at himself for running away. He should have seen it coming, been more careful. Unforgivable. He wondered now if his father's catatonic-like state was residual psychological trauma from the detention or whether it was directed at him, an expression of resentment and disappointment, which Fernando felt that he deserved.

Elena walked in, and Fernando saw that Antonio's behavior didn't change. He hated himself even more because he was sure now that what he was witnessing was a traumatized mind.

67

The sun was up a little earlier now in April, and so was Ines, just as the sky came out of darkness. She picked up the small bedside radio that had been Señor Luis's, unplugged it, and took it to the kitchen. She liked the fact that she was sleeping in his bedroom now, on his bed. Now that she was staying in the Leals' house she felt obliged to make them breakfast, not just clean up the remnants of it.

She made coffee for herself and tuned the radio to the news. As she sipped the concentrated black liquid, she turned her attention to the announcer more fully. "The invading forces have been defeated," she heard the man say. "The Revolutionary forces suffered very few casualties. Hundreds of invaders have been captured, hundreds are dead. Long live the Revolution!"

Ines turned the volume down and went to sit on a small stool just outside the back door. The dawn was still cool, and she shivered. She wondered how her mother was doing alone these last two days, how she would react to the news that the American invasion had been a failure in just three days. Her mother was not a great fan of the Revolution. "Why did they close down the church?" she had asked. "I can't even find lard at the bodega." Her list of complaints was long.

A few months ago, a small skinny woman from the government had come to the house in the evening, wanting to know if Ines and her mother knew how to read. Ines had been proud to say "yes," and her mother had sounded defiant when she said, "No. I never learned, and I don't need to now." Making notes on a clipboard, the woman had not been deterred, cajoling Ines's mother into going to the local community center for lessons twice a week.

Ines saw the positive things the Revolution had achieved—she now owned the small shack where she lived with her mother. Because the town was poor, a certain amount of electricity was free. They now had two lightbulbs, one in the shack and one in the outhouse, which meant that at night they could check for scorpions and tarantulas before sitting on the toilet. The medical clinic that had often been closed when Pedro was ill before he disappeared was now open every day and free.

But there was no question there were problems, besides the food shortages. There were many changes. You couldn't be heard complaining about the food situation, couldn't be seen wearing a crucifix, or defending someone who didn't agree with the government, because the vigilance committee would call you names and lower your rations. The magazines and newspapers all had the same articles about how wonderful the Revolution was, how much it had accomplished. And Ines hardly watched the old TV anymore, because they didn't show American programs now, but newscasts and dull Russian documentaries. But, most important, this family that had been so good to her had been terribly mistreated and humiliated, and now lived in fear. This was difficult for her to watch.

She heard someone in the kitchen, and the radio's volume going up. The sun wasn't quite above the horizon yet, and the sky was a pale violet. She went inside to see Señor Fernando standing by the stove staring at the radio, mouth open with disbelief. The announcer was repeating the news about the failure of the invasion. "So," Ines said, "the Americans lost. Nothing's going to change."

68

In May, a month after his incarceration and the failed invasion, Antonio's health began to improve and his mental state was on its way to recovery. Elena began the application process to leave the country, which involved filling out forms at the Office of Interior Affairs to apply for an exit permit. For the American visa, an application needed to be made at the Swiss embassy, since diplomatic relations with the US had been suspended and the American embassy was now closed. Within days of filing the application, two of the neighborhood vigilantes appeared at Elena's door to take inventory of the household contents: furniture, kitchenware, linens, towels. As she had been warned by Betty, she was advised by the inspectors that the inventory had to be the same as the day before departure or the permit would be null and void.

She told no one outside the family. The canasta games had been suspended as the unrest preceding the invasion mounted. Large department stores had been bombed, sugar refineries were set on fire, and imported oil supplies blown up, all by antigovernment dissidents.

"Ariel and I are getting married soon," Fernando said to his parents on Sunday. He had just come from her house and found his parents in the living room. There was no expression of joy from either parent.

"When?" Elena asked.

"We haven't set a date yet."

"You know we'll probably get the exit permit this summer and we'll leave immediately," Elena said.

"I know. I hope we can do it before," Fernando said.

Antonio said, "You and Ariel haven't applied to leave yet?"

"No. We have to talk about that."

Elena shook her head. "I don't see what there is to talk about," she said. "You're not going to stay."

Fernando shrugged. "No. She wants to leave."

Elena stood up. "What do you mean, 'She wants to leave'? And you don't?"

Antonio said, "Elena."

With her lips in a tight line, she looked at Antonio before she turned to Fernando and said, "After what they did to your father, and all because you weren't here, by the way, I would think you'd want nothing to do with this country."

Fernando stood stock still and considered leaving the room. Harsh and self-centered as always, she had begun the process of emigrating without letting him know, without encouraging him and Ariel to do the same. No wonder Luis thought only of himself. He remembered the old Spanish saying *From this stick of wood comes this splinter.*

He thought back to her affair with Ramon, his own hand in the man's death, and found in some remote nucleus of his brain the possibility of bringing it all up now if his father hadn't been present. He felt no shame and no remorse for what he had done and would have been untroubled recounting it for her. But then he saw in her besieged face the terrible strain of what she had gone through—the armed intrusion into the house, her husband being dragged away as she watched, then nursing him back to health, as she had done for him.

"We'll set a date for the wedding soon and we'll let you know," Fernando said and then left the room.

69

Club Maxime, like all the other nightclubs, remained closed weeks after the invasion. Fernando and Gustavo had lunch once a week.

"I'm thinking of leaving," Fernando said, after the waiter had served their food.

Gustavo's fork stopped in midair. "You mean the country?"

Fernando nodded. "Ariel wants to leave. We're getting married in July. I want you to be my best man."

Gustavo looked away toward the other tables. "I'd be honored to be your best man. But you're leaving?"

Fernando nodded again and shrugged. He saw a disturbed look settle on his friend's face.

"You'll leave after the wedding, then?" Gustavo said.

"Of course. As soon as we get the exit permits and the American visa. We've applied for both."

Gustavo put down his fork. "I don't know what to say," he said. "I didn't think you hated the Revolution that much."

"I hate what they did to my father. And although I have to believe that things will get better, Ariel really wants to go."

Gustavo shook his head and said, "What they did to your father was brutal. Their tactics are too heavy-handed."

Very little was said during the rest of the meal. It was the most unpleasant lunch Fernando could remember, at least with Gustavo, with whom it was usually a congenial get-together.

When the nightclub reopened there was little for Fernando to do. Few customers came, none of them tourists, and most of the locals were still too rattled from the upheaval and the sabotage bombs that had gone off during the invasion.

Fernando had time to visit the club's terrace several times a day now. He enjoyed the breeze from the sea and the beautiful azure sky that touched the ocean in a thin line of ivory. The long fronds of the palm trees danced in the wind and mesmerized him. From the other side of the terrace, looking out over the city, wide avenues dotted with obelisks and parks created a sense of grace and civility. Despite the political upheavals, the terrible governance that repeated itself like a recurring nightmare, the magical splendor of the island endured. People who traveled, even foreign visitors, said no other country was this beautiful.

When he happened to see Julia on the terrace, he looked at her only after she turned away, not wanting to make eye contact, and he didn't stay long if she was there. Their last conversation had been devastating, despite her gentle manner, because she had made it clear that there would be no more discussion of a future together. He walked past the group of dancers on his way back to the office without a glance. He didn't know if she had looked or not, and he made it a point to nod and wave to Tony, the dance captain who had introduced him to Julia years ago.

On the rare afternoons when he played the charade on the terrace, he sat at his desk afterwards with his head in his hands. Minutes later, he would call Ariel at work to hear her voice and reassure himself that the energy and enthusiasm at the other end of the line was what was good for him, what he needed.

70

It was said that the sand at Varadero Beach was the finest and silkiest anywhere in the world, and indeed it felt to Fernando as if he were walking on talcum powder. The gleaming whiteness of the sand could be seen beneath the aquamarine ocean as it stretched out toward the horizon.

Their honeymoon would only be a week long. Two weeks later they would be flying to Miami, unexpectedly early. Not having residential claim to any property—no one had real estate ownership nowadays, of course—meant the exit permits had been processed in only a few weeks. They would be good for two months. In contrast, Antonio's and Elena's permits had not yet been granted.

Fernando was immensely happy. He touched Ariel at every opportunity—walking on the beach, out in the ocean, ambling to dinner from their fine suite in the luxurious hotel. Ariel's affection and good spirits, even on the morning when he had not been interested in sex, made the days of his honeymoon as precious as a string of sapphires. The only pebble in the exquisite necklace occurred on day five, when the memory of Julia intruded intermittently throughout the day, and his mood sobered. Ariel noticed and said, "Are you worried about leaving?" and he said, not entirely falsely, "A little." And, indeed, there were moments when he remembered that they'd be leaving the country relatively soon and he grew pensive about the uncertainties ahead. He tried not to dwell on it.

It had all been planned out the past few weeks. Both of them had given notice at work. After Varadero they would live with Ariel's parents until their departure. That house was bigger, and her parents were quiet people. Without saying so to Ariel, Fernando thought Elena's personality would be too intrusive. In Miami, they would stay with Ariel's cousin and her husband until they could find work and get their own place. Ariel spoke good English and Fernando's was passable. Ariel was enthusiastic, clearly not at all apprehensive about the future. Fernando used her positive outlook to give himself courage that everything would be fine after emigration.

A few days after they got back to Havana, Fernando went to visit his parents. He had already moved some things to Ariel's parents' house in preparation for staying there the two weeks he had left in Cuba.

For the second time in just a few weeks Fernando was taken aback at his father's appearance. He had finally regained his weight and skin color after the detention, but now he looked ashen again. There were dark circles under his eyes, and he seemed to be panting just sitting on the living room sofa doing absolutely nothing. His lips were blue.

"He went to see the doctor yesterday," Elena said. "He diagnosed pneumonia and gave him antibiotics."

"This was Doctor Ramirez?" Fernando asked. The physician had taken care of the family for years. Fernando would be forever grateful to him for the care he had provided after his assault.

"No. He's on vacation," Elena said. "This was a young doctor covering for him in another office."

He looked at his father again. Antonio's eyes seemed to be asking for help. "Let's go," Fernando said.

"Where?" Elena said.

"The hospital."

It took many hours to get the tests completed, and the emergency room doctor finally gave them the results as he stood next to Antonio's bed. A blood clot had traveled from the right leg to the lungs. The physician who took care of him later that day in the ICU said he likely would have died in another day or so had he not gone to the hospital. He was placed on anticoagulants to dissolve the embolus in the lungs and also the thrombus in the leg. He remained in the ICU for several days before being transferred to a general medical floor.

Dr. Ramirez, back from vacation, rounded on him one morning when Fernando and Elena were at his bedside. The physician said, "Did you have any trauma to that right calf in the past few weeks or months, any injuries?"

Antonio thought a moment. "Yes," he said. "When I was being taken away to detention, one of the men in the van accidentally stepped on my calf. I had a bruise and it hurt for days. It was hard to walk."

"I remember the detention. That's when you got parasites and you needed treatment," the doctor said.

"Yes, that's right," Elena said. "And now this. Those savages."

Dr. Ramirez nodded. "That trauma to the calf was probably the cause of it, then," he said, pointedly avoiding any further political discussion.

Elena said, "How long will he be in the hospital?"

"At least another ten days, until we're sure the clots have dissolved. This is still serious," the physician said. "He's going to need treatment and careful monitoring for months."

Fernando drove to Ariel's house from the hospital. He stopped at a traffic light in the Vibora section of the city. Havana was changing. Even in this fashionable neighborhood, houses were in need of repair, the paint peeling, neglected due to the scarcity of supplies that had always come from the US. Even at Club Maxime the festive garlands of lights hanging over the terrace had burned-out light bulbs. The formerly dazzling club was looking shabby elsewhere as well, the floors unpolished, the brass tarnished.

As the light turned green, it dawned on him that he should not go to the US in a few days, with his father seriously ill in the hospital. Perhaps once his father was out of danger. But travel between the two countries was limited and arduous. If he left, he would not be able to return in an emergency, or worse. Despite his growing passion for Ariel, he thought she could go live with her cousin in Miami as planned, and he could follow in a month or so. His exit permit and American visa would still be good for six more weeks. He felt this was the right thing to do, although of course he would have to deal with the heartache of being separated from her.

Ariel looked surprised and then sad when he told her, but she nodded and kissed him on his scarred cheek. "I understand, my love," she said. He felt blessed to have this reliably good-natured woman as his wife.

71

He drove Ariel to the airport four hours before the scheduled departure. Since the invasion, the government was demanding that travelers sit in a glass enclosure for three hours, within view but isolated from family and well-wishers seeing them off. Meanwhile, the officials inspected every piece of checked luggage and scrutinized every travel document. Some passengers were interrogated and strip-searched. Fernando stood by the glass partition the whole time, his heart troubling his chest with the separation he didn't think he should have to suffer so soon after his wedding. They mouthed phrases through the soundproof glass, mundane things that gave them the illusion of being closer than they were, that this parting was trivial, easily reversed. He watched in despair as Ariel blew him one last kiss when the two armed men in uniform called her name. They checked her documents and she went through the glass door out to the tarmac and up the plane's boarding stairs. At the top of the steps she turned around briefly and waved before she disappeared into the Pan American DC-6 for the one-hour flight to Miami. He felt no shame or embarrassment as he wept.

Fernando moved back to his parents' house. He watched his father recover his color and some of his strength. The right calf was still swollen, and Elena grew anxious about their exit permit, which still hadn't been granted. She fretted that the American visa would expire before the Cuban documents arrived.

He missed Ariel terribly. He wanted to talk to her, hear the sound of her voice, at least, but calls couldn't be placed to the US. Only someone in the States could initiate the process, which took hours. His mind replayed the two options he had faced: leave with Ariel and hope his father recovered uneventfully, or stay by his father's side and delay beginning his married life. He didn't know if he had made the right choice, and suspected either one would have seemed unsatisfactory.

He had lunch with Gustavo. "They haven't replaced you yet at Club Maxime," his friend said. "If you want to go back to work while your father recovers, I can ask them."

"Maybe I should," Fernando said. "It'll give me something to do for the next three weeks, until my father is well enough for me to leave."

He dropped Gustavo off at work at the Riviera Club and drove home. When he turned the last corner and saw an ambulance in front of the house, he knew a disaster had occurred. He pressed down on the accelerator and nearly slammed into the rear of the parked ambulance. In his parents' bedroom, two men were transferring his father from the bed to a stretcher.

"They think it's a heart attack," Elena said, her voice unrecognizable with trepidation. He put his arms around her and took her to his car as Antonio was placed in the back of the ambulance.

Fernando parked the Peugeot in the hospital's lot and they made their way to the emergency room. When he asked, a nurse said they could not see him. "His heart stopped just as they wheeled him in," she said. "They're reviving him now."

Fernando started to put his arm around his mother, a reflex to lend support before he dealt with his own dread, but she had turned away and put her face in her hands. He could not hear any weeping or vocalizations coming from her. He put his hand on her shoulder, but she ignored him and turned back toward the nurse. "I have to see him," Elena said. Her eyes were dry but she looked terrified. "I need to see him before he dies."

"Not now," the nurse said. "Let the doctors do their work."

Antonio survived, but this time the recovery was slower, the damage to the heart of much more consequence than what the lungs had suffered. The cardiologist was a little gray-haired man with a long pointy nose who came to see Antonio twice a day. His opinion was that the heart attack was a result of the residual clot in the lungs. The cardiac muscle had not gotten enough oxygen. Antonio would be in the hospital six weeks, the doctor said.

Fernando wished he could speak to Ariel, but all he could do was write her a letter in which he asked her to call him. When she called a week later and he had given her a rushed account of what had happened, he said, "I just can't leave them now." He pushed aside the knowledge that his exit permit would expire in four weeks.

"Oh, Fernando," Ariel said. "I wanted to tell you in person." Even with the static of the terrible connection he could hear her voice breaking with emotion. "I'm pregnant."

72

At last, Elena thought, the September stars are aligning. Antonio recovered and appeared to be his old self, although he limited his daily walks to two or three blocks now. Their exit permits from the Cuban government had finally arrived in the mail, just before the American visa expired.

"Leave as soon as you get your emigration permit," Elena told Fernando. "Don't delay." They were reading in the living room on a Saturday afternoon. Antonio was out at the bodega, although he had nothing to buy.

"Of course," Fernando said. "With you safely over there, I have no reason to stay. I miss Ariel."

He did not sound convincing to her. Elena had detected a lack of enthusiasm in her son about leaving the chaotic situation in Cuba to join his beautiful wife in Miami.

"What's here for you?" she asked him. She could not fathom that an attachment to his childhood surroundings could hold him with such a grip, and suspected another personal connection he hadn't spoken about. She remembered he had mentioned somebody named Julia, and she wondered if he wasn't still involved with her.

Fernando took a moment before he said, "This country is my home. Where I was born and grew up. I have faith that it will someday be a good place to live. I'll leave like you, yes, but part of me wants to stay and try to improve the situation, work to make it a democracy eventually."

Elena believed him, and although she was touched by what she saw as his naïve sentimentality, she shook her head. "Don't try to be a hero, Fernando. Only God and history make martyrs."

His reaction was to drop his chin and say nothing.

"And you and Ariel should come live in Tampa. Don't stay in Miami," she said. She and Antonio were going to join her sister, Isabel, and her husband, Alberto, in Tampa, where there was a sizable Cuban community. She wanted to preserve the close family structure as much as possible.

"We'll see," Fernando said.

"No, really. Miami is a nothing town," she said. "You'll see. It's all beaches and small hotels. It's nice for vacations, but there's not much there otherwise."

Her decision to join her sister in Tampa was also based on the question of adequate medical care for Antonio in the future. She wasn't going to trust his health to small hospitals of unknown quality. And the large university hospital in Miami had a reputation for being shabby and treating mostly indigents. She had heard from Isabel that Tampa had many fine Cuban physicians.

Elena went to see her friend Betty. She wanted to say good-bye in person, not on the phone. She hadn't seen or spoken to Nina in months and had heard from Betty that her friend now had a vigilance committee out of her stately home.

"Can you imagine?" Betty had said about Nina. "With all that money and that mansion that she would get involved with these thugs?"

Betty opened the door herself. She had a wide but sad smile, her eyes missing their usual sparkle. Her hair was now the dull flat brown of Soviet hair dye, which made it look as if she wore a cap made of tree bark. She hugged Elena hard.

Betty made the coffee herself. She had dismissed the housekeeper. "A communist, I confirmed finally."

When they were sitting in the living room, Elena said, "Betty, we're leaving."

Betty put her cup down on the end table. Her eyebrows flew up into her forehead. "Oh, Elena," she whimpered.

"Why don't you leave, join Rebeca and Samuel in New Jersey?" Elena said.

"I don't know, Elena. Maybe I will." She paused. "But Ramon is here. I'd be so far away."

A cascade of memories and regrets surged through Elena. She nodded and said nothing more about it. As she got into her car to drive home, she asked herself whether in Betty's place she would stay close to her husband's remains or join her children in another country. She looked at herself in the rearview mirror for no particular reason that she could discern and realized she would have no doubts about what she would do.

73

Fernando was back working at the Club Maxime. Because of the diminished business, shows were only Thursday through Saturday now. Still, Fernando worked his old schedule and he had time to wander around even more than before. He did not feel that he would have to avoid looking at Julia if they both happened to be on the terrace, and wondered whether that change was because he was now so attached to Ariel.

He wanted to forget the last, bruising conversation he'd had with Julia, but knowing that they were both in the same building made it difficult. She had been soft in demeanor but inflexible about their relationship being finished, no further explanations. It had been one of the worst days of his life. Fernando wanted to tell Gustavo about that encounter, exorcise the pain of it by telling his trusted friend, a confessor of sorts. But he knew Gustavo was smitten with Ariel. When the four of them—he and Ariel, Tania and Gustavo—spent time together, Gustavo normally agreed with Ariel's opinion about everything, whether it was the food they had eaten or the movie they had seen.

Eventually, Fernando saw the dancers rehearsing, but he didn't see Julia among them. He thought he could ask Tony, the dance captain he had been friendly with, but he wasn't around either. During one of the several lunches Fernando had with Gustavo, he brought the conversation around to the diminished amount of business the clubs were doing. "There are fewer dancers now, and I haven't even seen Julia rehearsing," he added, as if it were an afterthought.

Gustavo looked at him, sizing him up, Fernando thought, and he tried to keep a neutral, disinterested expression. "I guess you haven't heard," Gustavo said, "because you were away for a few weeks. She left the club."

Fernando's upper lip unexpectedly prickled with something like panic. "Hmm," he said. "A new job, I wonder?"

Gustavo hesitated. "From what I heard," he said, speaking slowly and in a low voice, as if he didn't want to release the words, "she's seriously ill." He paused. "She has lymphoma."

Fernando's vision left him for a few seconds. He could not have found the spoon on the table alongside his dish of rice pudding. "That can't be," he said, and his voice was raspy and soft. "She's too young." *That can't be. She's what I need, essential, the ground on which I walk.*

"No, that's what I thought too," Gustavo was saying, and his voice sounded very far away. "But it shows up in young people sometimes."

Fernando nodded, now back in the moment, but confused, even resentful that his usually reliable friend was telling him something that had to be erroneous. "Do you know if she's being treated or how she is doing?" he asked.

Gustavo shook his head. "I just heard this from administration when you were away, but that's all we know." He hesitated before he continued. "And how's Ariel?" he asked, the look in his eyes sharp, maybe with some reproach, and Fernando understood that his face had betrayed the depth of his dismay.

"She sounds fine in her letters. I only spoke to her once. She's looking for work." His mind was spinning, unfocused with the news about Julia, and he didn't mention that she was pregnant. He wouldn't have been able to stand Gustavo's judgment, especially after that look.

Gustavo nodded. "She's a fine person," he said. "She deserves the best."

After a moment Fernando said, "Yes, she does," and he knew exactly what his friend had meant.

74

The departure at the airport was uneventful and less emotional than Fernando had anticipated. Elena was uncharacteristically quiet, a frown dipping her eyebrows, her lips pursed. Antonio was the picture of equanimity, smiling at Fernando through the glass partition that separated them. He had become more placid since his medical catastrophes, his brow more relaxed and further away from scowls. He also moved more slowly, as if he had aged at an accelerated pace.

They had each checked a half-empty suitcase. Citizens leaving on an exit permit for an undetermined period of time, which was the vast majority nowadays, were allowed to carry no more than three changes of clothing, including socks and underwear, and only one pair of shoes. The rest of his parents' clothing still hung in their closet. "They're good clothes," Elena had pointed out. "Don't just throw them away."

When he arrived home from the airport his parents' absence felt enormous and obliterated all other thoughts and emotions. He went into their bedroom and sat on their bed. The concept—though not the image—of their parents making love on this very bed entered his mind. He missed Ariel terribly. He had never felt so alone before, and he felt desolation enveloping his heart.

Within days of his parents' departure, Fernando found a notice taped to the front door of the house when he got home from work. The one-page document, from the Department of Municipal Housing, was addressed to him as the primary tenant. He remembered his mother saying that they would sign that title over to him before leaving. The notice advised him that the house was too big for one person, and per regulations, he needed to show proof of two other people sharing the space as a primary residence or he would be relocated to smaller quarters. He had a month to show proof, which would be confirmed or rejected by the vigilance committee, or he would be locked out.

Fernando could not imagine being evicted from his home. The house was modest but comfortable and well-maintained. It had been his home since childhood. This was where he and Luis had played tag, making the best of the postage-stamp-sized front yard, the short driveway, the narrow alley that wrapped around the side to the back, and the laundry sink. The porch, with its terracotta floor, was where Antonio had taught them to read before they were old enough to go to school.

He didn't think he could face another loss, and considered asking Gustavo and Tania to move in. They were still squeezing themselves into his mother's house or her parents' apartment, and the more he thought about it, the more it made sense. But when he asked Gustavo, he said no; he didn't want his mother to live alone and was trying to convince her to move in with them when they got their own place.

He pondered Ines's situation. It would be a bit awkward, a young single woman living with a man, but he saw it happening all around out of necessity, even in this neighborhood. She had already stayed in Luis's room during the invasion, after all, and he knew the bus trips had become increasingly difficult for her. When he asked Ines, he approached the proposal by first explaining the ultimatum the government had issued a week after his parents' departure.

Ines thought a moment, then said, "I think I can do it. But I'd have to talk to my mother first to make sure she wouldn't mind being alone most of the week."

Fernando said, "Would that create a problem for her, because the house you share with her would be too big for just one person?"

Ines shook her head and looked like she was trying to hide her smile. "No. Our house is just one room."

Fernando frowned, not understanding. "You mean one bedroom?"

"No. It's just one room. A little bigger than the living room here."

He thought about this several times over the next several days. This quiet, capable young woman, who had become part of the fabric of the household, almost a member of the family, went home every day to what was probably a hovel. How did two people live in one room? He remembered mention of Ines's father dying some time back, and of the disappearance of her husband, Pedro. Had either of them shared that room as well? It took him several days to accept that, yes, this is how people lived, even in the suburbs of the capital. The picturesque mud and straw huts in the countryside that appeared on postcards were probably bigger and more comfortable than the shacks of the shantytowns he had seen on his outings out of the city. He had assumed that the people who lived in those slums were lazy or inferior in some way. And yet Ines was talented and industrious, and she was one of them. No wonder there had been so much support for the Revolution, and continued to be among so many people. It was completely understandable to him now that they could not possibly care about mere scarcities and authoritarian oppression.

And of course he thought of Julia. Not that he hadn't thought of her almost every day since their last, brief meeting several weeks ago, despite his growing love for Ariel. But now he understood Julia's enthusiasm for the Revolution in a more concrete way. And although he knew that her support of it had not been the cause of their breakup, he wanted to at least tell her that now he understood, on a visceral level, why the Revolution had succeeded. He called her.

75

She was on her fourth week of chemotherapy and her hair was beginning to fall out. The first morning Julia saw her pillow covered with tufts of it she felt lightheaded and had to sit back down on the bed. She shook the pillow out in the shower and ran the water to get rid of the sight of it. There wasn't one hour of the waking day that she didn't feel the weight of an uncertain future. How do you resume your career if you don't know how long you're going to live? When would she return to normal activity, take the bus to see her mother, go out and do her own shopping? She depended on her roommate for the food she ate. Cooking was out of the question because her feet were swollen and she couldn't stand at the stove long enough. Her roommate brought her empanadas, croquettes, and pork sandwiches from the bodega. And Julia was running out of money. She hadn't danced in six weeks and didn't know how long her roommate would be able to handle the living expenses by herself. Already the young woman had talked of disconnecting the phone, because her income as a singer was less than what Julia had earned dancing at Club Maxime. She dreaded the prospect of moving in with her mother into that tiny apartment.

Julia hadn't seen her mother in weeks, since the radiotherapy, the first treatment the doctors had tried before they discovered that the lymphoma was in more than one spot. She wondered how her mother was coping with the news that her only daughter would probably die before she did. On the phone, the old woman's voice now sounded ancient, weak, weepy. Julia felt like she was ruining what was left of her mother's life.

She thought it was her mother calling, and didn't immediately recognize Fernando's unexpected voice.

"Yes, it's true," she said. "Your friend Gustavo is right." She listened. "I don't have the energy to go out with you or anyone anywhere, and my roommate is here."

He was insisting, and she thought she was done with disentangling herself from this relationship. "All right," she said. "Come tonight while she's at work. But it has to be a short visit."

She wrapped a scarf around her mostly bare scalp. Fernando arrived exactly at eight. She noticed his look of surprise at her appearance when she opened the door, a stab to her pride. He was carrying a takeout container of garbanzo beans with pork, which she put down on the small table before he moved toward her. She understood he wanted to hug her, and she opened her arms and hugged him back.

She took out plates and utensils and served them the garbanzos. There was already rice on the stove that was still warm. Julia saw that he ate very little and looked down at his food repeatedly, as if bursting with the need to say something. She asked about his job, his parents, his wife. She had never mentioned Ariel before. His being married had not entered into their last conversation.

"Ariel left. She's been gone for months," he said. "I had to stay because my father was ill. And now they're gone too. They left the country."

"Oh, no," Julia said. "So you're all alone."

She saw him hesitate. "I came to ask you a favor," he said. "The government is going to relocate me out of my home. They won't let me stay in that house by myself. The housekeeper has agreed to live there, but I need one more person."

His eyebrows were high up on his forehead in an anxious plea. "And?" she said.

"Why don't you come live in my house?" he said. "It would be good for you to have Ines there all the time. She does all the cooking and the cleaning. And it would be good for me too, because then I can keep the house."

This was more complicated than she could consider in a short time. "I don't know," she said. "How can this work? With our history, and now you're married."

"You'll have your own bedroom, and there are two bathrooms," he said. "I don't want to lose the house. And between me and Ines, if there's anything you need, we're there."

"But aren't you leaving also? To be with your wife?"

"The exit permit won't be coming for months. And before I leave I'll transfer the primary right of tenancy to you."

"You can do that?" she asked.

"Yes. I can name you as the new principal tenant of the government if you're living there. And after I leave, you can bring your mother to live there as well."

Her head was spinning. "Let me think about it," she said.

76

The Riviera Club, where Gustavo had been named chief administrator, was designated by the Municipal Business Administration as the headquarters for all nightlife commerce in Havana. Gustavo was therefore the de facto director of all the city's nightclubs and any management decisions had to be approved by him.

A knock on his office door. "Come in," Gustavo said.

Vicki, one of the secretaries, came in. His own secretary was out sick. Vicki was a large light-skinned Black woman who wore skin-tight pants and low-cut blouses. Her cleavage and her thighs commandeered any room she entered.

"Jorge from Personnel is here to see you," Vicki said.

"Okay, let him come in."

A short, thin man with a large head walked in holding what seemed to be a letter. After he sat down, Jorge said, "I need your approval to dismiss Fernando Leal."

"Why does he need to be dismissed?" Gustavo couldn't suppress a frown.

Jorge held up the letter. "The government office says we have to reduce personnel at his grade level. He's the most recent hire."

Gustavo knew Jorge was right, but he said, "Yes, but he was a re-hire. He had been here for years before that."

"Just over two years, about the same as the other man at his level."

Gustavo said, "Let me have the letter. I'll take care of it."

Jorge appeared reluctant to hand over the letter, but did so and left. After Gustavo read the letter, he called Fernando. "Let's have lunch," he said.

They went to their usual spot, which was now a Cuban-style Italian restaurant, featuring pork cutlet parmigiana and spaghetti with chorizo. After they ordered from the stained vinyl menu, Gustavo explained about the letter from the government. "I don't want to dismiss the other man if you plan to leave the job soon anyway," Gustavo said.

Fernando shrugged. "I have no reason to leave. I'm not interested in another job."

"No," Gustavo said. "I mean if you're going to be joining Ariel and your parents in Miami in a month or two."

Fernando shook his head. "I can't leave. I can't apply for another permit for four months, because I let the other one expire."

"So you'll be around for a while," Gustavo said. "I'll dismiss the other employee, then."

After they had finished the main course, Gustavo said, "I really appreciate your offer for Tania and me to move in with you, but my mother needs to have somebody around. Did you find somebody else to move in and share the house with you?"

Fernando shifted in his seat. "Yes," he said. "I have two other people living there now."

Gustavo didn't know of any relatives whom Fernando had in Havana now, with his parents and brother gone. "Who?" he asked. He felt comfortable asking. The closeness of the friendship permitted the querying. But he saw Fernando squirming in his seat again.

"Ines, the housekeeper." He paused. "And Julia."

Gustavo's head dropped, chin on chest. He looked at his empty pasta bowl, the remains of the sauce congealing. Service wasn't what it had been. "You're not serious," he said finally.

"I won't have the exit permit for another six months at least, probably more. And I didn't want to be relocated and live somewhere else."

Gustavo covered his eyes with the heels of his hands. "You're going to ruin your life," he said.

Fernando said, "Julia is very sick. She's being treated with chemotherapy and needs a lot of help."

"Doesn't she have any family?"

Fernando shook his head. "Just her mother, who's old. And a cousin she doesn't like."

They were mostly silent in the car while Fernando drove Gustavo back to the Riviera. As they neared the club, Gustavo said, "I don't know what I'm going to tell Tania about Julia living with you. She's going to ask about our lunch. She talks about Ariel all the time, how she misses seeing her and working with her." He paused. "She's going to ask if you've had any news about her."

"Tell her the truth. That we didn't talk about her."

77

1962

After three months of chemotherapy, the lymphoma was in remission. The doctors were cautiously hopeful that the cancer would be suppressed for a year or so, they told Julia, possibly longer. Fernando accompanied her to the oncologist for the last treatment.

"What are the chances of a cure?" Fernando asked the physician in the consultation room, and Julia looked at him and then at the doctor.

The man lowered his gaze to the desk and said, "We're hoping for long-term control."

Fernando heard the words but couldn't process their meaning. "But cure?" he said, and Julia reached across from her chair and squeezed his forearm.

The physician shook his head, stood up, and said, "I'll see you in six weeks to examine you again."

Fernando held his temper. He was sure this renowned oncologist had the latest knowledge. How could he not be able to cure this? Was there another hospital they could try? Were things different in the US?

On their way back to the parking lot, Julia took Fernando's arm. She always did it now, her feet numb and unsteady from the neuropathy caused by the toxic intravenous medications. Her hair was completely gone, including the eyebrows. She didn't bother painting them on anymore, although she wore a scarf on her head.

When they got home she didn't want to go to bed like she usually did after a session of chemotherapy. She sat in the living room and turned the Grundig on. The radio was tuned to the news, and she changed it to a music station. From the Grundig's large speaker came boleros, many that the orchestra at Club Maxime played, some of which Julia had danced to. Fernando said nothing of this and watched as she changed the station again, this time to classical music.

Ines came into the room with a glass of pink liquid. "It's a papaya shake. Good for energy and for your appetite," she said. She left it on top of the Grundig and went back to the kitchen.

"I have to go back to the club," Fernando said. It was near noon and he had a meeting at two.

"I'll be fine," Julia said.

"You'll eat something?"

"I'll try. Ines makes good chicken soup."

Fernando went into the kitchen. "Can you make her some chicken soup?" he asked Ines.

"I always have it ready. It's all she eats for lunch most days," Ines said, and then added, "Her bed needs new sheets. The old ones are worn with so much washing, and some of the stains still show."

Fernando didn't want to hear about the stains. Stains from what? "I'll get new ones this afternoon on my way home," he said.

He considered, as he drove to the club, that he was feeling something like satisfaction, a harmony in his life. He was devastated that Julia could not be cured, would certainly die of the disease. The doctor had almost said as much. And yet he had a feeling of fulfillment in providing for her—a roof, all her material needs, emotional support. Absent was the romance, supplanted by a protective role that he would do anything to preserve. He imagined having that same feeling with his newborn son Armando, just a week old. If he could lay eyes on him, hold him, caress him, he imagined the same all-consuming need to protect and provide would arise in him. As it was, he had to be satisfied with the monthly calls his parents made from Miami. They had postponed their move to Tampa, as they had originally planned, to be with Ariel and help with the pregnancy and the new baby. "He looks just like you," Elena said during their last conversation two days prior, right after Ariel and Armando came home from the hospital. Ariel was too weepy to come to the phone, Elena said.

78

Everything, someone would say, had finally fallen into place. His exit permit had been granted by the Cuban government just before his American visa was due to expire. He had convinced Gustavo and Tania to leave his mother, Obdulia, and move into his bedroom, and he had signed the primary tenancy of the house over to them. Julia had agreed, had nodded and said "of course" when Fernando asked her about the house going to his friends instead of her. She was still in remission after several months and had gained some of her weight back, but they both knew it wouldn't last. She spoke of her health in temporary terms. Ines had gone back to live with her mother but would return to live in the household if Gustavo and Tania wanted her back. It was all out of his hands now.

He left the Peugeot to Gustavo, had signed that away to him also. And part of his heart, a big slice of it, was being left behind as well. He had seen it on the floor of the living room as he said goodbye to Julia, both of them knowing that this would be the last hug, the last sight of each other. He had been embarrassed to leave her shoulder wet when he rested his cheek on it during that last embrace. There were also fragments of him scattered throughout the house, specks of his being settled into corners and crevices like thick, clinging ashes from an existence that could never be cleared away.

Gustavo drove him to the airport. Sitting in the passenger seat of the Peugeot made him uneasy, like this trip—this entire day—was a mistake. He had to stop himself from nitpicking about Gustavo's driving, his clumsy use of the clutch, the inconsistent turn signal. It wasn't his car now.

"You must be crazy happy to be joining Ariel and your little Armando in Miami," Gustavo said.

"Yes."

Gustavo glanced at him. "But you don't sound so excited."

Fernando kept his eyes on the road ahead. "There's a lot to deal with."

"But it's all for the good, right?" Gustavo said.

"Well, it's a new life, different language. I've never been there." He paused. "I have to find work and I don't have a degree."

"But didn't Ariel say the museum where she works has an opening in administration?"

Fernando said, "Yes, but who knows if they'll hire me. My English is not great." Then he added, "There are many unknowns."

And, in fact, the biggest unknown was how life with Ariel would be. His parents had plans to go to Tampa after he arrived, although they would stay until someone could care for the baby while he and Ariel went to work. Once his parents left, it would just be him and Ariel and Armando. He really hadn't lived with her and hadn't seen her in over a year. His anticipation was clouded by a sense of loss, that everything he had known up to this point in his life was being ripped away from him. The future he had imagined for his country, that it would be a better place for his offspring and future generations, seemed like an unattainable dream.

"Well, it's a good thing you're leaving now," Gustavo said. "There are missiles with nuclear warheads that have arrived from Russia, and there's going to be big trouble with the Americans."

Fernando had heard about this, had read about the ominous retaliatory measures the Americans were preparing, but he really didn't care about it much. He had his own problems to deal with. The palm trees lining the road were waving their fronds, as if they wanted to say something to him, perhaps just *goodbye*.

Epilogue

1965

He flies back to the land of lights and shadows, bombs and music, blood and linen. He leaves behind his three-year-old son, who holds his heart, and his wife, loving and trusting and the object of his adoration. He has told her what he hopes will not be a lie, that he will be back soon.

Ariel has heard and believed the incomplete truth that Gustavo, now a quadriplegic after a car accident and not expected to live long, holds a premium position in his heart. "I have to go see him one last time," he said. She didn't question his vacillation when she asked how long he would be gone.

Of course, he has not told her about Julia, who has miraculously held on, but whose end is also near, Tania revealed in her horrific letter. Ariel doesn't know that Julia exists. He's never mentioned her because the utterance of her name would have made something seismic erupt, distort his face, and reveal a truth that would be as lethal to the marriage as a sword to a rose. And he has loved his wife with fidelity, a commitment her goodness has extracted from him. He had not suspected it would be so easily forthcoming, this surrender. But he has been ensnared by her emotional largesse these past three years, until Tania's letter arrived and pried open a critical link in their bond.

And his parents. He wonders, as the plane leaves the coast of Florida above the rippled cobalt ocean, whether he will ever see them again. They're not yet frail, but they had visibly aged the last time he saw them. He thinks that if he does go back to Miami at some point, it might be for a short period only, even after Gustavo and Julia are gone. He does not foresee going to see his mother and father, witness their fading further away from what they have been. Nor will he seek out Luis, whom he still loves as he always has, and his roommate, Pablo. The old admiration he has always felt for his older brother has turned into an even stronger bond, buttressed by Luis's candor after he explained that Pablo was more than a roommate.

The four chambers of his heart hold the ether of the important people in his life. One of the four spaces is for Ariel and Armando. His parents and Luis are in another. Julia and Gustavo each have their own. He has discovered a fifth secret chamber in which he hides his disappointment in the people he loves for abandoning their country. It is a chill, dank place where love does not enter.

He has come to understand that he is as much the product of his birthplace as he is of his parents' egg and sperm—cumulatively, ancestrally so. And that he can best exist rooted and thriving in his native terrain, essential for him despite its appalling deficiencies.

There is a nugget of fulfillment inside him at the prospect of seeing Julia and Gustavo again in his own homeland. He feels it, a joyful sprite dancing in his chest, even though he has left Ariel and Armando behind. He hopes his son can forgive him when he talks about his life many years from now.

The End

Acknowledgments

This book would not exist without my early life alongside my older, politically astute cousins: José Antonio (Tony), Jorge, and Teresita Hurtado. It was their involvement against the Batista dictatorship and their subsequent complete opposition to the Castro regime that fed my imagination and gave life to these pages. The experiences they endured were as harrowing as those that appear in the novel.

I am grateful to Roz Burd and Michael Leszczuk for reading the manuscript in its early stages and giving me priceless feedback. As therapists, they helped me define the motivations and nuances of behavior of the characters.

The copyediting of the manuscript was done by the singularly astute Cindy Hochman of 100 Proof Copyediting Services in Brooklyn. I don't like to compose even an email without her help.

I am thankful for her discerning eye and surgical precision with my words.

Finally, my husband Donald Schwab was not only supportive—he was absolutely saintly in his acceptance of my remove from our life together while I became submerged in writing this story.

Other fine books available from Histria Fiction:

For these and many other great books visit
HistriaBooks.com